The
Secret
of Spring

TOR BOOKS BY PIERS ANTHONY

Alien Plot	*Isle of Woman*
Anthonology	*Letters to Jenny*
But What of Earth?	*Prostho Plus*
The Dastard	*Race Against Time*
Demons Don't Dream	*Roc and a Hard Place*
Faun & Games	*Shade of the Tree*
Geis of the Gargoyle	*Shame of Man*
Ghost	*Steppe*
Harpy Thyme	*Triple Detente*
Hasan	*Xone of Contention*
Heaven Cent	*Yon Ill Wind*
Hope of Earth	*Zombie Lover*

WITH ROBERT E. MARGROFF
Dragon's Gold
Serpent's Silver
Chimaera's Copper
Mouvar's Magic
Orc's Opal
The E.S.P. Worm
The Ring

WITH FRANCES HALL
Pretender

WITH RICHARD GILLIAM
Tales from the Great Turtle (anthology)

WITH ALFRED TELLA
The Willing Spirit

WITH CLIFFORD A. PICKOVER
Spider Legs

WITH JAMES RICHEY AND ALAN RIGGS
Quest for the Fallen Star

WITH JULIE BRADY
Dream a Little Dream

WITH JO ANNE TAEUSCH
The Secret of Spring

WITH RON LEMING
The Gutbucket Quest

The
Secret
of Spring

Piers Anthony
& Jo Anne Taeusch

TOR®
fantasy

A TOM DOHERTY ASSOCIATES BOOK
NEW YORK

This is a work of fiction. All the characters and events portrayed in this book are either products of the author's imagination or are used fictitiously.

THE SECRET OF SPRING

Copyright © 2000 by Piers Anthony Jacob and Jo Anne Taeusch

A Tor Book
Published by Tom Doherty Associates, LLC
175 Fifth Avenue
New York, NY 10010

www.tor.com

Tor® is a registered trademark of Tom Doherty Associates, LLC.

ISBN: 0-812-56487-1

First edition: March 2000
First mass market edition: July 2001

Printed in the United States of America

0 9 8 7 6 5 4 3 2 1

This book is dedicated to
the memory of my Mother,
who loved life, laughter, and me.

—J. T.

Contents

viii ● Contents

The
Secret
of Spring

❧ 1 ❧

Playmate

Wiping the perspiration from his brow, Herb Moss looked with admiration at Holly, the beautiful, fresh green Veganette resting next to him. She was a busty blossom, with luscious strawberry lips and long, thick emerald hair that fell enticingly to her hips. It had been tied up out of the way for greater freedom of movement, but the ribbons had worked loose with exertion. Now she was busy knotting a tighter bow. Finishing up the small task, she whirled around to grace Herb with a winning smile. His heart pounded faster at the flash of even white teeth.

Infertile pollination? Was that all life meant to him? And yet, why else had he travelled to this remote and expensive resort? It had seemed like a good idea at the time, but like so many of his spontaneous decisions, it had resulted in much less than he had anticipated. Herb knew he wasn't above a little discreet Ip, given the improper circumstances. And Holly was more than another attractive girl, she was quite a woman.

Her soft voice brought him back to reality. "Let's do it again!" she said breathlessly.

"Again?!" he protested. "Wasn't five times enough?"

"Oh, I know! But, you are so good, Herbie! The best! Why, I've never known anyone like you before!"

Herb flushed at the generous praise; he couldn't deny he was flattered, but a man could only go on for so long.

He hedged. "Thank you, Holly. But aren't you feeling a little bushed?" He hoped!

"Me? Oh, no! I could go on like this all day! Just try me!"

Herb's hopes of an honorable out wilted in the hot afternoon sun. He sighed audibly.

This was Holly's signal to wheedle. She put her arms around his neck, heedless of the fine view of her bust this afforded Herb. Herb was not heedless. He heeded for all he was worth.

"Please Herbie," she said with the sweet pout her lips formed with such expertise. Her fresh breath tickled his ear, and his firm resolve melted down to a watery puddle that seemed to form in his knees. It was all over.

"You win," he said weakly. "But this is the last time today—or at least until after lunch." He braced himself. "Take your position!"

Holly squealed with girlish glee and scampered to the other side of the nets to retrieve her stringed bat. "My serve!" she called gaily, giving the small yellow ball a swat. It bounced neatly up and across to meet Herb's bat for a quick return. Their sixth match of the day was on.

Holly was one of several playmates Herb had met since coming to the city of Avocado for an extended vacation. Elite Club Algae was a small resort spa by Sea Weed for the idle, rich, and bored of this part of P#23. Herb added "the confused" for his category, for now that he was here, he hardly knew why.

The club had been touted in the colorful brochure as a hotbed for singles, but the actual selection, in his opinion, left much to be desired. First there was Rosy, who had attached herself to him the first day he arrived. While she was a sweet, friendly girl with a pretty face, she also happened to be there for the serious purpose of dropping over a hundred and fifty pounds at the exclusive spa. Clearly, too much woman for him.

Then, there was the dark exotic Flora, a winsome widow, who kept dropping hints of Ip. Tempting, yet he had the uncomfortable feeling that she regarded the resort as a shopping center for husband number four. Or was it five? And what had happened to the other three anyway? There was covert talk of poison ivy. Probably just pool gossip, but why take chances? True, she was mysteriously attractive, yet there was something in her eyes when she looked at him. Something unsavory that reminded him of the hungry glance of a big garden spider patiently awaiting the right moment to pounce.

Most of the others he had met had been the usual garden-variety types one would expect to meet at a singles resort. Just pretty, pleasant girls, hoping to meet a cute boy they could take back home to meet their parents. They claimed to be there for the moment, for a good time, but Herb was not deceived. He had seen that look before, on girls at home. On the face of one girl in particular. Those girls were just like her. Herb was getting thoroughly disgusted with his big adventure. If he had wanted a "nice" girl, he would have stayed at home and dated Lily.

He had left to find more. Whatever that was. Since his arrival a couple of weeks ago the wildest thing he had swung with had been a gourd club on the neatly mown greens. Holly had been the most promising of the group. Had been. Just his luck, that she had turned out to be a ten nets nut. These daily marathon matches had to stop! By the time he satisfied her insatiable lust for the silly game he was too tired for more pleasurable recreation. A thing like that could stunt a man's growth.

He had Ip with Holly only once after a long, romantic boat cruise beneath the misty tri-moons, and that had been almost a week before. They had stopped into the Algae Bar afterward where she had quaffed down more than a few drinks of distilled water before Herb had noticed the effect they were having on her. Oh, they looked harmless enough with their carrot sticks and little umbrella trees, but cumulatively they packed quite a punch.

By the time he realized what was happening, Holly was wilted. Like the gentleman he was, he had guided her back to her own bungalow and put her to bed with every intention of fading quietly away until morning.

Holly, however, had different ideas. Unused to strong drink, she implored Herb to remain until she fell asleep, but somehow she never did, and eventually nature took a fascinating course. Herb felt only mild guilt, which had soon faded to a fond memory, and progressed to outright lust as he looked forward to more of her company. Not letting any grass grow under his feet, he called the next morning. They met for a game of ten nets, and his beauty turned into a back-hand beast. There had been, regrettably, no rematch of their night game.

Herb had come to the end of his rope, deciding to give it just one more day. If there were no improvements, he planned to push on down the coast and catch the Party Grass Festival at New Oleanders. There should be profusions of wild flowers there.

A ball whizzed by his ear, as his bat swished impotently in the air. "I win!" Holly exclaimed triumphantly, crisscrossing through the nets toward him. "Got that one right past you!" Then she frowned slightly. "Oh, you didn't let me win, just to be a gentleman, did you? I want a rematch!"

"Blight, no," Herb muttered, thinking how tired of the stupid game he was, in more than one way. "I mean, of course I wouldn't do that, Holly. You won because you're a good player, that's all."

And because his mind had wandered. She was enthusiastic, but he had all the moves; a pity, considering that she cared more about it than he did. Looking at her bosom heaving from the combination of happiness and exertion, he was glad she was the winner. Herb watched that lovely structure quiver beneath the thin material of her ten nets suit as she continued to bask in the glory of her victory.

"That's what I love about playing with you, Herb. You are a real natural at this game, and I knew if I could beat you, I would really have accomplished something. So I said to myself, 'Holly, you are going to play until you win, or drop.'"

Herb cursed silently. That was all it would have taken? He would gladly have thrown the match long before if only he'd known. But no, his male ego sprang up like an ugly weed, and what had happened? Nothing, that's what. How was he to know she hadn't expected him to win all the time to impress her? She was always going on about how great he was. Women. Did they never mean what they said?

Herb looked into her beaming eyes and felt a tinge of guilt. After all, men didn't always mean what they said either. Hadn't he been the one to say how he loved ten nets, while in reality he wanted to play a more intimate game?

"Congratulations," he said wearily. "How about that lunch now? Nice cool melon?"

Holly ventured a coy smile, lowering her long green lashes. "Are you really hungry, Herb? I'm still so excited over winning the game, and hot, too!" She stroked a manicured hand across her bust line. "Before lunch, wouldn't you like to relax? Come back to my bungalow for a nice shower?"

A cold shower would be in order at the moment, Herb thought. What was going on now? He was beginning to warm up from more than the game.

"On second thought, no shower. Why don't we make use of that hot tub? I'm paying enough extra for it. It's cozy, but roomy enough for two," she said huskily.

Herb decided that the Party Grass Festival could wait another day. Maybe two.

Indeed, things finally were going right. This time Holly wasn't intoxicated on distilled water, but she was actually more ardent. The excitement of the ball game translated nicely into enthusiasm for the bedroom game as played in hot water, and Holly was a real delight.

"Too bad we didn't think to do this sooner," she murmured. "It's even more fun than balling!"

Herb didn't answer. His sentiments about timing were mixed. If only he had caught on to the key days ago . . .

Later that evening, Herb Moss was a mildly contented being. He'd reluctantly put Holly aboard the last transporter home. Her vacation was over, but she had left him with at least two nice memories.

There was nothing more for him at the resort, however. The time had come for him to move on. But not to the Party Grass Festival. Whatever he had been searching for was definitely not to be found in yet more places like Club Algae. The interlude with Holly had been fun, but he still wanted the elusive "more." It was time to go home.

Snuggling down within the cool cotton sheeting, he

drifted off to sleep with dreams of ten nets that were more like hot tubs, and a most accommodating Holly. He did not dream that in less than ten days he would become a pawn in a far deadlier game.

❧ 2 ❧

Secret

Spring was perplexed. "Father, you want me to what?" Magician Gabriel made an ineffective pacifying motion with his hands. "Just to help me test my equipment, my dear, as you have before."

"Your equipment is fine, father. Nothing's happened to it. Meanwhile, I have all these crystals to catalog. Can't your routine tests wait?"

Gabriel looked pained. "I don't think they can, dear. Something has, um, come up." His hands twisted together in the way they had when he was disturbed.

She looked sharply at him. "Father, is something wrong?"

"Oh, no, no, no, of course not, dear." But his hands continued to writhe.

Spring realized that she would have to humor him, and try to find out what was bothering him. She loved her father deeply, even if he did annoy her on occasion. "Of course I'll help," she said.

"Very good." He sounded relieved, though his hands

still quivered. "If you will just sit in the testing chair, and I will adjust the helmet—"

She didn't remind him that she was well familiar with the routine; she had occupied this chair many times before. She set aside her collection of crystals and took the seat. She looked around while he somewhat fumblingly adjusted the helmet and connections. It was important that her emotions be neutral while the monitors were being placed, or the baseline settings would be slightly wrong. So she pretended that she was a first time client, to whom this was a novelty, and ran her father's job description through her mind as if it were an announcement:

This was the office of the Magician Gabriel, one of Planet New Landers' more prestigious healing practitioners. Not only did he enjoy a thriving local practice and the respect of his peers, but he had recently received wide acclaim for his work in Crystallography from both magical and scientific communities. His name was becoming known over the planet, and many new patients were arriving for the special treatments they believed only he could provide. His was a most profitable practice, to say the least.

Given the present circumstances he should have been a happy man. But she knew he wasn't. Because his wife— oops. That would foul the setting for sure! So she carefully neutralized her thoughts again, thinking of pretty crystals, and soon he had things set.

"Now it is ready," he said unnecessarily. "Except for a blip when you thought a naughty thought." He forced a chuckle that only increased her concern. What *was* bothering him? It had to be pretty serious, for he was not a temperamental man. "If you will just recite some ancient history of a routine nature—"

So he hadn't completely zeroed it in yet, and needed

more ground neutral mental activity. Spring smiled, and re-cited the ancient canon, using a singsong voice:

"Lightships, Freezers, and Floaters faded in the sunlight of a former ultra-society that existed in those earliest of days when man had sown his seed from the Milky Way to the constellation Corona Borealis and beyond to galaxies now unknown."

"Very good," he said. "The registration is perfect. Continue."

Perfect? Then why did she need to do more mindless recitation? The equipment should not take this long to get tuned. But she smiled, and spoke the next paragraph of the standard history lesson. "Earth, renamed New World at that time, had one great Central Government, utilizing the finest combination of scientific minds available from all former nations. They banded together, achieving breakthrough after phenomenal breakthrough. That union was in many respects, more feared than the gargantuan military machine. For all their might, it was no secret that the real power of New World rested in the hands of the super scientists."

"Yes, yes, excellent, excellent," Gabriel said, wringing his hands again. "Just a bit more—"

"Father—" she started, allowing some annoyance to show in her tone, though it was really concern that motivated her.

"Oh, no, quite routine, quite routine, very good, no problem at all, just a tiny—a little—nothing to be concerned about, no need to inquire. Merely a trace aberration in the—the attunement. Don't be concerned."

Spring sighed mentally. She had *better* recite some more mind-numbing rote material, to calm her rising concern for her father's state of mental health.

"The entire island of what was once called Japan was designated as the NWSL, or New World Science Lab. It was so for several generations after the Great Migratory

Act was rigorously enforced. Separate countries ceased to exist. Mandatory integration throughout many centuries eliminated most physical racial differences as New World became one large Family of Man." She glanced at Gabriel again, covertly. He was watching the indicators so intently that she knew something was amiss. Had the equipment suffered a software virus infestation?

Rather than challenge him on this immediately, she continued the recitation, though her limit of tolerance was approaching. "Individualism was ostracized as differing cultures were assimilated into the whole, with none taking precedence above another. This did not come about from any ideal of brotherly love, but by decree from a firm dictatorship, determined in its zeal, that might would make right where morality had failed." Even as a child she had questioned that, though her classmates had seen nothing wrong with it. Thus she had become aware that she was different, intellectually, from ordinary children of New Landers, and not just because she was the daughter of the planet's leading magician. And there was the charged concept: magic was an accepted aspect of reality, but there were still those who looked askance at it, as if there were something wrong or strange about it. So she had felt the dawning isolation of her heritage.

But she preferred not to dwell on that, so she resumed the oration. "New World language became Unispeech, a simplified monophonic pattern of sounds based on mathematical equations. A child of three could communicate fluently in six weeks when aided by a computotech implant." She herself had learned to speak that way, of course, and had become mistress of many other disciplines similarly, thanks to equipment simpler than what they were testing right now. By the same token, there was nothing extraordinary about it, and there was no need for a prolonged testing session. She glanced yet again at Gabriel.

He remained fascinated by the indications. Enough was enough! "Father, something is amiss. I know it. What—?"

"No, no, no, please, please, no problem," he babbled, his hands threatening to twist their own fingers off. "Just a little more, and it's done, it's done."

So she yielded, one more time. "The average life span increased to approximately two hundred and sixty years. Most women waited well into their seventies to bear children, and a woman of fifty was as attractive as a young girl in ancient times. Thus, the planet did not populate more rapidly than before, and with the last phases of the Great Migration in progress, natural resources were replenished by discoveries on bountiful distant worlds." Of course the old technology had been mostly lost now, but lightships still transported beings to the more distant stars. Perhaps in a few more centuries the ancient techniques would be rediscovered; knowledge seemed to grow in patterns, ebbing and flowing in the tides of time.

But she had had enough of this. "Father, I demand to know what this is all about. Why are you so upset, and what does it have to do with this equipment? I won't recite another paragraph until you tell me."

"Quite all right, quite all right," he said, looking quite all wrong. "It's done now, and everything is in order. Now you must emigrate."

"Emigrate? What are you talking about? I have no intention of—"

"Please, we must be off immediately. Do you have your purse?"

"My purse! Father, girls haven't carried purses for centuries! What's this all about?"

"There should just be time to catch the last ship out. We must hurry."

Now she put her foot down, literally. "Father, I will not move one single solitary step until you tell me what is going on! What's wrong with the equipment? Why do I have to leave the planet I've always lived on? Why are you so disturbed? Look me straight in the face and answer."

He gazed at her. Then she saw something that completely unnerved her. His eyes were bright with tears. She had never before seen him like this. Something was terribly wrong.

"Very well," she said, shaken. "I will go, if you want me to. But please, father, tell me why."

"If I must," he said reluctantly. "But on the way to the lightport. Time is of the essence. I must dial a taxi."

"But why not use your own car?"

"I fear my private car could be under surveillance." He fumbled with the vidphone, but his hands were shaking so much that all that showed on the screen were the symbols for planets, numbers, and punctuation. It was as if the screen were swearing at him—which it was, in its way.

"I'll do it, father," Spring said, having mercy on him. She punched in the code for a rental portacar, immediate use. Then she took what she suddenly realized might be her last look around at the office, suffering a siege of nostalgia. She knew that Gabriel would never boot her out like this without compelling cause, and that she had given him no such cause. Something had happened, something awful.

Then they hurried out to the arriving taxi and piled in. She was about to touch the LIGHTPORT symbol on the panel, but he stayed her hand; "Random course," he said.

So she closed her eyes and touched a button blindly. The vehicle lifted and flew across the surface of the planet, going nowhere she cared about.

"Now tell me," she said. She had known the research they were doing was highly secret and probably dangerous, but most of the time she had not understood anything beyond the surface procedures he gave her to complete.

"Until this day, I have not felt it necessary to reveal the entire truth of the project to you," he said. "Now I fear I must, with deepest regret. Do you remember Zygote?"

"Zygote! He's involved with this?" The mysterious magician named Zygote had been coming around to speak with her father, but she was never allowed to remain during their discourse. She knew that he was no friend by the loud voices emanating from the lab. Whenever she questioned her father about him, he had told her not to be concerned, that it was only professional disagreement. Yet, when she had been alone with Zygote during times her father was detained with a client, he had shown an uncommon interest in her personal life that made her flesh crawl.

Once, during one of those unfortunate times, Zygote had pressed the limits of her patience. Though he had not said it in so many words, she was certain he was trying to discover whether she was a virgin! Small difference that could have made to him; he was her father's age, but resembled Gabriel in no other way, aside from the power of his magic. He struck her as malignant, not benign. The very notion of those long, swarthy fingers touching her made Spring recoil with disgust.

It was not that he was ugly or so old, for she did not regard her father as ancient; in fact mature men could be quite interesting. Though Zygote was neither handsome nor young, he had a charm that would appeal to most women. No, it was just an uncomfortable feeling that she got whenever near him. He was not a man to be trusted, of that she was certain. She couldn't imagine the nature of business her parent could possibly have with such a creature, and was doubly careful to make herself scarce when he appeared thereafter.

Gabriel had given her time to reflect. Now he changed the car's route again, randomly. "Yes, unfortunately. He is very much involved, and your suspicions of him are amply justified. He seeks power for its own sake, without regard to the harm it may do. And I have found a key to power. What I have discovered has the potential for tremendous mischief in the wrong hands, and I have no intention of allowing Zygote to obtain the information."

"Well, of course not," Spring agreed emphatically. "What is this thing, father?"

Gabriel shook his head. "I have no time to elaborate on the actual nature of the information, but it is the gate to great riches, absolute power, and forbidden knowledge. Reason enough for any number of ambitious, would-be tyrants to become interested in my project."

"Such as Zygote," she agreed. "But how does this concern me? I know nothing of it."

Gabriel's smile was chillingly compassionate. "You do know it, my dear—and you do not. That is your secret."

"Father, I assure you I haven't snooped on your—"

"Spring, I have used you, perhaps more cruelly than any man could have. I used a magically enhanced form of hypnotic spell to project secret information too sensitive for my files into your subconscious mind. It now contains the awesome knowledge which will activate only under certain conditions. Brainwashing or other forms of extortion will not gain access to the secrets, though they would most likely leave you mindless. You will not be aware of the buried knowledge at any time, as I feel the burden is too great."

"I have the secret to absolute power?" she asked, dazed. "But if it can never be revealed, even to me, what's the point?"

"There are two ways to release the secrets. Either I could say a code spell that would trigger a transference, or someone else could receive the information another way."

"Another way? How?"

"It, ah, um, I, that is to say—"

"Out with it, father! I need to know."

Gabriel struggled to voice the concept. "When you find a suitable young man, and are interested in, er, in a manner of speaking—"

"What are you trying to say, father?"

"When a young man and a young woman, the bees and the birds, romance—"

"What does love have to do with it?"

Gabriel made a supreme effort. "The secrets will activate and transfer telepathically to your partner when you make love for the first time."

Spring was shocked. "Carnal knowledge?"

Gabriel blushed. "Very nicely put. But, knowing you, I feel confident with this safeguard."

"Because you suppose I'm too unattractive ever to get that close to a man?" she demanded indignantly. "Thank you so much, father!"

"Oh, no no, no, Spring, no!" he protested, flustered. "I believe you are supremely attractive! It's that I trust your judgment. I did not do this without some long and careful thought. If anyone but myself is to activate the secret, it must only be by the permission of my most trusted daughter."

Suddenly Spring understood Zygote's attentions. It was not her body he was interested in, but her mind. Or rather the secrets it contained. Somehow Zygote had discovered she was the key. If he caught her away from the protection of her father, it was doubtful he would be gentle in his extraction.

"And now you fear that Zygote will try to kidnap me," she said, not even phrasing it as a question.

"Yes. I have reason to believe he intends to strike soon. Therefore I must hide you, until this threat has passed."

It did make sense. "Where am I going?"

"I would prefer that you not know, until you are actually aboard the ship. That should help protect your location from discovery."

That, too, made sense. So she let it be. But as they zipped randomly in to the lightport, she inquired about one other thing. "Why all the business with the equipment, today?"

"I was verifying that the information remains in place, together with its guardian routines. My equipment will no longer access the information itself, but does attune to certain marker keys I implanted. They are all in order. I had to be sure that no error had developed, no unprogrammed access. I am only approximately pleased that all remains in order, because of the threat to you it represents."

"I'm like a bomb wired to detonate if anyone tries to disarm it," she said with a wry smile.

"An unfortunately apt analogy." Then he kissed her, and she saw the tears in his eyes again as he gave her the coded ticket. "I hope that some year you can forgive me for what I have done to you."

"Of course I forgive you, father! I would have done anything you asked to be of help in your quest. I know it is all you have lived for since my mother's passing." She knew of the circumstances, yet still felt an unreasonable guilt as the destroyer of their happiness. She had always hoped he would find another woman to replace his loss, but he had not, saying there had been only one such as she. Spring found that touching and hoped to one day be as fortunate. To find that one true love, as he had felt he had in his Laurel.

That would have to wait, now. Perhaps forever. "Beware of whom you trust," her father warned. "Zygote's spies are everywhere, and they will stop at nothing." She promised to be alert, and then they embraced, saying a last farewell until they met again. But she feared that was not to be.

Nevertheless, she held her chin high as she entered the port and boarded the ship whose code matched that of the ticket. No one would know that her heart was breaking.

❦ 3 ❦

Sharing

T housands of solar years after the Age of Light, and for as many more before the descent of the Great Darkness, in those wondrous days when men traversed the distant galaxies, not in spaceships, but as one with the energy of light itself, was P#23 born!"

Thus spoke the ancient Vinese Elder, his vines trembling both with age and pious fervor as the rapt congregation of Vinese, Treeple, and Veganoids clung, boughed, or knelt respectfully in separate rows.

The sacred sowing season was upon them, and it was on Founder's Day at sunrise that the most holy of all the spring rites were performed. On that day alone did all three species of intelligent life inhabiting the small planetoid come together, leaving the temples of their diverse denominations to meet in the Great Hall on common ground. There, ethnic, cultural, and personal differences were put aside as all gathered as one for the Sharing.

The Great Hall, a huge outdoor temple, was resplendent with fragrant spring foliage and blossoms. The sandalwood trees exuded a musky scent while the muted sound of reeds played lightly on the breeze. It was truly a majestic and inspirational setting for the most hallowed of days.

Herb Moss squirmed in his secluded spot on the fifty-third row. He hoped neither Elder nor fellow worshiper would notice, but the truth was he had been kneeling in one position for so long that his knees were asleep. It was hard to concentrate on lofty matters of the Light with tingling joints. But that was only one of his problems.

Herb regarded himself as an ordinary Veganoid and was not particularly religious. He felt awkward as always when suffered to attend these days of commitment. First came the interminable sermon, The Reminder, hailing the Founder and recounting the long history of their small planetoid. The sacred rites of Renewal followed. Another long and clinging ceremony.

It was not that he was a disbeliever. On the contrary, he had much respect for the Founder. It was these organized theological pantomimes he objected to, with their rigid, greener-than-thou attitudes. Let each grow in his own way! That was Herb's motto. And at Herb's age, spring after spring, it was all worn soil by now. He could quote the history of his home planet by rote.

Herb ceased pondering his beginnings as a young Treeple passed cups down his row for the Sharing ceremony. He accepted his, observing a bunchy Vinese female as she rolled to the pulpit. The rite of Rebirth was about to begin.

The Elder extended his vines, assisting her onto the hard earthen mound, and then led the faithful in the first of the traditional chants.

"Praise the Light! The Light is life!" He opened his leaves in acceptance as the congregation mimicked the gesture, repeating the chant in unison.

The Elder raised the cup and poured the clear cool liquid over the tender leaves of the female.

"Praise the Water!" he began. "Water is life!"

The female quivered with emotion, her blossoms losing a few soft petals. She was in full bloom, as was the proper state for the ceremony.

The congregation deposited their cups over their foliage in like manner as all chanted away. Herb hoped no one had seen him as he quaffed his down instead. He was terribly thirsty.

Reaching into the earthen mound, the Elder gathered and threw a scoop of soil onto the female's roots, signifying growth.

"Praise the Soil!" chanted the believers, dipping their own limbs into the tilled rows before them.

At last the Elder reached into the center of the Vinese female's foliage, clipping gently with his shears. He held the tender green cutting up for the congregation to admire. It was a strong and healthy shoot. Carefully, he placed the cutting into the soil, poured water, and extended the Founder's Day blessing, "Grow and flourish!"

The ceremony ended with an invocation, and many went forward, reaffirming their belief. At last it was over.

"Amen," said Herb, slapping his thighs in an attempt to bring life back into his aching limbs. Growing pains were nothing compared to this!

Yet Herb was glad he had observed the rites. They were a pain in the nether section, but they did serve to refresh his heritage. But for an unusual series of past events, his kind would not exist. It was proper to appreciate this.

Just previous to the forming of the Human Conception, as it was dubbed by the devotees, Dr. Ni Gell, one of New World's foremost genetic programmers, made a tremendous breakthrough by creating intelligent life hitherto believed impossible: the successful grafting of plant and animal tissue.

The doctor believed the new form could possibly inhabit those planets with a large carbon dioxide–based atmosphere. With time, the new life would flourish, giving out sufficient amounts of its waste, oxygen, to transform the environment, eventually changing the inherent atmosphere of such planets to a breathable ratio for Earthlings. Herb had only an elementary grasp of the theory, but it had been hoped that the forms would adapt through evolution, and in that way open new worlds to future generations.

It was a long-term project at best, but one considered feasible enough to gain support from Central. When words of the NWSL experiment leaked out, however, Humanite followers screamed heresy, denouncing NWSL and the doctor as a vile blasphemer. But Dr. Ni Gell did deserve credit. If not for his lone sacrifice, Paradise would be just another green ball in space.

After the return of the other humans to New World, only Gell had remained to carry on. The few plant/humanoid mutations he had successfully developed which had somehow managed to survive the terrible blight, served as his assistants and companions.

Without a fresh supply of cells, for all the inventory had been stripped and returned along with the other scientists, he had been forced to use the only tissue available to him: that of his own body. He had feared, after deliberately contracting the blight, what such contamination would mean for the future strain.

He need not have. Miraculously, his cells when injected into a living mutation proved to be the very vaccine he needed to exact a cure. By reinjecting those same cells into himself, he was able to arrest its progress for longer periods of time, though never achieving a total cure upon his human system.

Years later at the time of his death, he had left prototypes of sufficient health and intelligence to carry on his work. His greatest contribution, however, was of a more personal nature. He had taken one of the female prototypes as a companion and she had successfully born him a son. Spiritually and physically he was truly the father of them all.

Eventually, three main intelligent offshoots came to inhabit the green sphere: Treeples, Vinese, and Veganoids such as Herb.

Treeples were of a dark wooden hue, with supple bark-textured skin. Their general appearance was that of a young maple, with eight branches spreading above a face which was inset into the upper portion of the trunk. Leafy branches served the same purpose as arms, and twigs as fingers. From a distance the foliage gave the appearance of a great head of hair towering above the small face.

Their trunks were divided into two sections for legs beneath the torso, allowing for upright locomotion on a strong root foundation, the equivalent of human feet. Females grew small mounds approximating human breasts, which contained sap during gestation or arousal. Depending from which branch they descended, Treeples reproduced by cuttings, buds, or seeds.

Vinese had the least overt human properties of the three species, resembling a large green tumbleweed. Hundreds of leafy vine tendrils grew from a round ball body, covering it completely. They moved by rolling, clinging, or climbing, spoke from an elongated mouth tube in the upper region of their sphere, and peeped out through narrow slits of golden eyes.

Male and female Vinese had the same overall appearance except during gestation, when the female blossomed. They reproduced by the sole method of cuttings.

Veganoids like Herb most resembled their human ancestors, following the normal human pattern except for a few modifications. While Veganoids had human skin, it was a pleasing shade of green, as was their hair which grew to great lengths in both sexes, but usually kept trimmed to ear level by the males. Some females let it twine to their ankles, but this was uncommon, since it was impractical to care for. There were other differences as well. For example, fingers and toes could extend to root into the soil for energy in case of emergency. This was a throwback to the time before their kind had evolved into the human habit of eating rather than absorption.

Herb's predecessors had been equipped to pollinate in much the same fashion that insects pollinate flowers. It was a short cut to bypass a missing element, for there were no insects on Paradise at that time. Until NWSL introduced new varieties, plants depended upon the winds to carry drifting seeds.

In those days, the prototype ate by absorbing nourishment from the soil and procreated by means of a retractable stamen in the mouth. Through years of experimentation and evolution, the sexual function came to be served by a fleshy root located in the usual human region. Veganoids still had the stamen, though it came to be considerably smaller and located far back in the upper roof of the mouth. It was employed only under certain questionable conditions, and was no longer capable of reproductive qualities. Otherwise, Veganoids had standard mouth equipment, and consumed nonsapient vegetable matter.

Female Veganoids were also cut from the general pattern of their human ancestors, with the same inherent differences. Female sex receptacles were positioned in the proper junction of the legs, but opened like the blossom of a lovely flower when aroused. Naturally they did not possess the stamen; that was strictly a male property.

And so Herb had been strongly reminded again of the

origin of his subspecies. The ceremony bored him, but it did instill in him the pride of being a Veganoid. Surely his kind represented the best attributes of both animal and plant.

The ceremony having concluded, Herb moved slowly along with the departing throng toward the exits. A smaller figure stepped quickly, pushing through the crowd toward him.

"Herb! Herb Moss!"

He turned to see who had called out his name, and felt a dainty female hand caress his arm. It was Lily, a sweet blossom, but a rather strong-willed young Veganette. They had been childhood friends, growing up together, and later keeping close company for several seasons as prospective union mates. All their friends and family had naturally assumed they would eventually put down roots together, but Herb had not been ready for a permanent commitment.

He had left the parental garden to go out on his own to grow up a bit. He was hardly the green sprout she had known, yet he realized how he must have hurt her with his abrupt departure. He did not regret leaving, but knew he could have let her down more softly. He had departed without any goodbye, simply because it was easier that way.

Time had not changed much. He was still at a loss for words, but a confrontation could not be avoided this time. The least he could do was try to explain why he had done it. Of course, that might prove as difficult. At the moment, he was not sure he understood it himself.

They walked out through the rock gardens beside the Hall for a short while in silence.

"Herb—"

"Lily—"

They had spoken in unison, then laughed nervously together.

"Please, you first!" said Herb, gesturing for her to speak. At least she had something to say, perhaps.

Lily looked up at him, nervously twisting a leaf of her woven skirt in her hands. It was the custom of Founder's Day to dress in natural fibers. Herb had compromised with a grass shirt over cotton trousers.

"I was surprised to see you in the Hall, Herb. It has been half a season. Of course, I am glad to see you again."

Had it been so short a time? It seemed much longer to Herb. A lifetime since they had been this close. Physically, yes, but emotionally he suspected they were as far apart as ever. If he should reach for her now, would she intertwine or pull back? Did absence make the heart grow fonder? Or only wiser?

Herb found he was too much the coward to test it. Without moving he sensed the invisible barrier that was still there, holding him at arm's length. Was it worth it? He could not look directly at her, but concentrated upon the patterns of the rocks. If he met her gaze, he was afraid he would still want to tear down the barrier, and doubted he had the strength for the siege. The quiet of the moment seemed to roar in his ears.

She was waiting for him to say something. "The Sharing," he said.

"Ah yes. Obligatory attendance. Otherwise you would not have returned." It was a statement, not a question.

Herb colored. He knew it was true. He would not have returned home this soon just for Lily. It was the timing that seemed right. She had not come into it. But he did not want to hurt her feelings, so he said nothing at all.

"You weren't always so reticent, Herb. I can remember when you had quite a bit to say on the subject of you and I. But to go without a word! I kept believing that I would hear from you day after day, but eventually I saw the light."

She had almost exploded in her sudden vehemence. Then abruptly, in a softer tone, almost a whisper, she asked, "Why, Herb? Why did we grow apart?"

Herb felt a rush of anger toward her for making him the villain. He wanted to hurt her back. "How can I explain it to you, Lily? I felt stunted! I couldn't go on seeing you as things stood. You wanted roots, a unionized status. I wasn't ready for that then."

"And now?" Lily said, green tears gathering at the edge of her eyes. "You have been away to see more of the sphere, to encounter new varieties, to taste strange nectar. Tell me, in all your travels, was there ever a quiet moment when you contemplated our situation? No, I suppose you were much too busy to—"

Lily stopped speaking as Herb suddenly shook her. "Stop it!" he snapped. "Of course I thought about us! That's all I thought about. That, and my life here. Where it was all leading. Frankly, I didn't like what I saw."

Lily had composed herself somewhat. "But Herb, all young men have doubts. It's a natural part of the growth process. You can't just pull up and leave each time things aren't the way you imagine they should be."

"I know. That's the reason I've returned." He rubbed a hand across his forehead. He was getting a headache. He hadn't had one since—since the last time he saw Lily, as a matter of fact.

"Oh Herb, let's forget all this foolishness. Why don't we see each other again, and go from there? I know it will be better this time."

She was grasping at straws. Herb hated seeing her this way, doing this to him and herself. Yet he couldn't walk away. She meant more than that. He suddenly realized his anger had been directed toward himself, not at her. Perhaps it always had been. Lily was a lifelong friend. She was a wonderful girl, and he was undoubtedly some breed of locoweed for turning down her offer. But something about their proposed union had never grown quite true. He wanted to care for her as much as she obviously did for him, but he simply didn't.

Looking away, Lily asked, "Is it someone else, Herb?" She paused. "Or was it because I don't believe in preunion pollination?"

"No!" Herb quickly replied, taken aback. "I respected your feeling about that. I still do. And, in answer to your question, no, there is no one else. I am still unready to plant a commitment with you. Or with anyone."

The tears sat in the corner of her eyes, but did not run. They caught the morning light and sparkled like sad emeralds.

"I still work at the Mothers Day Nursery, Herb. If you should wish to speak with me about anything, well, you know where to reach me."

With that, she turned and walked swiftly away, then stopped short and called back over her shoulder without looking.

"Grow and flourish!"

It was the Founder's Day blessing. "Grow and flourish!" Herb returned as she disappeared around the corner. He suspected that she had not turned because she didn't want him to see that her tears were now falling. Indeed, he had hurt her, and she didn't deserve it. He felt like a ripe stinkweed.

❧ 4. ❧

Gabriel's Trump

Gabriel was depressed as he returned to his office. He loved Spring as he had loved no other since Laurel, yet he had had to send her away, and he doubted that he would ever see her dear face again. But there was nothing to be done about that, so he did his best to distract himself with sedate thoughts about his profession. The alternative would be to brood on the likely disaster he feared was coming, and that was pointless.

After the setback of the Great Darkness had isolated so many worlds of the galaxy, recovery had been sporadic and uncertain. The new order, as it gradually emerged, was not the same as the older order. Science had not sufficed to maintain civilization; now a number of disciplines of magic buttressed it. Thus, the current scene had spaceships and sorcery, in a sometimes uneasy association.

Medicine had advanced once again to a comforting level, but the occult arts had also achieved a new status, being revered by the general society as much or more as science. Both such establishments often existed side by side with equal respectability, as many of the planets regarded the ancient practices a science in their own right. Many wondrous works were performed that could not be explained away by the strict scientific standards of the past, and what cannot be readily explained must necessarily be magic.

Astral projection tours were conducted for those adventurous enough to crave something beyond mere planetary travel. Channeling and reincarnations clinics were available for others interested in genealogical research. There were any number of Forecast centers which dealt with the fundamental teachings of tarot, I Ching, palmistry, handwriting analysis, astrology, numerology, and all the lesser divinations. This did not include foreign institutes specializing in Egyptian magic, Celtic Runes, Voodoo, and alien based future castings so numerous and obscure that it would be impossible for any student to become proficient with more than a few.

Schools of Witchcraft were also in evidence on a few planets, but not as popular as they used to be with the new spoilsport galactic regulations forbidding sacrifice, human or alien. Most of the so-called "old religion" establishments were now more cultural than magical in nature. Of course, there were stories of unexplained disappearances, but none had been directly linked to known witchcraft universities. There was one planet said to "overlook" many of the regulations, but it was not a member of the Galactic League and therefore not open for visitation by the general public.

Within the circle of healing artists were White Witches, herbalists, yogis, visualists, color therapists, mentalists, experts in all fields of meditation, and psychics. Medical men often relied upon the mystical powers of these healers as backup for harmonizing the physical and mental balance of their patients. The mind/body connection was an established fact, and often was the thin line between death and recovery. MD stood as often for Magical as Medical Doctor. No longer were such ideas or their proponents considered to be lunatics. It was an era of free belief.

He arrived at the office, and stepped out of the cab. The charge for his travels would be debited from his account. With luck, no enemy would have spied the particular destination, or realized that his daughter had not returned with him. Above all, he wanted her to be safe, and not just because of the precious information she carried.

It was no longer safe for Spring to remain with him on New Landers, so he had decided to send her away to New Moon where she would be cloistered among the secluded Companions of Comfort Society. They were a peaceful female meditation order, located in a remote sector of the Moon known as the Crater Tycho. She was to travel there by a roundabout route under an assumed identity. He hoped it would be the last place Zygote would ever think to look for her.

Gabriel didn't know how much Zygote had learned about Spring's involvement, or how much he only guessed, but it would hardly be in his best interests to spread his suspicions. No, if anyone was searching for Spring, it was only Zygote, he was certain. One formidable enemy was more than sufficient, however.

Gabriel regretted having used her at all, but in the event something should happen to him, he needed to be certain that she would have the information. It was his legacy to her. Now that word had leaked out, all he could do was attempt to protect her and hope that she would come to forgive him one day. Of course she had said she had forgiven him already, but that was her sweet impulse; she had not yet fully appreciated the gravity of what he had done to her.

He looked warily around, but saw no sign of intrusion. But surely it was coming. He had been afraid that it would strike before he managed to get Spring clear; his arts had shown its malign incipience. Now all he had to do was await its arrival. Meanwhile he would continue business as usual, so as to pretend that he suspected nothing. He resumed his musings.

Some planets were freer than others, naturally, and it was the wide diversity of cultures and faiths which made travel in this age so rich an experience. New Landers was a pleasant planet, with strong, Old World roots. It had been inhabited by a conservative group of Free Thinkers following the great purge on New World. They brought some of their radical democratic ideals to their new home and they had stood well against the test of time.

Fair Dale was an average small metropolis. It had a centralized downtown district with shops and public establishments, surrounded by a wide scattering of homes and farms. New Landers was one of several planets in orbit around one central sun, with a rotation time providing approximately thirty-hour days. Seven or eight were spent working, and the remainder used for sleep and recreation. Not so different from the old Earth days. Earth, or rather New World, was of course now little more than a grey molten cinder.

His residence was nice enough. At Number Thirty Bay Lane the early morning sunlight filtered down through the stained glass windows in colored beams. They reflected softly off sparkling clusters of amethyst and quartz, causing multicolored dots to dance around the bare walls.

Shelves filled with clear dishes contained sprinkles and chips of jaspers, sapphires, agate, and garnet. Darker col-

ors of onyx, turquoise, and emerald shone with a rich lus-
ter in shallow trays on the table. Soft pouches with more
precious stones were hidden from sight in a wall safe.

But now he couldn't stop the personal memories. Well,
perhaps it was time to indulge himself, for even the painful
ones were precious in their way.

Gabriel's wife had died in childbirth less than two
decades before; a rare occurrence even then. Although he
had known many satisfactory liaisons with beautiful and
accommodating companions, he had yet to find her like.

Even so, he had been content with his life; he enjoyed
his chosen practice, and doted upon his only child, Spring.
Less generous men might have felt ill disposed toward such
bitter fruit, blaming the child for the demise of the mother,
but he had a firm grasp of reality.

His wife Laurel had been a beautiful but delicate girl.
The doctors had advised them against having children,
fearing for her health. Yet, so great had been Laurel's desire to bear a child that she had foregone her birth control
prescription and become pregnant. Even then, it could
have been aborted, but she had willingly chosen to risk her
own life in the hope that it might live. Gabriel loved her too
much to stand in the way of her decision, and agreed to
gamble against the odds. In the end, they had lost, for Laurel had not the strength, and he was left with Spring. To
disown such a gift would have been to disown Laurel and
their love as well. That he would never do.

Gabriel did the best he could to bestow enough love for
the both of them upon his motherless child, and he could
honestly say that he'd never found cause for regret. He
had taken in Tete, a native of Vertro, as housekeeper and
nanny for Spring. She had remained with the family until
Spring's thirteenth birthday, when she decided it was time
to retire and return to her home planet to have a litter of
her own. Tete's kind were an intelligent race of lovable

teddy bear creatures. They were understandably popular for positions in the child rearing field.

When she left, Gabriel decided he was sufficient to the task of raising his daughter alone. Spring never ceased to be a joy to him, though he was still uncertain if he had raised her or the other way around. She was ever a precocious child and had stepped in to help out almost as soon as she could walk. At the age of five, she took a serious interest in her father's work with the crystals. The colors and sparkles fascinated her so that she could not learn fast enough. By ten, she was capable of reading the chakras with surprising insight, and could select exactly the right gem to prescribe for most ills.

Yet, as complete as was her understanding of the stones, her greatest talent lay in a different field as an herbalist. That had been her mother's great love. Spring had discovered Laurel's thick book of pressed leaves and flowers and began to make a deep study of herb medicine and botany. There was hardly a plant in the League of Planets she could not now identify at a glance. When she was fourteen, she had set up a small corner area in Gabriel's shop with vials of dried herbs she had gathered and prepared herself, and soon had her own loyal clientele.

Gabriel had joked that she was stealing his patients away. Spring protested it was nothing against the crystals, but only a supplemental help for the most difficult cases. So serious, so loyal, even then. What a treasure!

When Gabriel began to delve deeper into his metaphysical studies with the crystals, she had been an able research assistant, working long hours without a murmur of complaint. He was well aware he owed much of his progress to her devotion.

Now he pondered his wisdom regarding his daughter. Were those pangs of guilt he felt for not insisting she get out more with young people of her own age? A bit late, if so. He knew he should have encouraged her to enjoy her youth more, to have been less serious, more carefree, to see young men more often. She was not too young to think of marriage. Oh, he knew that marriage was an antiquated custom on many planets these days, but it was still alive and well on New Landers, and he was thankful for that.

His short but precious union with Laurel had meant quite a lot to him through the years, and he was certain Spring would feel the same once she had found the proper young man. Whenever he had broached the subject, however, she usually laughed in that impish way she had, and said he was the only man in her life that mattered. That she had lots of time for that later on.

No, Gabriel had not encouraged her, and he regretted that now. Didn't it please him to have a devoted and lovely daughter by his side? Didn't she honestly enjoy the work they did together? And time did not go on forever. Who should know that better than he? He had been so intent on perfecting his discovery that it soon became all he could think about. He had referred many of his patients to an associate, to give more time to his research and it had paid off. He had discovered a way to tap secrets from the crystals, secrets that could change the world.

Cursed secrets! If he had only seen where it was leading, had only known then what it would mean for them now, he would have done many things differently. Would he not? Would he not? That question frightened him, for he still was not certain of the answer.

Lovely Spring! She was the very image of her mother at the same age; lithe and small with soft amber tresses that turned golden in the sunlight. He missed her immensely, his lovely shadow. But the secret—now that Zygote's spies were beneath each rock, behind every tree, she was far and away safer where she was. Spring's wellbeing was all that was important to him now. He could not bear to lose her as well. It would be like losing Laurel, all over again.

Gabriel reached for a small piece of polished lepidolite and pressed the cool ridged surface against the proper chakra, hoping to restore some peace to his nerves before the next client arrived.

Looking down his list of appointments, he proceeded to assemble the necessary stones and wands he would shortly be using. This was a sad case. A young man traumatized by a Turbocar accident. Those vehicles were dangerous and should be recalled, in his opinion. Both the client's parents had been killed instantly, but he had escaped unharmed, physically. Emotionally, it was another matter. It would be a long road back for him. A complete cleaning would be called for, followed by daily visualization. Gabriel wished Spring were there to consult about some medicinal teas to relax him, but he could probably find some mention of them in her record book.

He set out the cleansing stones, then selected several others. Red jasper should improve the immune system, jade would help dispel negativity, a moonstone for calming, and rose quartz for love. That young man would have to learn to love himself again; grief and guilt were terrible burdens for one so young to bear. For anyone to bear. Gabriel paused, remembering.

As he held the chunk of pink quartz in his palm, his thoughts returned to a day not so long ago when he had commissioned a jeweler to carve an especially fine piece into a heart shape to be mounted and hung on a golden chain for Spring's sixteenth birthday. She was so delighted, and had sworn never to take it off. She had been wearing it today.

Gabriel started in surprise to hear the door chimes ring

so soon. The client was early. Laying aside the quartz, he paused long enough to pull on his silk robes and adjust the golden half-framed glasses upon his nose. He took time to survey his appearance in the mirror.

He was an imposing figure with his six foot frame, and touches of grey at the temples. Even at his age, he could turn a lady's head for a second glance. Clients tended to respond better when he was properly attired for their sessions. So much of healing depended upon faith, and they felt a doctor should look like a doctor and a magician should look like a magician. He did indeed look every inch the magician.

Parting the inside curtains, he went out into the front of the shop to unlock the door. It was not his girl's regular day off, but she had called in claiming illness. He had offered to help, but she assured him it was a mundane problem best looked after with bed rest. He deduced it was most likely her time of the month and did not press for details. Since his schedule was lighter these days, he had decided not to cancel any appointments. He was capable of opening a few doors by himself, after all.

Gabriel reached for the lever and swung open the door. He was immediately hurled across the room into his secretary's work station, knocking off most of the contents and overturning a large potted plant.

His glasses went flying from his face, lost in the action, and he winced from a sharp stabbing pain in his left side where his body had violently connected with the corner of the desk. He had just enough time to orient on his attacker before going down. It was gratifying to know it was not his client, but shocking to see the hulking form of a huge yellow Martian amazon crouched above him.

The woman gripped him at the collar and yanked upward, slapping him hard across his face with the back of her free hand. It was the size of a ham, and felt like a rock.

Martian females were no dainty breed, but the dominant sex on their home turf. No strangers to physical violence, they easily kept their less robust men in line. The Men's Liberation League had sent emissaries to Mars for several years, but to no avail. At least that was the conclusion, since none had ever returned. Such events were the subject of crude jokes, but it was hard to see the humor in his present situation.

Gabriel's head was ringing from the savage blow as he slumped down thankfully into the seat where she had flung him. His sight was bleary from more than the loss of his spectacles, but he finally made out that his assailant was not alone. Standing behind her were two more foggy forms, one tall and angular, the other smaller, almost effeminate. He hardly needed much vision to recognize that nefarious pair. It was the mad Magician Zygote, and his strange Ki companion, Elton.

"Zygote," Gabriel said slowly, trying to focus. "Welcome to my establishment. You must excuse me if I don't rise." He wiped away a trickle of blood from his split lip, his expression feigning apology.

"We will soon cure you of your insolence, Professor Gabriel," whined the small young man beside Zygote. It was, of course, presumptuous to refer to Elton as a man. He/she/it was neither, being a Ki. Kis were multisexed, being capable of mating with male or female or most alien species. They were simply whatever they wished, and adapted accordingly. Since Elton had dressed in male attire when Gabriel had met "him," he tended to regard the Ki as male for convenience of reference.

Elton's facial features were rather neuter as well; what one might describe as sensitive. That was delusion, of course, for there was no sensitivity in the distorted creature as he addressed Gabriel. He accented the magician's name as if it were a slur of the vilest sort. It was not hard to imagine the nature of service he performed for his master.

"Never mind, Elton," Zygote said. "I'm sure the good doctor realizes this is not a social call." He pulled out a folder from the inside of his robe and held it up for Gabriel to view. "Does this look familiar to you, Doctor?"

Gabriel stared back in stunned horror. It bore his personal seal. "Where—where did you get that?" he gasped. His private research papers, kept in his secret files under lock and key and protected by a confidence spell of the strongest potency. No one could have possibly gotten in unless they knew the magic code. Debubrah? He had trusted her implicitly.

"Yes, I see you've figured it out already, Doctor," Zygote said. "Your little secretary. But she's off today, isn't she? Shopping, I imagine. Bribery is so old fashioned, but still effective. She wasn't cheap, you know. Still, I tend to believe it was the love spell that did it. Young women remain romantics at heart, despite their independence, don't you agree?"

Elton snorted in derision. Zygote, suddenly bored with light conversation, spoke coldly. "But enough small talk, Doctor. You know why we're here, and what we want."

Gabriel sighed with the resignation of a man who knows what he says is not going to be popular. "You won't get it."

Zygote raised a brow quizzically. "Oh? I think I shall." He nodded to the Martian who had been glowering none too patiently in the corner. Now her face contorted in a smile, exposing ugly yellowed teeth, a healthy color for her kind.

"Augah!" she snarled, moving in. Conversation was not her forte either. She obviously adhered to the maxim that actions spoke louder than words.

The sounds of hard brutal punches rang out clearly in the quiet office. They drowned out the sharp words of Zygote, or perhaps it was Elton, as all sounds became garbled to Gabriel after a few moments. All that was left was the pain.

Gabriel was no longer a young man, nor was he well. When the giantess reluctantly ceased her battering, he lay limp and bleeding across the cold surface of the office floor. His breathing came in shallow, painful rasps as he tried to speak.

"Zygote—my heart. Can't take this," he said, clutching at his chest. "My medication. In the cabinet in my office. Green label."

"Get them!" Zygote snapped to Elton.

"No, make him talk first," Elton said sadistically.

"Get them!" repeated Zygote. "He can't say anything if he dies, you imbecile!"

Elton sulked off into the other room and returned with the bottle which he flipped to the prone magician. Gabriel fumbled with the cap and finally managed to slide one tablet beneath his tongue.

"Feeling better, I trust, Doctor?" asked Zygote. "This sort of violence appalls me. I am a physician, too, you know. Come, give me the information and we can surely work something out like civilized beings. There is enough in this for both of us. We can work together."

Gabriel eyed Zygote contemptuously, if blearily. "You shall never have the Secret. Never!" The blood had gathered in his throat, forcing him to cough violently. He tried to stand, but slid back down the wall, closing his eyes against the pain. Then, realizing that there could be no compromise with such ilk, he played his trump. He swallowed the rest of the pills. It was a relief. The pain faded, leaving only his hearing, for a while.

"Talk, you doddering old fool!" Elton screamed, kicking

him viciously in the rib cage with his pointed shoes. "I can make you talk!"

Zygote gave an exasperated sigh and shut his eyes momentarily before glaring at his companion. "I seriously doubt that, Elton," he said dryly. "This man is dead."

❧ 5 ❧

Polli Parlour

$\mathcal{H}$erb had been wandering aimlessly, trying to focus his swirling thoughts into a coherent pattern. The encounter with Lily at the Hall still weighed heavily on his mind. He wondered if he would find himself returning to her to propose a union after all? All this time that he had been so certain that it was over between them, Lily had been patiently biding her time, not giving up on him.

Herb began to lose conviction. Seeing her again had triggered a chain reaction. See Lily, want Lily. There had been a time he had not thought her so unsuitable. Even though he had been the one to transplant, deep down he knew she would be waiting should he decide to commit. Not fair, but true. Was that the real reason he had never officially ended it? Had he wanted her to wait?

From their last conversation, it was plain the door was wide open, the ground still fertile. Lily was a nice girl. Perhaps too nice for her own good. Herb would choose to remain friends, but knew in his heart that was impossible. Lily was a union-or-nothing girl.

Herb felt suddenly lonely. It was growing late. The tri-moons were rising. He had been walking without noticing where his feet had taken him. It had seemed important only to keep moving. Now as he turned the corner, he saw it was one of several streets in a seedy part of town. Potted plants leaned against doorways of disreputable establishments or sat along the curbs talking to each other. One specimen came toward Herb from the opposite direction, wobbling uneasily on his feet, and reeled into him as he passed.

"Par'n me—" he slurred, weaving drunkenly onward.

Herb moved aside to give him ample passing space, then continued on. As he approached one of the local polli parlours, a top heavy female Treeple boldly beckoned with her branches and called out to him.

"Evening greetings, Sugarcane. Come on in." Her leaves waved most enticingly.

Herb paused, amused, but shook his head. He had never been inside one of those places, considering them a haunt of last resort for males unable to satisfy their needs within normal relationships.

"Oh, come on. Don't be so shy," she coaxed. "There's a free show inside, and you don't have to spend a scent. Costs nothing to look." She stuck out her mounds, which were blatantly outlined beneath the tight, thin garment. "You do like to look, don't you?"

Herb allowed curiosity to overcome embarrassment for the moment. "What type of show?" he asked.

The Treeple girl beamed. She could tell when she had a ripe one on the vine. "No, no, you have to see for yourself, Hot Pepper," she said, pushing him inside with her branches and closing the door behind him before he realized what had happened.

Herb decided to look around, since he was there. On the surface it looked like an ordinary book store, but on closer examination of the stock he realized he'd never seen books like those in the Public Botanical Library.

There were rows and stands of books and magazinias with lewd photosynthegraphs of all Paradise varieties in every imaginable pose. "Ip! Ip! Ip!" read the covers. Herb blushed deeply as he opened a zinia portraying his own Veganoid species in graduating steps of infertile pollination, or Ip, for short. A lovely green Veganette lay with her limbs fully spread, tied up to stakes, revealing the open blossom. He slammed the zinia shut and put it quickly back on the shelf. He was no prude about Ip, as his recent vacation had proved, but there was a better way to express it than in these degrading zinias.

He almost fell into the stands as a young Vinese girl sidled up to him, allowing some of her tender firm vines to brush against his leg. He moved back, thinking he was in the way. She repeated the action and he realized it was intentional flirting on her part.

"Greetings, Green God. Want to go get potted? Afterward, we can roll together. Wouldn't you like that?" she asked seductively.

The strong fragrance of her blossoms assailed Herb's senses. He had never cross-pollinated, but she was alluring in a strange, foreign sort of way. It was a temptation, but he reflected sensibly that he probably couldn't afford her anyway. His prolonged vacation had depleted his savings, if not actually rendering him financially barren.

"How much?" he asked, more from curiosity than intent.

"Only five merrygolds," she purred, wrapping her slim vines possessively around one leg.

Herb wished she hadn't done that. Even though they were quite different in appearance, he had chlorophyll in his blood. Her close proximity was evoking automatic male reactions he wasn't prepared to handle.

"Sorry. I'm unscented," he said apologetically.

Her scent faded as she abruptly removed her vines, shrugged, and moved on to better prospects. She was a working girl with no time for dead beets. Herb watched her roll away with a sigh of regret. He saw her attach herself to an aging Treeple with dried leaves. The old bark pulled some yellow coins from his trunk and they left together.

Herb wandered over to the counters containing union aides. There were hoes and spades of all sizes for every need of each species. Sprinkling cans and small bags of "Fertilize Her" were piled high. Rubber plants were also popular items. Herb had never seen so many varieties. He reached out curiously, stretching a leaf. It snapped back with a loud pop. He looked up to see the eyes of nearby customers leering at him. Ducking his head, he moved quickly to another part of the store, his ears glowing emerald.

Pausing at a new counter, he discovered he was no better off there. It was devoted to appliances for self-pollination, or Sip, as it was crudely termed. Narcissus powder, kissing tulips, clinging vines, sweet-scented potpourris, and leaf wax lay blatantly beneath the bright lights of the display. Herb's color expanded to his lower regions. How could anyone find the nerve to purchase such items he wondered.

Just then an attractive Treeple woman reached past him and gathered up a variety of the tulips and other items in her branches. She winked at him.

"Polli Party tonight," she explained, and looked Herb up and down appreciatively. "We can always use an extra male, if you're free?"

"Uh, sorry. I have a date," he lied.

She sighed with regret and carried her selections off to the clerk. She was joined by a couple of her friends who helped carry the purchases. Herb noted their attire and decided they were Ippies, members of a sexual cult that believed in free Ip, roaming from place to place in brightly painted conveyances, smoking weeds and using potting soil. His friend, Cling Ling, had joined such a caravan briefly, and told him all about it.

He started to leave, then noticed a concession stand at the back of the shop. Wandering over, he saw it sold potting soil and distilled water, though he doubted seriously if they had a license for it. The Patrol were lax these days. Maybe he should buy a pint of water and save a trip to the liquor shop.

"Finding what you need?" asked the proprietor, appearing at his elbow. He looked as if he didn't care for browsers. It was a hard business and those who ran it had thick stalks.

"The girl outside," Herb stuttered, "Uh, she mentioned a free show. No obligation." He felt ridiculous and out of place. He wished he had kept walking.

The manager became more friendly. "Sure, we have two shows tonight. Good for business." He blew the smoke of his suspicious-smelling leaferette into Herb's eyes. "The shows put the customers in the mood. Know what I mean?" He winked.

Herb didn't know, but he winked back. He didn't want to seem like a sapling.

"I know what you want," the manager said, putting a finger to his lip, and looking around cautiously before reaching beneath the counter for a small zinia. He handed it to Herb, winking again.

Curious, Herb accepted it and flipped open the cover. He gasped in disbelief. It was a seed catalog! The Patrol might be tolerant of most of these establishments, for sex played a large role in many of the new imported offworlder religions, but this was incredible. Child pollinography was an instant cancellation of license and closedown. Herb handed it back, disgusted.

"No?" The owner took it back, disappointed that his top

draw had come up losers. "Just don't talk it around, huh, Sprout?"

Herb grimaced. As if he'd tell anyone he had looked at that filth. He turned to leave. The clerk grabbed him by the sleeve.

"Hey, you haven't seen the show yet. Two tender young sprouts, hardly out of the hot house." He noted Herb's frown. "Oh, wait. The second show is just the ticket for a sophisticate like yourself, sir. Vivacious Violet is performing in the Orchid room." He grabbed Herb around the shoulders before he could speak and guided him down a dimly lit corridor and shoved him through a curtain of wallflowers.

Herb was left at the back of the small dark room with hard chairs filled with different varieties of males. He took a seat near the exit and slumped down, hoping no one there knew him. But if they were there, he was seeing them too, he reasoned. Even so, he kept low as the strains of the Chlorophyll Harmonica orchestra began. The harmonicas whined in rhythm as the main attraction entered and began her bump and grind.

Herb's eyes popped out on stems, figuratively speaking. He had never seen anyone like her. Not only was she a fully matured Treeple, but her leaves had been pruned, revealing the smooth dark bark of her branches. They swayed wantonly above her head in a scentual rhythm. Sap oozed from her exposed mounds and ran down the torso of her bare trunk. Her hips moved wildly to the music as it ended in a building crescendo. The crowd of males cheered and stomped while Herb sat in shock.

And then it happened. Herb gasped as the Treeple peeled back the bark opening from the center of her trunk to display the tender bud beneath. Never had he been exposed to such lasciviousness! Even as he was repulsed intellectually, he could feel his stamen unrolling. Herb clenched his teeth together and swallowed, forcing it to the back of his mouth, and stumbled out into the bright light of the store front.

The manager, swift to observe the effect his acts had upon the customers, offered him a private room upstairs with one of several passionflowers, retained for such purposes. Herb almost wished he had the merrygolds, but declined with a shake of his head. It was difficult for him to speak at the moment so he shrugged and gestured to his pockets. The manager got the message but wasn't ready to give up yet.

"Then how about a booth? You know. For a green thumb," he said, leering.

Herb was appalled. It was a long walk home, but self-pollination was not something to be indulged in public houses. He had heard about such booths in school. They called them Sippers. They were provided for the exclusive use of unruly stamen. The practitioner would place the distended member over his thumb and blow until the yellow pollen erupted in a cloud of ecstacy. It could happen to the best of Veganoids, but was not something one spoke of in mixed company.

"These are class A booths. For a little extra we can run a hologram show while you enjoy your privacy," the clerk pressed.

It was a sick proposition, and more than he could stand. Herb shook his head violently and dashed through the front door. All he wanted was to get out of that hot house.

Easier said than done. Two seedy pollitutes latched onto him as he descended the steps outside. One was a plump Vinese, the other a Treeple. The Treeple brushed her branches against him. Not again!

"Ever had it with a Treeple, Veggie? Eight limbs give a crazy massage," she cooed.

Herb drew back in disgust. Her rings betrayed her advanced age and her leaves were withered. Dried sap clung to the material over her mounds. "No!" he snapped, and ran before she could get a better grip. She probably had root rot.

"Up your Aster," she yelled after him, and rejoined her sister by the shop.

Herb felt sick to his stomach. What had he been thinking of to get mixed up with that bunch? Was that the life he preferred to an arrangement with Lily? As he turned the corner, he saw the symbol of a Vegetarian Temple ahead. On impulse, he went inside where an old Treeple Elder was standing by the altar.

"May I, uh, make admission, Elder?" he asked.

The Treeple nodded him toward the booth. Entering, he sat facing the Elder with a curtain of wallflowers between them. He began the ritual.

"Forgive me, Elder. I have erred."

"In what manner, my son?" asked the Ancient.

"I was wilted this past week," he confessed.

"Is it your habit to indulge in potting soil, or in distilled water?"

"Not usually, Elder. I mean, no, I never use potting soil. But I did absorb the water."

"What caused you to err?"

"I've been depressed. Lonely."

"Nonhabitual. Absolved."

"Tonight, Elder, I don't know why, but I visited a polli parlour. Infertile pollination establishment," he added for the Elder's clarification.

"I see. How do you feel about that?" asked the Elder.

"Low. I didn't mean to. I was walking by and a pretty Treeple called out to me. I was weak."

"Not premeditated. Absolved."

"Wait. I watched a show there. A bare-limbed passion-flower. My—my stamen was unruly," he blurted.

The Elder sighed a long sigh. "If you plant the seed, you must harvest the fruit."

"Oh no, no harvest. But, my mouth was full," he admitted.

"Unforeseen circumstances. Absolved."

"Thank you, Elder. I feel much better now." And he did. The dirt of the polli parlour seemed to wash away, leaving him cleansed as after a spring shower.

"Perhaps you should consider putting down roots, my son," the Elder suggested.

"I had a girl, but we grew apart. I don't know if she is the right Veganette for me."

"Must it be a Veganette? Cross pollination is no sin within a compatible union. I have grafted many such couples in my time. True happiness can be found in variety."

"That is not the problem, Elder. I have not limited my interest on the basis of species." He thought of the young Vinese girl he had met in the polli parlour. "I just don't know if I'm ready to plant a commitment yet."

"You will be sure when the time comes, my son. My advice to you is to plant your seed in a sanctified union, raise a family, and take vitamin C."

Herb went on his way, vegetating on the Elder's words of wisdom. He would turn over a new leaf. He would certainly try!

❧ 6 ❧

New Moon

Spring dried her eyes and accepted the cup of hot clear broth from the gentle servant girl standing solicitously by her bedside.

"Thank you. What is your name?" asked Spring, waiting for the broth to cool.

"Companion Iolanthe, my Lady." The girl smiled shyly. Her dark straight hair was tied back primly, and she was dressed in the long loose tunic uniform of all the Companions of New Moon. Spring guessed her age somewhere between fourteen and sixteen. She was a humanoid, and a rather pretty one, at that. Spring wondered what such a young woman would be doing devoting her life to service in this secluded Order? Well, they all had their reasons.

"Iolanthe," Spring repeated. "Yes, Flower."

"You know the meaning?" the girl asked, pleased. "It's an Old World name, from the ancient times."

Spring nodded. "Greek. I've made a study of botany, plants, and flora. It's sort of a crossover study, though most of the scientific names are in Latin. Another ancient lan-

guage from that era." Spring sat down the cup and leaned
back against the pillow.

"I should not be taxing your strength with questions.
Companion Alma is always admonishing me for my glib
tongue. You need solitude after your ordeal. I will return
later for the cup." She turned to go.

"No, stay. Actually, I would appreciate some company.
My father was the only family I had, and I feel so alone
now."

Iolanthe looked at the older girl with compassion.
"Have you had any sleep?" she asked.

"I don't know. Yes, I think so," Spring answered. Awake,
asleep, what was the difference? Nothing would change,
she thought.

"I don't think you have slept at all. I am going to request
some medication for you right now," the young girl said,
and opened the door.

"No, please don't do that," Spring said. "I don't like to
take drugs of any type. But, if you will hand me the small
pouch from the tray on the table, I will do some relaxation
exercises with my crystals. That works just as well."

Iolanthe brought the pouch, and stood by curiously
while Spring removed several small stones and held them
in her palm.

"Jewels!" Iolanthe exclaimed, obviously impressed.

Spring smiled. "Not exactly. These are healing stones.
They aren't worth all that much monetarily. Their value
lies in their application. My father—my father was a
renowned crystallogist. I assisted him in his practice on our
home planet until—until I came here," she finished, tears
glistening in her eyes.

"How do the stones work?" asked Iolanthe, hoping to
take Spring's mind off the sad subject for a few moments.

Spring held up a small purple gem. "This is an
amethyst," she explained, pressing it to the small space on

her forehead between the eyes. "I place it here, on my sixth chakra. Chakra is a term for an energy center. Some people refer to this spot as the third eye, because it is the center for intuition and spiritual awakening. I don't want to confuse you. Let's just say there are chakras that correspond to various parts of the body, and different stones work for each."

"But, what do they do for you?" Iolanthe pressed, glad to have Spring expressing an interest in anything again. For days, she had stayed alone and silent in her room, hardly acknowledging Iolanthe's presence.

"To put it simply, they contain energy, and so can project thought, heal, protect, whatever the intent of the user. Now I will visualize a peaceful scene, and attempt to sleep."

"Yes, that is good," Iolanthe said. She stayed for a short while watching as Spring shut her eyes and breathed deeply, closing out her surroundings. The servant girl walked quietly through the door, closing it behind her.

Spring tried to concentrate on the visualization, but all she could see was her father's face. Her father. He had always been her strength. How was she to go on alone without him? The deep sorrow swelled up to sweep over her again as she remembered the last time they had been together.

Word had reached her through the Society that her father was dead. The official version was that he had been fatally injured in a Turbocar accident, but a trusted source revealed that his office had been found in shambles and traces of blood were definitely his. Spring knew it had been no accident.

It had to be Zygote. He had friends in high posts who could have easily initiated a cover-up. Of course, her father had friends also, and that was why she had learned the truth despite their efforts. But his friends could not help her now. No one was to learn the secret, so that left it all up to her. Zygote would never profit from her father's death!

She needed no warnings now. Her father need never fear she would betray him for one foolish night of passion. Love was the last emotion she was capable of feeling at this point.

It was late when Iolanthe completed her rounds and remembered to look in on Spring to retrieve the cup and see how the young lady was resting. It was with surprised consternation that she found Spring not only wide awake, but poring through some questionable reading matter spread across the bed covers.

"You promised to rest," she scolded gently.

"Rest?" Spring laughed mirthlessly. "Yes, I will rest, but not until—" she stopped abruptly, finding the page she wanted in the index. "Here it is."

Flipping to the page, she read hastily, then spoke. "Will you post a letter for me, Iolanthe?"

"You know the rules, Lady. No outside communication while under the sanctuary of the—"

"Yes, yes. I've heard all that before. But I also know you have posted letters for others here at the sanctuary." Actually, she didn't know this, but felt it likely from observation of the kind hearted girl. Her bluff turned out to be correct.

"I should not have done so," Iolanthe answered contritely.

Spring scribbled on the sheet of paper and copied the magazine's address onto the sealer. She tucked in the paper along with some standard Planetary Payment notes and sealed it, passing it over to Iolanthe.

"Lady—" the girl began to protest.

"Please, Iolanthe. This is important. I know you don't understand, but my life may depend on the answers I receive from this letter. This is no time to balk."

Iolanthe sighed, but tucked it into her tunic, then looked

with disapproval at the lurid magazines scattered across the bed. "I don't see how anything sent to that type of publication could be so important."

"And how would an innocent young thing like yourself know about such magazines? Don't tell me you Companions have your own secret library? I found these here, under the bed."

Iolanthe looked scandalized. "Here? I don't know how they came to be. This room was that of a former Companion."

"Could be why she's former," Spring teased.

"That is not for me to say," Iolanthe answered primly. "But I do know that no good can be coming from this." She patted the sealer beneath her tunic as if it were tainted, and excused herself.

Spring looked after her departing figure, thinking aloud. "I hope you're wrong, Iolanthe. I'm betting my life on it."

• 7 •

A Tangled Vine

The tri-moons were just peeping over the horizon. It was a peaceful summer evening with only the sound of the soft warm breeze playing in the trees. A lone dogwood barked in the distance. It was a night made for romance in Paradise.

Herb and Lily sat entwined in the swinging vine on her parents' front porch. His arm rested comfortably around her shoulder. Her head reclined against his chest while they swung gently to and fro in thoughtless pleasure. Lily was the first to break the silence.

"It feels so natural being with you again, Herb. I missed you while you were away. All my dreams were tied to you. My heart withered, and I simply went to seed."

Herb shifted and sat up straight. "You weren't—!" His heart plunged into his stomach.

"Of course not; don't be silly." Lily smiled in embarrassment. "You know as well as I that we never," she paused, "never."

"Yes, I know," Herb said, but he still felt a wave of profound relief at the negative confirmation. At the time, it had been a major source of annoyance to him, but now he was honestly glad they had waited. What if she had become with child? Lily was an innocent, and probably didn't even know about proper prevention. It very well could have happened. Thank the Founder for her high morality.

"I thought we should see if we could grow together again," Herb said. "But, union is a serious step, and I don't think we should plant in haste. You do understand, Lily? I wouldn't have suggested we see each other again if that wasn't understood?"

He was babbling and knew it well, but he had no intentions of being pushed into something again.

"Yes, Herb, you've made that completely clear. It's just that we've known each other for so many seasons, and if you don't know how you feel about me by this time, I don't see how another season will change that."

Herb could see that strong will beginning to surface again. "It's not the situation which must change, but me," he said. "And who can say? You may be the one to call it off. You may grow tired of waiting."

"I will wait, Herb. I believe the fault was mine that you felt you must transplant. I was raised to hoe a straight row. There are many wild flowers out there to tempt a man, and if you have wandered, I must accept my share of the blame." She sighed.

"No," Herb said uncertainly. "That was not the only reason."

"Then you admit it was a reason," Lily exclaimed, pouncing upon his lack of conviction.

"It was," he reluctantly admitted. Herb hated to think he was so shallow as to discard seasons of a good relationship simply on the basis of sexual frustration. "I always admired your strong principles. It proved to me that you were a nice girl."

An odd look came over Lily's face. Herb wondered what he could have said wrong now. After all, he had just paid her a compliment.

"You mean," she pondered briefly, "if I didn't bed with you, then you knew I wasn't bedding others?"

She certainly had a way of getting to the root of the matter, Herb thought. "Yes, I guess so. That is what I meant." He was beginning to feel decidedly uncomfortable with the turn the conversation had taken.

"And, what if I had bedded another?" she asked softly.

Herb looked surprised. That notion had never crossed his mind. He had always assumed she was unsoiled. The arrogance of the male ego had dismissed any possibility that she might simply have preferred someone other than him.

"I see. Well, that makes no difference to our friendship now, Lily," he managed to say. He noticed that odd look was still on Lily's face.

"Oh," she said. "You forgive me?" Was the tone slightly sarcastic?

"No. I mean, yes. I mean, there is nothing to forgive." What was she trying to do?

That answer seemed to satisfy her at last. "Yes, Herb, that is so, for I have not bedded with any other."

That stripped away the last of his patience. "Then why the blight did you even bring it up?" he asked in exasperation.

"Because I know as a man you must have bedded others, if not before, then in your absence. It also makes no difference to me. But, I didn't know if that was an issue still between us. Now I see it is not. We can make a fresh start together."

She smiled possessively and squeezed his hand in hers. Herb began to see light dawn. It was her way of saying that she would overlook his past, but now expected fidelity since she was pledging hers. Smart girl.

"We can begin fresh," he agreed, acceding to their unspoken pact. Lily smiled up at him with a pleased expression. She had neatly won her case. He took both her hands in his and gave them a kiss. Lily was a good woman, and if she was willing to take him back and wait upon his decision, the least he could do was give their relationship every chance to flourish.

Herb did not stay long after their talk. Though her family was prosperous, she was a dedicated working girl who had to be at the Nursery early the next morning. Herb felt a bit drained from the emotional confrontation, and decided to make an early night of it himself.

He was soon home in his small apartment, stretched across his water bed, thumbing through the swimsuit issue of *Play Plant* magazinia. The photosynthegraphs of scantily clad passionflowers leaped out at him from the scented pages. He almost regretted his promise to Lily. While not prone to hop from one flower bed to the next, he did regard himself as a normal young Veganoid. His magazinias were a far cry from the raunchy trash he had seen in the polli parlour, but they still had lovely blossoms, and were not helping matters.

He flipped to the classified section instead, and browsed through the personals; the seed of answering one was growing in his mind. Why not? Responding to an ad would fill up a dull evening, and it wasn't as if he would actually meet the girl. Just writing a letter could hardly be considered disloyal to Lily, especially if she didn't know about it. It might be amusing to see what kind of reply he got.

Some of the ads were blatant, while others were obscure. He wanted to know something about whom he was contacting, but was put off by the aggressive ones. An ad near the end of the page at last caught his eye.

"Attractive, human Moon Maiden with botanical background seeks correspondence with interesting male. Species no obstacle. Object?"

A botany student? Herb thought girls in these magazinias were more interested in body than mind games. He was certain she had never studied his species of plant. Paradise was off the beaten path for vacationers, not without good reason. "Moon Maiden." He liked the sound of that. It was romantic, rather than sexy. "Object?" probably meant friendship, but the door was open for exploration. Herb decided he would answer this "Moon Maiden." Anything to relieve the monotony.

On New Moon, Iolanthe slid another letter beneath Spring's door and walked quickly away. If any of the Companions saw her do such a thing, it could mean expulsion or at the very least, solitary penance.

The Companions were quite strict about some of their precepts and outside communication was one of them. It would not matter that Lady Spring was only in their temporary care; she was still expected to abide by their tenets. It was, after all, for her own good. Hadn't her father made it a matter of extreme importance that none were to discover his daughter's presence? He did not explain why, but that was of small matter. The Companions were not curious. They wished only to lead a quiet life away from distracting outside influences. What he had requested was no more than they required.

Under ordinary circumstances, Iolanthe would never have agreed to such complicity. It was only that the sad-eyed young woman had been through so much and now had no one at all since her only parent had passed away. If this covert communication afforded her a measure of peace, then who was she to deny that request? Peace and comfort were the goals of the Companions, were they not? And it was plain the letters she had smuggled in to Lady Spring did provide her with a strange comfort.

She also admitted to herself that the harmless intrigue spiced up an otherwise too peaceful existence for Iolanthe. She went on down the hallway, reminding herself to do extra kitchen duty for the worldly thoughts she had been plagued with of late. And perhaps there would even be the chore of discarding the extra portions.

While Iolanthe contemplated pudding, Spring was thinking of her dearest enemy. "What is on your mind tonight, Zygote? Are you warm and secure in your mad magician's bed, or can it be you will toss and turn, wondering where the daughter of Gabriel has eluded you?

"Do you dare dream of holding her in your thin arms, penetrating her soft young body even as you penetrate the deepest secrets of her mind? Or could the ways of the flesh hold any allure for one such as you? I think not.

"No, a woman's heart is but an organ. To know a heart, you must possess one, and yours is cold hard lead. Power is your love, wealth your desire. How could a mere woman compete with that?"

"Dream on, Zygote, and sleep well. All your fond desiring, anxious waiting, patient planning, will avail you nothing. Yet, we will meet. But at a time of my choosing, and I fear, your dreams will become a nightmare."

The sound of the letter thrust beneath the door jarred Spring back to reality. Her face still reflected the hatred for the man who had destroyed her father, as she retrieved the missive. Another of the growing assortment she had received in answer to her ad.

Most were from smut-mouthed aliens looking for thrills with a pretty human female. They minced no words detailing descriptions of their incredible desires. Many were unintelligible to her, of course, as she had no idea what it meant to "gibrate with her dorlinta as she comarited his nobila." Or to "swing the ten patos to contact her ba ba." But one could imagine a full stomach would be a no-no.

She had assembled three piles of replies to go through. The truly depraved were tossed aside, the mixed bags sorted through, and the handful of best possibilities carefully considered. She went through these again, noting they came mainly from lonely males on distant or rural planets without many females of their own age or status to choose from. They seemed genuinely interested in forming a friendship. She lingered over one in particular.

It was from a tiny planetoid called P#23. Wait—it stood for Paradise. How quaint. It was very secluded. A point in its favor. The young man who was writing called himself a Veganoid, a part human, part plant person. As a student of botany she found that concept intriguing rather than repelling. She had a vague recollection of such beings, but as the plant folk were not space travellers and of comparatively noncompetitive technology, they were largely unknown. Certainly she had never met one nor knew of anyone who had. Interesting.

Spring set the letter aside and ripped the rest up, tossing them at the bathroom disintegration unit. Considering their foul content for the most part, it was an appropriate way to dispose of them.

Reading through Herb's letter again, for that was the plant man's name, she discovered he had mentioned enclosing a picture. Could she have overlooked it when sorting? Probably he had intended to, and then forgotten before posting it. Now she was more curious than ever. What would a plant man look like? A walking bush?

Taking out a sheet of floral-scented note paper, a nice touch, she wrote thoughtfully for a few minutes, then placed the note in its sealer and tucked in a photograph of herself in swim apparel. While it was common on many planets to swim in the nude, body suits were still used on her home world. She had on such an outfit in the photo, a transparent affair except for big daisy designs at the proper places. It was actually quite concealing, but the illusion was otherwise. She had had quite a discussion with her father over that selection. How she wished he were still with her to argue! Sighing wistfully, she closed the sealer.

The object of her interest, Herb Moss, sat in a shady bower in the Paradise Public Gardens reflecting on his life. He and Lily were getting on well. At least, they never disagreed. Maybe that was because Lily always deferred to him whenever the least hint of discord threatened.

While it was all very well to have one's way all the time, such a relationship lacked stimulation and exchange of ideas. She was giving in for the sake of peace, not because she agreed with him. Now that he thought of it, they didn't discuss much of anything outside of their upcoming union plans and his work at the firm, or other safe subjects.

Lily's family had forgiven him for his temporary transplant, and his father had offered him a good position at the firm of Moss and Ivy, Inc. It was an old company with a spotless reputation and would assure them a good financial future. It was uneventful work, but secure, with his father for his boss.

Herb was just the sort of steady young man most parents hope their daughter will meet, and Lily's parents were thrilled that he had at last decided to plant a union with their daughter. Financial considerations aside, they had always felt he was right for her. Likewise, Herb's family approved of Lily and felt she was the proper type of girl for Herb. One who would stand him in good stead as a company wife. She came from strong roots, her family had run a thriving cottonwood plantation for several generations, and they were frequently mentioned in the local society column at this or that charity function. His father thanked the Founder that Herb had not taken up with any of those spa blossoms he'd spoken so fondly of.

The families were happy, Lily was happy—well, that was two out of three. Everything was coming up roses and he still could not feel right about it. He had it all, and yet something was missing.

True to his unspoken word, Herb had not strayed from the narrow path. It took some getting used to, but he had faithfully confined his interest in the opposite sex to lofty thoughts of Lily, and the not so lofty thoughts to the pages of some men's zinias he had picked up on a whim from the corner newsstand.

Lily might not exactly approve of *National Galactic Girl, Interstellar Stud,* or *Spicy Aliens* as reading material, but he was certain she wouldn't like the alternative. Yet, compared to his long distance friendship with the Moon Maiden, she might not care at all.

One bright spot in his life had become his secret correspondence following the answer he'd sent on impulse to a personals ad one night. He saw no reason to discontinue it yet. He and Lily had not set the final date for their union ceremony. She agreed with him it was wise to wait until they could afford a down payment on a home. Now that she was certain of him, there seemed no end to her patience.

The Moon Maiden had enclosed a photosynthegraph with her first letter, revealing she was well grown and as pale as her namesake, yet every bit as lovely as any normal, green Veganette he had known. Lily was also a fine grown woman, but something about Moon Maiden caught his eye as never before. The human girl was, in essence, forbidden fruit, and he was sorely tempted.

It was more than her beauty that held such allure for him, however, for he found her letters as enticing as her form. More than once he found himself recalling the Elder's words to him about cross-pollination. But that was only foolish fancy. What matter how intelligent or pretty she was since they were light years apart?

Plant folk were not disposed to planet hopping, and even had he the unlimited merrygolds required for such a trip, other societies were not generally compatible with his kind. Most did not even recognize them as people. Herb recalled horror stories of past visitors who had actually uprooted saplings. It was nothing less than the murder of innocents, yet those who committed the acts claimed all ignorance of wrong doing, saying they had only "picked a few flowers."

Because they were protected by the code of Intergalactic Immunity, there had been no punishment for the heinous crime, but the government had made entry to Paradise difficult to obtain thereafter. A native had to vouch for any visitor that set foot on P#23 soil.

With the new restrictions in force, interest in the small sphere as a vacation spot soon waned, and the little planetoid eventually shrank from public notice. No one appeared to mind very much. The few offworlders that did venture here, did so mainly on business. The home grown atmosphere was tame for more adventurous travellers.

Moon Maiden was cut from a different vine, Herb was convinced. For one thing, she had studied all manner of plant life and respected it greatly. A pity more of her kind did not share her open-minded views. Not only was she extremely interested in hearing about Dr. Gell and the history of Paradise, but she urged Herb to reveal more about himself, as she thought he was "fascinating."

Lily had never told Herb he was fascinating. In fact, she

was not the type of woman given to ready compliments. The nearest thing to flattery she had ever said was that he was "tall, green, and healthy." But that was so cliche, anyone could say that. "Fascinating." He liked that.

❦ 8 ❦

Kamalot

*T*he planet wasn't always known as Kamalot, nor was it actually a planet, but a large meteorite of some hundreds of miles in diameter that had been trapped in orbit around Tarnaria, one of the obscure stars near the Cone Nebula.

A pheric generator had been placed in the core, making a breathable atmosphere. This was a device of enormous expense, and only a few large companies would go to such extremes for exploration, most still preferring more economical life suits or oxy bubbles. It was considered a waste of money and resources; therefore, no such company had done so. But the local Tarnarian government had.

It was their theory the meteorite would be useful as a combination observatory and military base, and they had stationed troops there for a short time. As closer moons were later made available, they discovered it was unnecessarily wasteful to maintain, and all in all, there wasn't that much to observe either. Eventually it was abandoned and placed on the market.

The pheric generator was left intact as the base wouldn't be worth much without it, and once installed, such units were virtually a part of the planet with all the underground connectors. The cost of removal was prohibitive. The new administration had all but given up hope of finding someone to appreciate the property's unique possibilities, when a very rich, eccentric magician made an offer that was ludicrously low. But it was an offer.

In order to erase the blot of the previous administration's foible, it was quickly and quietly sold to one Zygote, who was of unknown origin. In matters of that sort, in effect cash in hand, it was not prudent to pry too deeply. Doubtless he would put the base to good use.

Zygote set about using all the scientific and magical powers at his command to decorate his new home, and they were considerable. He was rather traditional in taste, and built a fine medieval castle for his home and headquarters, making it resplendent with tall towers and secret passages.

He landscaped the exterior with loving care, adding a forest here, a mountain there, and tied it all up with rocks and rills for a flawless fairy tale setting. Just the right sort of environment a magician could comfortably wave his wand over.

Zygote's planetoid was peopled with unusual beings, some from far planets, and some from imagination. He envisioned a world of his own where all were loyal subjects, ever ready to do his bidding at the drop of a spell. It might have been strange, odd, eerie, and even extravagant, but to Zygote it was simply "home."

Magic could take one only so far, he soon discovered. An undertaking of that magnitude also required a certain amount of hard, cold cash. Magically produced Planetary Payment notes were regrettably detectable. Every establishment was equipped with a Forgery Scanner for all incoming notes. Zygote had been forced to travel extensively, from planet to planet, plying his trade, and earning an honest living. A sorry lot for one of his talents.

Now it was there on Kamalot, in one of the high towers containing the library of his magical tomes, that Zygote sat gazing out the window, master of all he surveyed. There was a great deal he could not survey, of course, but that small deficiency was taken care of by the two large eyes set into the front gate of the castle walls overlooking the moat. No one could enter unseen, as that was the only access to the castle. The surrounding moat was filled with beasts and unpleasant spells that made it undesirable for swimming. Zygote felt ever so secure.

Now he thumbed thoughtfully through some of Gabriel's papers stolen from the late magician's files. Most of the files were protected by confidence spells and written in magical codes. Some were protected by curses as well. It was not an easy task to pry into another magician's private papers. He reflected for a moment on that challenge.

Once, Zygote had invoked a counterspell, thinking the code broken, only to have a vicious wasp fly through the tower window and attack with supernatural fury. Fortunately for him, he had been wearing a protective amulet, rendering the stings painless and impotent.

Another time, he almost had one seal broken when it suddenly burst into flame, destroying the entire document. He made a note to be far more careful in the future, or the valuable information he sought would disappear into smoke before his eyes.

If it wasn't so annoying, he could almost admire the late Gabriel's efforts to protect his secrets so zealously; it was hard to properly appreciate such steps when one was dodging balls of fire, hosts of ghosts, and tar and feathers. Gabriel had been a cunning old devil despite his angelic namesake. In fact, Zygote was sorry that the ornery cuss had rebuffed his offer of friendship and cooperation. He was truly sorry that the man had died rather than yield. Because he really did respect what Gabriel had done.

Zygote had fallen upon news of Gabriel's work by a stroke of sheer luck. When attending the last New Landers Magicians and Medical Doctors conference, Gabriel had been so secretive about his projects, he had inadvertently piqued Zygote's interest. If it was that good, it had to be profitable. He had tried to worm his way into the good doctor's graces, but to no avail.

While rabbits feet and four leaf clovers were all well and good, a well concealed microphone in Gabriel's lab had yielded a far better harvest than expected. It was in that way he had detected that the doctor's daughter, Spring, was somehow connected with the vital information he sought.

Unfortunately, Gabriel discovered the technical device, and that tipped his hand. He managed to spirit her off the planet before Zygote had a chance at her. He regretted not using a magical device instead, a spy spider, for instance. But no, that fool Elton had installed the microphone without his instructions, and it was too dangerous to go back.

Too bad Gabriel was no longer around to lend assistance, but that heavy-handed female he hired had gotten carried away with her duties. Then Elton had finished the job. He was young, and the young always grew impatient. Now he was attempting to make up for his blunder by tracking down Gabriel's elusive daughter to return her for interrogation.

Zygote had made it clear he would brook no violence in her case. If the key to the information was as he had surmised from pieces of broken codes, it might be the most pleasant interrogation he had ever conducted.

Zygote ceased his reverie and bent once more to the task of removing the troublesome spells, cursing anew as a three-headed snake slithered across the floor toward him. He took off all three heads with one quick slice of his enchanted sword. Preparation. That was the key to a magician's long life. Smiling, he replaced the sword in its scabbard as the snake puffed into smoke and disappeared.

His smile was replaced by an expression of surprise as he felt a sprinkle of wetness. A sudden storm brewing? He glanced to the window but no rain was blowing in. The sun was shining as brightly as it always did unless he decreed otherwise with a rain spell.

He looked upward, then brought out a kerchief and wiped some sticky residue from his eyelid. He held the cloth beneath his nose and sniffed. Really—Gabriel had pressed the boundaries of good taste this time. Zygote pulled an umbrella from beneath the table and sighed as he opened it above his head. There was nothing to do but wait out the shower of bird dung.

❦ 9 ❦

Discovery

Spring paced the floor of her small room awaiting Iolanthe's return. She had another letter to send and knew the lightship had landed. There wouldn't be another one for three months, so timing was critical. It went on alternate cycles of coming every other week for three months, then skipping three.

She had been lucky to have timed her first inquiry on the frequent cycle because it allowed her to have answers quickly. It was vitally important that Iolanthe smuggle this last one out.

Spring had decided to visit Herb of P#23 in three months when the ship returned. That would give him time to prepare for their meeting and for her to plan her departure so that Zygote would be none the wiser.

She had pushed her luck by remaining in one place for so long. Now that her father was gone, for all she knew Zygote might have found clues to her hideaway among Gabriel's papers. That wasn't too likely, as he had been so intent on strict secrecy, but there was nothing more she could accomplish by staying on with the gentle Companions of New Moon now.

It was time to be getting on with her plan of revenge. Zygote had been spared her wrath far too long. There was not a moment of the day that she did not feel the bitterness of her father's loss. Zygote must be made to suffer as she was suffering. It wasn't much to live for, but it would have to do.

Yet, Spring did not feel right plotting such mayhem among the peaceful people of New Moon. They had granted her refuge when she was in need, and in return she had defied their rules and betrayed their trust. Now she was corrupting poor little Iolanthe by having her post letters to the outside. And she must do it again one last time. It was necessary the letter to Herb get to that lightship.

By mid-afternoon Spring began to worry in earnest. Where could Iolanthe be? It was not like the girl to be absent for so long. Spring began to have premonitions of disaster, but tried to push them aside. Nerves were her worst enemy. If she began to worry about her safety she would never get the job done. Poking around in the small pouch of crystals, she brought out a polished white moonstone. She must calm down.

It was not until the dinner hour that Iolanthe entered, carrying a tray of fresh bread and vegetable chowder. She seemed distraught.

"Where have you been?" Spring exclaimed accusingly. "I was frantic. I was afraid the lightship would leave before you posted my letter." She pulled it from her pocket and thrust it at Iolanthe.

The girl took the letter and sat down beside Spring at the small table. "Oh, Lady. What a day this has been. Usually, we only have supplies from the ship unless there is a Pledge."

"Pledge? Oh, you mean a new Companion?" Spring said.

"Yes, but—" Iolanthe sighed.

"What happened? Is something wrong?" Spring asked worriedly.

"Yes and no. There was a man, a visitor."

"A man?" Spring said in surprise. "I understood no men were allowed to enter the Companion's sanctuary?"

"Yes, that is so. Companion Alma explained and explained to the captain of the lightship that it is not permitted, but the visitor was a very important, rich person and he kept insisting. Still, Companion Alma refused. She did agree, however, to meet with him at the lightport where the supplies are unloaded."

Spring took a spoonful of the thick white soup and a bit of the bread. Simple fare, but delicious. "And did that satisfy the visitor?" she asked.

"No, but it was the best he could do. You know Companion Alma. When she says a thing, she means it."

"Oh yes, I know," Spring agreed, smiling. Companion Alma was a short, little white-haired woman in her late sixties. She had rosy cheeks and the face of an angel, and had never raised her voice in her lifetime as far as Spring knew. Yet, all the Companions jumped to her least command as if she were Attila the Martian. "So, was she able to help him?" she asked.

"Not really. He said he was seeking his cousin, a young woman who had journeyed here about five months ago. He said her mother had fallen gravely ill and it was needful for the daughter to return home before it was too late. A sad story."

An uneasy feeling began to come over Spring as she picked at the food. "Did Companion Alma know this girl?" she asked.

"No, she couldn't be of any help. Obviously, that girl must have gone to some other retreat. No one has joined us since you. Until today. We had one new Pledge aboard, also. But Companion Alma is aware that your mother is deceased and now your father, so of course, it could not be you."

Iolanthe babbled on about how rude the visitor became at not being allowed to come see for himself, and how Companion Alma made short work of putting him into his proper place. Spring felt a chill run down her spine. It was odd timing that a stranger, a man, would come asking questions . . .

"Iolanthe," she interrupted, "Do you know what this man looked like? Was he an older man? Tall and thin with a sharp grey beard?"

Iolanthe laughed. "Oh no, Lady."

Spring breathed easier. Perhaps she was unduly nervous. For one awful moment she had been fearful that Zygote had managed to find her. Still—

"How do you know? Were you there?" Spring asked.

"Well," Iolanthe said, scooting her chair closer and looking conspiratorially at Spring. "I really should not mention this."

"Go on. You have me curious now," Spring urged.

"It could not have been such a man as you describe because I did see him. Companion Alma was so long at the lightport that some of us grew worried and went down to join her. This man was not old at all. He was youthful and clean shaven. Yet, we could not help but laugh at him, though that was surely not a kind thing to do." She laughed again in remembrance, and quickly put her hand over her mouth.

"I don't understand," Spring said. "A young, clean shaven man. What was so funny?"

"Well, he was so upset. He would not believe Companion Alma at first. He was absolutely positive that his cousin was here."

"Oh, he made a scene, did he?"

"And how. But, he was so funny. He had such a high voice for a man, and even went so far as to stamp his feet. He was a small, little man, yes, but he acted more like a girl. One of the Companions, Leah, said she had seen such men, and that they really aren't men. Or women. They come from a distant planet—Oh."

Iolanthe stopped and reached out to catch the water glass as it tumbled from Spring's hand, crashing to the floor. It broke into scattered fragments as Iolanthe cried out and jumped back, but Spring had not moved. She sat staring straight ahead as if she didn't even notice.

"Why, you're as pale as a ghost, Lady," Iolanthe exclaimed.

❧ 10 ❧

Unsuitable Suitor

$\mathcal{A}$re you certain that little man is as evil as you say?" Iolanthe asked. "He was strange, but seemed harmless."

"Yes, well. So did Dr. Jekyll until he turned into Mr. Hyde," Spring said.

"Who?" Iolanthe asked, puzzled.

"Never mind. It's an old story. I have to get away before he finds me."

"But the only way out is on the lightship, and he is on it too," Iolanthe protested.

"But if I don't go, he'll be back. Probably with goons like the ones who killed my father. Somehow they'll find a way to get in, now they suspect I'm here. I don't want anyone else hurt on my account, and they aren't the sort to care who they have to step on to get to me."

"We will protect you."

"No, you can't. I've already imposed on the Companions far too long anyway. I won't endanger you. There has to be a way to get past him." But what way could there be?

Iolanthe thought for a moment; then a mischievous smile spread across her features. "Maybe there is." She clapped her hands. "Companion Alma would put me in solitary a month!"

"Why, Iolanthe," Spring said, smiling. "Just what did you have in mind?"

Spring took her seat on the lightship toward the rear of her compartment, trying to look unobtrusive and fade into the woodwork. There was no wood on lightships, of course, but it was the thought that counted.

The dark stain on her arms had blended in beautifully and her face was painted in blue with white stripes in the custom of Tyranian males. The hood partially covered her face, and her hair was wrapped tightly in a turban-like swath of cloth beneath it.

It was a little hard to breathe naturally after Iolanthe had bound her breasts flat with more cloth and adhesive strips, but it would be worth it all if she could pass for a man until reaching her destination.

Iolanthe had sewn the costume using a photo from one of the magazines Spring had found under her bed. They picked out the Tyranian because it was the most concealing look they could find. Many of the offworlder males wore little or nothing to conceal their muscles, but for Spring's purpose, the less revealed, the better. The shoulder pads gave her body a more masculine look, and the boots added height. The hardest part was when they had painstakingly cut and glued on a moustache from the milk goat's tail. All things considered, it was not a bad disguise.

She had to remember not to cross her legs in a ladylike manner when sitting, and to watch how she walked. The natural feminine swing of her hips could easily betray her gender if she wasn't on guard. Spring hoped she had entered with a proper male swagger as she slumped down in the seat, unconcernedly letting her legs fall apart. It would almost be fun if it weren't so serious. One slip and all would be lost.

Elton might be slime, but he was no dunce. He might even suspect she would try to escape on the ship after his attempt to enter the sanctuary. She had not seen any sign of him so far; he was probably in one of the expensive compartments. That was the main reason she had opted for simple accommodations in the budget section. All she needed was to be stuck in the same compartment with him all the way to the next stop.

There was an attractive redhead in the seat next to hers giving her the once-over. In theory, it was easier to deceive a man about her sex than another woman. A female might recognize another however well she contrived to conceal herself. Spring averted her eyes and closed them as if resting.

This lightship, like many others of its ilk, concealed a modern technology in a shroud of nostalgia. The USS *Orion, Universal Star Ship,* resembled a luxury coach train, an archaic mode of transportation employed by the wealthy ancients who must have had much time to spend in travelling to their destinations.

Quaint it might be, but it presented another unwanted aspect to the trip. She would have to go to a common dining facility for her meals. That would put her on display before more people than she cared for. Perhaps even Elton.

While that was one confrontation she relished, the timing was not yet right. She needed time to formulate the method of her retaliation, and she would have none should he discover her true nature now. She was confident he would be travelling with a goon or two to do his dirty work for him.

Spring avoided the dining area for as long as possible, but a gnawing hunger finally forced her to risk it. She ordered what she hoped was a fast preparation dish from the robot menu at her table. When it came, she ate without pause so as to vacate quickly. She finished and had entered the narrow corridor leading back to her compartment when someone came bolting around the corner, stopping just short of crashing into her.

The young man muttered a quick and insincere apology, then looked up scowling to see who had caused his inconvenience. Elton. The one person she hoped to avoid. She was not a tall girl but with the boots she was almost on an even eye level with the small Ki.

"Sorry," she muttered roughly, hoping her voice would not betray her. She had managed to avoid all speech until now, even to punching in her dinner order on the robot to bypass a waiter. Elton did not move aside, however, but stood looking at her appraisingly. Spring perspired beneath the paint and costume. Her heart was pounding like a hammer. All this trouble and he knew.

"Oh, not at all, young Sir," Elton said. "It was clearly my own fault, charging through these narrow passages like a rocket." He laughed and gave her an odd look. Suddenly she realized. He was flirting with her—him. She had forgotten he had no gender preference, so anyone was fair game. She tried to look indifferent, and moved aside to let him pass. Still he lingered.

"You know," he continued, "there aren't many passengers aboard of our age, and these trips can grow monotonous after a bit. What say we meet in the Smoker later, since you've had your meal and I am about to have mine?"

A date with Elton? Swallowing her fury and revulsion, she opened her mouth to decline. "I—"

"Now, I won't take no for an answer. You can't have anything better to do in that cramped compartment." He had noticed the ID badge labeling her for the economy section, and evidently knew what space that allotted. Hardly any. "I will even share my Havanoz with you," he offered magnanimously.

Havanoz. That was a brand of very good, very expensive, very hard to obtain cigar, much prized throughout the system. Even Spring, a nonsmoker, had heard of them.

"How—kind. But I couldn't allow you—" she began again, and was again cut off.

"Oh, but I insist. What pleasure do the finer things afford any of us, if we cannot share them with others?" He smiled sickeningly.

Spring was in a quandary. Elton was determined to share her company. If she protested too much, he might get suspicious and look for other reasons for her rejection. Reluctantly, she chose the lesser of two evils.

"Very well," she agreed in her fake voice.

"Splendid. Shall we say in, oh, an hour?"

Spring nodded and pushed by him, escaping with relief to her tiny compartment. The girl had stepped out and she was alone. That was also a relief. She wished no further testing of her disguise for the moment.

The time flew by on sonic wings and before she had fully assessed the situation, it was time for the meeting with Elton. Elton, the loathsome little snake who had in all likelihood been a part of her father's murder.

She wished she had her crystal pendant to touch and calm down with, but Tyranian men did not wear jewelry. Painted symbols on the face were their only adornment. The pendant was packed carefully away in a small travel bag along with her other stones. It was the first time in many years that she had been without it, her favorite gift from her father. The image of his face now flashed before her, giving her new incentive. She decided to get the unpleasant meeting over with.

When Spring arrived in the Smoker, she spotted Elton seated in a booth toward the rear of the large compartment. She sauntered over with her best male gait and bowed slightly to him in greeting. He rose and politely motioned for her to take the seat across from him, then drew out an elaborate case from inside his apparel.

Opening it, he offered her first choice of his prized cigars. She looked at them dubiously. Did he actually expect her to smoke that ugly thing? Naturally, as he had said as much earlier, but she had been so concerned with her close proximity with him, that she had completely blocked out the pretext for their meeting.

"Don't be shy, my friend. Your choice." He shoved the case under her nose. She looked them over and selected the smallest and thinnest among them. They were all hand rolled, so differed slightly in size, but it was still a brute.

Spring was not a smoker, even though tobacco had been refined to a nonlethal version of its ancient ancestor. There was no danger of cancer or lung disorders, but it remained a questionable occupation in her mind. She had studied tobacco as well as other recreational plants, but considered smoking to be a silly, rather nasty habit, used to waste time by those with nothing better to do than light a fire beneath their nose. She observed as Elton picked out a somewhat fat one, wet the end, and bit off a tiny piece.

She tried to emulate his actions, then paused as he offered her a light from his golden case. Spring wasn't sure what to do, but drew in the flame and puffed out the smoke as she recalled others doing. Elton then lit his, miraculously not noting how awkward she was with the process. At least she didn't have to converse while puffing on the abominable thing.

Elton took the lead in conversation, however, remarking on the service of the lightship and mentioning that although a seasoned traveller, he missed the companionship of friends and how glad he was to have met Spring.

This brought on late introductions, as they had not done so in the hallway. She gave a typical one syllable name of the Tyranian man from the magazine, Mank. Elton introduced himself as "Zygote, the Great. Magician extraordinary."

The little twerp! He was trading on his master's notorious reputation to make himself more appealing to her. Fat chance. Neither of that distasteful duo could have been more repulsive if they had been Venusian devil fish.

"Magician?" She smiled insincerely. "How impressive." Liar. "How is it you came to be on this voyage?"

"I had some unfinished business to conclude on New Moon," he answered suavely.

She just bet he did. "And did you conclude it successfully?"

"That's hard to say. I may have. Time will tell."

Yes, thought Spring. He was probably running home to Zygote to report she was stranded at the sanctuary, then would return with a force of goons to take her by force, if need be.

"How fortunate for you," she said insincerely.

"Yes," he agreed, smiling. "And unfortunate for others. But I am more interested in you. Care for another smoke?"

Spring hadn't noticed how fast the thing had shrunk with her constant puffing. "No. I mean, no thank you. It was, uh, excellent." Actually, it was like sucking on a burnt dish rag.

"I am so pleased you enjoyed it," Elton said. "The aroma is delicious, is it not?" He blew a puff her way.

Trying not to gag, she inhaled, and forced a smile. "Ah yes. Indeed." For those who liked the smell of fried cat fur, she thought.

Spring listened vacantly as Elton talked on and on, finally hoping she had spent sufficient time with him in order to leave gracefully. She was beginning to feel a bit woozy, and attributed it to tension. Even so, she would feel better back in her own compartment, away from the little toad.

It wasn't his sexual adaption that appalled her: after all, aliens had different standards of morality that could not be fairly compared with her own. No, Elton earned her disgust as a slime sucking lowlife on his own merits. As she arose to depart, she felt herself sway slightly and reached out to grip the side of the booth.

"Are you ill?" asked Elton, solicitously, reaching for her arm.

"I do feel somewhat strange. I did not have my usual rest last night," she said, concerned, "and am doubtless fatigued."

"Then I must see you to your compartment." He beamed.

Wonderful. "No, it is nothing at all," she protested, turning abruptly and causing her head to swim violently. Elton steadied her so she did not fall.

"Now, I must insist, dear fellow. In fact, why don't I take you to my private compartment instead? It's such a long way back to yours, and I know that I could make you," he paused, "very comfortable."

Spring panicked at the thought. Venusian devil fish were looking better all the time. This meeting had been disastrous. The last thing she needed was to be incapacitated and alone at the mercy of that little leech. ·

If he tried making a pass, and it was inevitable under the circumstances, she wasn't sure she had the strength to fend him off in her condition. Her mind was racing, but she could think of nothing to stop the chain of events. Suddenly, she felt another hand touch her shoulder. It was the redhead from her compartment.

"You seem ill, sir," she said. "I would be glad to assist you back to our compartment as I go."

Blessed break for the home team! Spring opened her mouth to accept.

"No need, young woman," Elton said, looking daggers at her. "I am taking my friend to my compartment, as it is much closer."

"Oh, but I am a trained nurse. I think he should go straight to bed for the night." She tugged Spring in the opposite direction. Now Spring knew how a wishbone felt.

But she had to assert herself, or she would be lost. "I think that is wise. I should turn in. But I thank you, sir," she said, holding on to the redhead like a lifeline, hoping not to swoon before she could exit.

There was nothing more Elton could say, but his tone betrayed his annoyance. "Very well. Perhaps we could meet tomorrow, after you have rested?"

"Perhaps," answered Spring. And perhaps she would run naked through the corridors juggling oranges, but the chances were just as remote. She clung gratefully to her rescuer as they proceeded at a slow pace toward their mutual compartment.

"You don't look good," observed the girl. "I think you shouldn't smoke any more of those weeds you were puffing like a smokestack."

The cigar. They might no longer be a health risk, but they did have side effects for the uninitiated. No wonder she felt so awful!

"I'm not a smoker," she confessed.

The girl opened the door and led her inside. Spring looked up in surprise. "This isn't our compartment."

"No, it's a private lounge. You know, for businessmen and rich old biddies to meet and gossip."

"Then why are we stopping here?" she asked.

"That little priss was right about one thing. You need to lie down." She led Spring to the narrow chaise longue, where she collapsed, thankfully. It did feel good to get her head out of the sky. She turned onto her stomach and shut her eyes.

"How did you get mixed up with that Ki anyway? It's obvious he had designs on you, but you don't strike me as one to prefer that type."

"I don't prefer him, or her, or whatever it is. He disgusts me."

"I thought so. That's why I horned in like I did. I have a confession. I'm not a nurse at all. And I will take you back to our compartment when you feel a little steadier on your feet."

"Thank you," Spring said, shutting her eyes again. "I'm sure it will pass."

Suddenly, she felt two feminine hands at the back of her neck, massaging her padded shoulders. Spring's eyes popped open. "What are you doing?"

"Just trying to relax you," said the girl. "You know, you have small bone structure for a man."

It did feel good, but she couldn't risk discovery of her phony muscles. "Thanks, but I'd rather you didn't—" She didn't finish the sentence for at that moment she felt not hands but lips kissing the back of her neck.

Leaping from the chaise longue, head reeling, she turned on her companion with wide eyes flashing.

"You kissed me," she accused.

The redhead stood bemused for a moment, then burst into laughter. "I don't know what your game is, but you are no man, sister," she said.

"Maybe not, but I do prefer them," Spring said, backing toward the door.

"Yeah? Me too," said the girl.

"But, if you knew I wasn't a man, why did you do that?" she asked, confused more than ever.

"To test your reaction, I guess. I thought there was something different about you when you first came on the ship, but I couldn't figure it out. Aliens are different, so I could have been wrong. But I wasn't, was I?"

"I guess this disguise wasn't such a good idea," sighed Spring.

"Oh no, you make a great Tyranian. You sure fooled that Ki creep, right? It's just that I am the suspicious kind. I like to know what makes people tick. It's kind of a hobby of mine, human nature."

"Can I ask you to keep your discovery private? It's very important," Spring said.

"Are you in trouble? Or maybe you just want to avoid male attention on a long trip?"

"Yes," Spring said.

"That's a definite answer. Well, I don't believe you're a criminal. Too naive. Tell you what. If your unwelcome Romeo comes calling again, just signal and I'll come running." She smiled and held out a hand for a shake.

Spring accepted gratefully. It could be the edge she needed to get past Elton until she could reach her plant man.

True to her offer, the girl stayed close by Spring for the remainder of the trip, keeping an eye out for Elton. It looked as if he had lost interest, for he didn't approach her in her compartment, nor had she run into him in the dining room.

But one evening when she was returning from the evening meal her luck took a sudden dive.

Elton was coming straight down the narrow corridor toward her. His eyes were glued to papers in his hands so he had not yet spotted her, but there could be no escape this time. Her friend usually accompanied her, but was resting this evening with a headache. Spring had given her a gemstone with directions to help eradicate the pain.

Spring knew she would be hard pressed to put Elton off a second time. Especially when he had her cornered alone. And of course, if he was expecting a male reception, there was no way she could comply, even had she so strangely desired to do so. The fact was, her disguise wouldn't go that far. She lacked the basic equipment, and he would find that out quickly and then realize who she really was. The fox hunt would be over.

He was still engrossed in whatever it was he was reading, so was advancing very slowly. There was no time to run back, though, and that was his destination besides.

Suddenly, she spied a small hatch at the side of the corridor. Spring shoved and it gave. Bending down, for it was only about three feet from floor level, she pushed against it and ducked inside. Instead of stepping out on the opposite side as expected, however, she plunged straight down into darkness.

❀ 11 ❀

Down the Hatch

𝓘t was a shaft. Now she'd gone and done it. "Out of the frying pan into the fire," as her late father was fond of quoting. It was an Old World saying that until that moment she had never fully appreciated.

Fortunately, it wasn't a straight drop. It slanted forward toward the center of the ship, causing her to slide down, rather than plunge the descent.

She came to an abrupt stop on something soft. It was alive. Giving an indignant squeal, it scurried off into the dark with scratchy feet. With the unquestionable intuition women have about such things, Spring immediately identified it as a smouse. Those were small, fuzzy rodents considered more as pests than a danger, but the thought of touching one still gave her the shivers.

Where in the universe was she? Her eyes were slowly growing accustomed to the darkness. Objects began to come into focus as her night vision increased. It didn't especially help. It looked as if she had landed on top of a huge room full of junk.

Paper and debris of all kinds made a sort of mountain upon which she tried to stand. It wasn't easy, for the footing was slippery, and worse, she nearly slid down between a loose section. If not careful, she could end up buried under all that trash. Trash? Had she mistakenly jumped into a garbage bin? How brilliant! The question was, how to get out of it.

More smouses rustled in the loose papers nearby, but seemed as content to avoid her as she was glad to have them do so. She tried yelling at the top of her lungs, but realized no one would hear her in there. Who would be listening to a pile of junk?

Besides, the noise of the ship's mechanics were rumbling like thunder at the moment. It would be virtually impossible for anyone to hear over the din that the machinery was—

Machinery?

Spring was no expert in the dynamics of spacecraft, but she did know that lightships were practically soundless. They ran on waves or something. There should be no rumbling engines to make those kinds of sounds. But if it wasn't the engines, then what was it? And more than that, what was happening?

Added to the present noise was the sound of swirling papers. Looking upward, she saw some of the top layer of the junk begin to rise. It followed a spiraling pattern upward toward the center of the high ceiling where it was being sucked into some type of—shredder? No, it would have to be a disintegrator. So that was how they disposed of all the garbage in space. Interesting. And if she didn't find a way to escape very soon, she would see its workings close up.

The lighter materials and papers were drawn up first; it was probably put on a lower suction to start, and then given more power for the heavy debris like packing cases, old furniture, and stupid people.

That meant there was still a little time to try forming a

plan. There might be a way to climb back up into the chute, at least until the machinery abated. It must run in cycles since it wasn't running when she first landed. If she could avoid this cycle, it might be several hours until the next began and that time would give her a fighting chance to escape.

Spring finally located the small opening she had tumbled through, but it was now far over her head. The level of the mountain was slowly diminishing while more papers flew up into the giant vacuum. How to reach it?

The suction increased again with a roar, and papers flew violently by her toward their demise. She had to bat them from her face as they swarmed around like angry bees. They stung, too. Her hands already showed tiny beads of blood from the sharp edges. It was a slow process, but given enough time, she could probably die from paper cuts.

Spring tried vainly piling up armloads of the trash to rebuild her mountain beneath the opening. It was futile, for the suction undid her work as fast as she built it up. What she needed was more heavy material, but that was buried under the lighter papers, their weight sliding them down as they lost support. There was simply no easy way of reaching the portal.

Well, maybe not that particular one, but the ship was on several levels. It should have chutes at each. There were two more levels beneath the dining area, so if she positioned herself directly beneath the present opening and rode the mountain downward, eventually she should find a second shaft to dive into.

The roar of the machinery was growing deafening as the suction increased for a third time. Some of the lower debris flew up and around the center, resembling an indoor tornado. It was all she could do to keep her position next to the rim as the papers beneath gave way.

At least the suction kept new arrivals of trash from falling on her head, as they were quickly sucked up into the swirling torrent. Fortunately it had all been lightweight trash.

Pieces of boxes and broken dishes slammed into the walls around her. She squatted as low as possible while most of the rubble was drawn above her head. She took a blow to one arm from the edge of a box, but it would leave no more than a nasty bruise. The worst part was that her support was disappearing and she was beginning to feel lighter. She needed more weight.

Squatting and digging about desperately, her hands struck something solid. It was an ugly old chair, dirty and natty, with the fibers hanging out. It was beautiful. Spring wrapped her arms around and under the sides of it and ceased her assent. It had worked.

For a while. She descended faster, but the suction grew stronger and her position more precarious with each passing moment. Suddenly, she felt herself beginning to rise. Her foot struck a hard object at the side. It was an old nutrition robot.

Holding on to the chair with her left arm, she slid her right one into the ejection slot of the robot. Ugh, she touched something fuzzy. A smouse. Spring dropped the unit as the rodent leaped out, landing near her foot and scrambling off. She shot suddenly upward.

Quickly kicking out with her foot, she jammed it into the slot before it was out of reach. Bending back down, she replaced her foot with her right arm again, and this time there were no resident rodents to chase her out. The upward thrust had ended.

Safe once again, she reoriented on the now distant hole above, making sure she was still on target. According to her calculations she should be nearing the second chute, if there was one. But what if they weren't evenly aligned?

What if it was in a completely different spot? She should have been watching the other walls as well. What if she had already passed by it?

"Spring, this is not the time to panic," she said aloud. Inwardly, she realized there was probably not going to be a better one. All at once, she stopped her downward slide as one of the chair legs caught on something at the side. The chute. She had almost missed it in her panic.

Crawling past the chair into the shaft, she gave it a kick and it joined the nutrition robot in an upward spiral as it succumbed to the now fierce suction. When she had a house of her own someday, she would get a chair just like that one, and damn the decorator.

It was a relief to be in out of the trash storm, but it was time to begin the next challenge, the climb up and out of the shaft. It should not be too hard. It was at a slanting angle, and not straight up until the very end. Removing her shoes and letting them fall down through the slot, she braced her toes against the hard metal. They gave a better traction than her thick-soled slickers. Good name for them.

Progress was slow, but with patience and proper positioning, she made a steady headway. Then there was a distant scraping sound from above. Sound? Maybe the exit was closer than she thought? Spring strained her eyes in the darkness. There was a darker shadow closing in with the noise. No. That was the source. A looming shape sliding directly for her. A huge unit of some type—a cooling unit? Some of the reflective light tubes were still working. Those things weighed a ton.

Hardly thinking, she edged back to the wall of the shaft and turned on her side, pressing in as closely as she could. In seconds it whooshed past, missing her by centimeters. She stayed frozen for a minute. It was a miracle it had missed. It could have sent her flying back down into the junk heap, probably crushing her skull in the process. She lay trembling, realizing how close she'd come to a senseless death.

Spring moved carefully forward, listening for sounds as if her life depended on it. Because it did. No more missiles came shooting from above, though, and with slow deliberation she at last reached the opening and pressed outward.

It wouldn't give.

"Idiot," she screamed. Of course it wouldn't open. It needed pressure from the outside, but was static from the back.

She banged with frustration on the inside of the small door as hard as she could with only one hand. She needed the other one to grip the edge of the shaft, while scotching her feet against the sides. The drop was straight down from the entrance.

She tried yelling, then screaming. Even Elton would be welcome at this point. It was soon evident no one could hear her, and she couldn't hear anything from the outside either. What if it was sound proof? To have come so close to escape and gain nothing. Tears of frustration and fear began to form, running silently down her cheeks in the darkness.

She winced as light flashed brightly through the open door, almost releasing her tenuous grip on the edge. Luckily, she was holding with both hands, having given up on banging. Two strong male arms reached down and drew her up and out into the ship's corridor. Her redheaded friend stood looking on anxiously as the maintenance ensign helped to steady Spring on her feet.

"How did you know?" she asked the girl, while holding tight to the ensign's sleeve and bracing against the wall. Her knees still wanted to wobble. Her bare toes cramped as they straightened.

"When you didn't return to the compartment, I searched for you everywhere. I even knocked on the door of a mutual friend," she said, giving Spring a knowing look. "There was just no place else to try. Then, I found this gem next to the trash bin upstairs." She held out a small glistening bit of quartz in her hand.

Spring remembered absently placing it in her pocket after finding the healing stone for her friend's headache.

"I knew it was part of your collection," the girl continued. "Since I couldn't locate you, I asked where the chute led and learned that the disposal unit was in progress. Then I just panicked and notified the maintenance crew. They shut it down, but you weren't there. So much had already been disintegrated that we were afraid." She swallowed hard. "But I knew you were resourceful, so we decided to check all the openings on the chance you'd clung on and not fallen the entire way down. I see we were right."

"Not exactly. I did go down, but managed to climb out," Spring said.

"But sir! That's impossible. The suction," the ensign exclaimed.

Spring was now able to stand on her own two feet again. "Improbable, Ensign, but not impossible, for as you see, I am living proof."

"Sir, I do not wish to pry at such a time, but how did this accident occur? These chutes are well beneath head level and must be pushed forcefully to open wide enough for something, someone, as large as yourself to squeeze through. I only wish to avoid any more such, uh, accidents to our passengers, you understand." He wasn't buying it.

Spring drew herself up to full height, wishing for the built-up slickers. "As you say, it was an accident. I dropped something. My jewel, there. Very valuable. I was looking for it, and bending over. I leaned up against the wall. The chute. And well, that's the way it happened."

The ensign still looked dubious. "Sir, that is highly un-likely—"

"Yes, isn't it?" she interrupted. "But that's an accident for you. Don't worry, Ensign. I have no intentions of press-ing charges." She'd give him something to think about.

The ensign's face fell. "Charges, sir?"

"Why yes. For negligence."

"But, but—"

"No, not at all. Accidents do happen. Why cause inno-cent parties such as yourself additional hardship?"

The ensign backed off. He had not considered that turn of events. "Yes, of course. Right you are, sir. Clearly an ac-cident. Thank you, sir."

Spring took her friend's arm and walked quickly away while the ensign was sufficiently grateful for his narrow legal escape. She needed to get private before she collapsed from fatigue and reaction.

The rest of the voyage seemed destined to pass unevent-fully, thanks to Spring's providential companion. They had yet to exchange names, since Spring could not truthfully reveal hers. They simply referred to each other as Friend.

There was only one last incident with Elton, which took place in the dining area. Spring was finishing her meal, when he suddenly appeared from nowhere and seated himself beside her without an invitation.

"May I?" he said, not waiting for the answer.

Spring was so shocked she could say nothing. Before she had to, however, her watchful friend arrived and seated herself on the other side, placing a possessive arm around Spring's shoulders. She followed the gesture with a swift kiss to Spring's cheek.

"So here you are, my beloved," cooed the redhead. "I couldn't bear to stay away a moment longer. What a night we had," she said, wiggling closely next to Spring. "I can hardly wait for a repeat performance."

Spring looked at her friend in amusement. Were she a man, she might have blushed at such a declaration, but as it was, she just wanted to giggle.

Elton took in the implication as he was meant to. His romantic hopes dashed, he bit his lip and quickly arose. "I regret I have business elsewhere," he said curtly, departing in a huff. It was all the girls could do to keep from bursting out in laughter while he was still within earshot. Free at last!

🌹 12 🌹

The Visitor

Herb's life had proceeded uneventfully. Each day he reported to his father's firm of Moss and Ivy, Inc. and went through the motions of corporate life, Paradise style. It was as good a job as any, and paid better than most. He would soon have the necessary merrygolds for his union to Lily. The work was not hard, though that may have been partly due to the fact he was the boss's son, and his immediate supervisor had no desire for complaints. But Herb had no complaints. Not really.

In the evenings he usually stopped by Lily's where they would sit in the swinging vine on the veranda or go for long walks down the garden path, observing the subsapient plant life.

Lily loved the roaring dandelions, tiger lilies, screaming wild flowers, and smoking snap dragons. His own taste ran more to the domestic varieties of dogwoods and pussy willows. They would look them over and speculate which sort of pet they wanted to buy once their union was settled.

Lily preferred pussy willows, saying they were happy

with just a saucer of milkweed, while dogwoods ate too much and were noisy. Herb argued that their bark was worse than their bite, and insisted the first choice should be a puppy plant. Lily gave in as usual, and so it was decided.

His only diversion from the set routine had been an occasional letter from his secret correspondent, "Moon Maiden." Secret, because Lily would never understand why he wanted contact with any other female, even on an intellectual level, and he had no wish to hurt her.

Also, he felt a bit juvenile about the whole thing. Pen pals were for sprouts, not full grown Veganoids. Yet, he had to admit the correspondence had grown increasingly important to him. Only that morning he had received one Special Star Ship Delivery. Unfortunately, he had been in a rush, so tossed it aside for later. Lily had met him at the firm after work and they had eaten dinner at a new place she'd heard about.

It was pleasant enough with simple fare. He had chosen the breadfruit and honeysuckle, with jumping beans and eggplant. The beans were good, but the devil to keep on the plate.

Lily had only ordered corn flowers and buttercups, wondering that he could consume so much. She teased Herb about his appetite, saying it would be a full time job feeding him, envisioning herself chained to the garden.

For dessert, they both had the tapi okra pudding with sugarcane sauce, followed by steaming cups of coffee beans and tea roses. They capped off the evening with a lazy garden walk.

It was still early when he arrived home, but it had been a full day all the same. All he wanted to do was kick off his shoes, have a drink, and take a nice hot shower. He went into the kitchenette and took down a bottle of distilled water, pouring a small amount into his glass. To that he added a dash of watercress and mint, stirring it with a celery stick. He carried the concoction back into the combined bed and living room, flopped down on the bed and sipped.

Herb began to wonder. Was this how it was going to be for the rest of his life? First work, then Lily, then bed. Well, after the union it would change a little. First, work. Then home to Lily. Don't forget the dogwood, man's best friend. Then bed. Perhaps there would be little seedlings later on, as well. He would never be lonely. Or, would he? Sometimes with girls like Lily who had waited so long, they really had no interest in—no. It wouldn't be that way at all. Lily wanted a family, and she cared for him. Still—

"Oh," Spring squealed, bursting into the room from the shower stall. She hadn't heard him come in and was attired only in a small towel which now fell to the floor in her surprise.

Herb was surprised, too. Who was this vision? He knew it must be a vision. She wasn't even green like a real girl.

True enough. Spring had used one of her father's magic keys to gain entrance to Herb's apartment, and had taken advantage of the bath to wash away the dark stain of her Tyranian disguise. She stood revealed for the moment in her natural color. She had come out of the shower to towel dry her long hair, when she discovered the apartment was now occupied.

Herb could not avert his eyes from the lovely intruder. She was certainly well grown, and her skin was as soft and pale as a moon. Moon Maiden. Now he recognized her from the photosynthegraph she'd sent. Of course, he had not been privileged to view as much as of her then as now. He might have recognized her more rapidly if his eyes had made their way up to the region of her face sooner, but they had had difficulty getting past the intervening terrain.

Spring had regained her composure and grabbed up the

towel, blushing with a slight pinkish tinge that Herb found delightful.

"Moon Maiden?" he asked.

"Yes." She wrapped the towel tighter and backed toward a chair. As her upper calf struck the edge, she lost her balance, sitting down abruptly. The action caused the towel to slide from the upper portion of her torso. Herb's eyes lost their purchase on her face and got lost again amidst the marvelous hills and valleys below.

Spring retrieved the errant towel, this time tucking it securely. "Peeping Tom," she accused him.

"No, my name is Herb."

"I meant, you didn't have to stare that way. Haven't you ever seen a naked girl before?"

"No. I mean, not like you. I mean, there's nothing wrong with—I'm sorry. Uh, why are you here?"

"I wrote you a letter," she exclaimed, squirming in the chair, trying to keep everything concealed, with delightfully imperfect success.

"Oh. Yes." The letter he had not opened. He found it on a table and ripped it open, reading swiftly. "Yes," he nodded. "It says you will arrive for a visit. In three months."

"Oh. Well, there was a slight change in my itinerary. I hope you don't mind too much?" she asked, still struggling with the unruly towel.

"Well—" He hesitated, distracted yet again by the towel. Or whatever. Herb hadn't even thought of such a thing happening. Writing was one thing, but a strange girl here in the flesh—and what flesh it was!

Spring noticed his reticence, but she wasn't ready to be kicked out into the streets yet. She allowed the towel to slip down just a bit more.

The subtle gesture had its effect. "That is, of course I

don't mind. And if you don't mind my asking, how did you get in here?"

"Oh. That. You must have forgotten to lock up," she said with wide-eyed innocence acquired from dealing with Elton. "I just walked in. It was a long trip. I didn't think you'd mind if I had a shower?"

Herb made a note to double check that lock in the future. "I, uh—" It was so hard to focus on anything other than that slowly sliding towel.

"So, Herb. I hope I didn't come at a bad time? Do you mind if I rest here a bit until I can find somewhere to stay?"

"No."

"No?" she repeated, disappointed. Drastic times called for drastic measures. She dropped the towel.

"I meant, no, I don't mind at all," Herb said, putting his eyeballs back in their sockets. She was amazingly clumsy, but he liked that in a woman. "Would you care for a nap? I only have this room, and the kitchen, and the shower."

Spring sighed with relief, retrieving the towel. "That would be wonderful. I'll just go slip into a robe now."

Herb watched as she minced out into the shower stall. She must have put her belongings in there. Moon Maiden in his apartment. She was even more lovely in person, he thought, recalling those quick, illicit glimpses.

She returned in only a moment, having dried her hair with a towel. It tumbled in a golden brown profusion over her shoulders, and she had changed into a robe of clinging material in a pale pink shade that complemented her fair complexion.

"Herb," she began uncertainly. She badly needed a place of refuge, but had done a bit of flirting in her letters and now after that towel business, well . . . She didn't want to risk him becoming overly attentive while she was vulnerable. He was probably very nice, but after all, he was a man.

It was possible he could be anticipating more than she was willing to offer for a night's lodging.

"Yes, Moon Maiden?"

"Herb, I feel as if we are friends. I must tell you up front, so you won't think there can ever be more than friendship between us, that there was someone else very close to me. He, uh, lied to me, and now we are separated, but I still think of him. So I'm not ready for another attachment yet, and I can't fully trust another man because of that. Do you see? I hope you do." She paused to see how he was taking it.

She had thought it would be safe enough with a plant man, but he wasn't that different from a human. If she had seen his photo, she might not have come. He was not only human looking, but darn good-looking, human or otherwise, and his reactions were exactly typical of a garden-variety human male. "Herb, you don't look the way I expected," she said accusingly.

"You are disappointed? But I sent a photosynthegraph," he said, taken aback by this declaration.

"I didn't receive it. Either it was lost or you forgot to put it in. I don't know. I didn't mean it the way it sounded. You look very attractive. I was just expecting someone more—more bushy."

"A Vinese," Herb agreed. "They look like bushes. We have Treeples here, too. They look like trees. But Veganoids are the most human. There are differences."

"And I want to know everything for my thesis. And of course, about your planet as well," she added.

Herb brightened. "I will be glad to help. But, is something bothering you? You seem agitated."

"I just wasn't expecting to have to worry about us. Herb, I can't sleep with you."

"Oh. You thought when I asked you to have a nap—?"

Herb blushed. "No, I just thought you might be exhausted."

"I'm sorry. I misunderstood. It's just that, the other man, I haven't gotten over him, and all his lies. Lies. Trust is everything in a relationship, don't you agree?"

And that was all lies, naturally. She wasn't carrying a torch for anyone. As long as she carried that dreadful secret, she could never allow herself to care for anyone that way. Whoever she touched would become another target for Zygote.

But she couldn't spend the rest of her life running, either. It was time to make a stand. She hadn't figured out how to do that yet, but with some time to think, perhaps she could ensnare Zygote in his own trap. He might be a magician, but she was a magician's daughter and that magician was a hundred times the caliber of Zygote. Why else would he try to steal from her father? Now the thief was a murderer as well. But he would pay.

Herb mistook the anguish on her face for the pain of losing her human lover. There was no misreading heartache.

Spring climbed upon the water bed and settled down on one side. "Oh. Where will you sleep?"

"Sleep? Oh no, I'm a night person. You rest. I have some, uh, reading to do." He only had to be up at the crack of dawn, after all.

Spring shut her eyes, and relaxed. Herb strode awkwardly over to the only chair in the small room and settled down, reaching for the letter again. Why had she decided to pay a visit if she had no interest in encouraging a romance? Not that he could afford to be encouraged. There was Lily. Still, not even to be considered? Male pride was not easily put to rest.

He found the answer on page two. "Your letters have made Paradise come alive for me, Herb, with your wonderful descriptions of the plant life there, not to mention the chance of meeting someone as nice as you. I have some time and have decided to work up my thesis there. I know this will assure me a confirmed place at the Jupiter Science Institute next year."

Nothing strange about that. Paradise would be a botanist's dream to study. Naturally, he would have wanted to meet her, and been glad to find accommodations for her.

Accommodations. He checked the time. It was too late to hunt for a room tonight even if they left immediately.

He looked toward the bed. She was sound asleep. It would be a shame to waken her. What the harm if she stayed the night? He could sit in a chair for a few hours. Not the most comfortable way to spend a restful night, but the only sensible solution. She would sleep right through, poor girl. She looked totally exhausted. He went over and pulled the light coverlet over her exposed limbs. Much as he enjoyed viewing them, he didn't want her to catch a chill.

Herb then went quietly about preparing for the night, taking a quick shower and returning in a loose robe. He clicked out the flowerbulb and settled back in the darkness. It wasn't all that bad. In the morning he could give her directions to a nearby boarding home or two. So few visitors came to Paradise that they didn't have conventional rooming for vacationers, but certain families would provide accommodations for a small fee. He would explain all that to her in the morning.

The light from the tri-moons shone through the window, casting a beam across the bed where Spring lay. She was quite lovely, Herb thought. He would show her the Crystal Gardens. She would love that because of her interest in such stones.

Perhaps they could go to the Sandal Woods. They could lie beneath the sunflowers enjoying a pinecream cone.

Maybe she would wear that fetching bathing suit she wore in the photosynthegraph? And they said daisies don't tell!

What was he thinking of? Naturally he would be helpful, but she was not there for his enjoyment. He could not squire her about town. What would Lily think? He must think of something to do about all that in the morning, though. He was very tired now.

Herb had not been asleep very long when the insistent tapping at the front door awakened him. For a moment he wondered where he was until remembering that Moon Maiden was in his bed. But first, he had to answer the door. Who would be knocking so late at night? He went quickly and opened the door a crack, not turning on the bulb, as he didn't want to disturb Moon Maiden. He peeped through the crevice. It was Lily, of all people.

"Lily! Of all people," he exclaimed nervously. "What are you doing here?"

She held up a small black case. "Your briefcase. You left it at the house." She smiled. "I saw it when I got up for a drink of water. I remembered you had that important meeting in the morning and knew you'd need it."

"That's right." He had forgotten all about the meeting, what with everything else that had happened. Moon Maiden! Lily must not see her. He took the case and began to close the door again. "Thank you for the case. I don't know what I'd do without you, dear."

The bulb snapped on behind him, flooding the room in bright light. Spring sat up in bed, sleepily rubbing her eyes. "Herb? Is that you? What's wrong?" she asked.

Lily pushed the door open, then stood perfectly still, wide eyes taking in the scene over Herb's shoulders. Herb in his night robe; a strange, foreign girl sleeping in his bed. She looked at Herb angrily, tears beginning to seep out the corners of her eyes. "It looks as if you do very nicely without me," she snapped, running away into the night.

Herb called after her. "Lily! Wait!"

"Herb?" Moon Maiden said again. "Is something the matter?" Her first thought was that Elton might have found her again. "Herb!" she called, upset.

Herb shut the door and returned to her. How would he ever explain this one to Lily?

❦ 13 ❦

Lies

"These are lovely flowers," Elton said.

"Children," Lily said, wondering who the off planet visitor was and what business he had at the nursery. "I don't mean to be rude, sir, but it is obvious you are new to our sphere. Do you seek directions?"

Elton looked nonplused. "No, I know where I am. Actually, I wished to speak with you, if you have a few moments?"

"Me? Yes, there is time before the next feeding. Step into the office, please," Lily said, more curious than apprehensive, now.

Elton pulled a picture from his coat and presented it to Lily. "Have you ever seen this girl before?" he asked.

Lily drew in a breath. It was the passionflower! Who was she that so many men were drawn to her?

"Who is this girl?" she asked casually, examining the photo with trembling hands. There could be no doubt. She would know those pale limbs anywhere.

"My wife," Elton answered.

Lily almost dropped the picture. "Your wife?"

"Yes. She is missing, you see. This is somewhat embarrassing to admit, but we were on vacation and had a silly quarrel. When the starship landed, my wife got off without telling me. I discovered she wasn't aboard only moments before take-off."

Lily listened in shocked silence. Herb bedded a unionized woman? How could he do such a terrible thing?

"It was a disagreement over nothing, really," Elton continued. "But my wife is a very impulsive individual. That was always part of her charm for me, of course. But I'm sure she must be frantic by now, alone here on a strange planet with unfamiliar ways."

"I'm sure. But why ask me?" Lily hedged. His wife was impulsive? She looked settled in last night!

"Oh, not only you, dear lady. The lightport is near this area, and I have since discovered that rooms are not easy to come by. I thought to inquire at the local business places, in case she had asked information there. You see, I fear I took your establishment for a flower shop," he added apologetically.

"Yes, most offworlders aren't familiar with how our different species reproduce young. This is indeed a nursery, but not in the way you thought," she explained. "We raise the offspring of working mothers while they are at their jobs."

"My sincere apology for the error. I have no wish to offend anyone, I assure you. I wish only to locate my wife."

Lily was torn. While she had no love for the young woman in the photo, she was sure her husband would not be pleased to learn that his wife had bedded with another. A unionized woman. She certainly did not take her union vows very seriously. True, offworlders had different values, but how could she tell this to the offworlder?

He might even hurt Herb. She had heard stories of how violent foreigners could be. While not approving of what Herb had done, Lily did not want to be responsible for him being beaten or even worse. In spite of it all, she still cared for him.

She pondered going to Herb and explaining what she had learned. It was possible he did not even know that the woman was unionized. If she was so impulsive and charming, she may have pressed herself on him. Forcing him beyond what any man could reasonably endure. Men were only human. And Herb was half human. She could have easily taken advantage of poor Herb. Lily began to realize what a jealous fool she had been to storm off in Herb's time of need.

"I see you recognize the photograph," Elton said. "Do you know where she has gone?"

"Recognize it? Oh, no. Forgive me if I gave you the wrong impression. I was only looking so intently because I have never seen a pale offworlder woman before. I will ask some of the others in this neighborhood for you, and if they have seen her I will let you know. Come back this evening." She was trying to buy time.

"That is very kind of you," Elton said, tucking the photo back into his pocket. "Until then." He made a slight bow and left.

Once outside, Elton smiled broadly and gave himself a mental pat on the back. He could tell she believed his story; he could see it in her eyes. Spring had eluded him aboard the starship, but he would soon find her out.

He had almost believed she was not at the Moon sanctuary until one of Zygote's other spies had successfully infiltrated the compound and found proof that a girl of Spring's description had been there until the day the ship left. True, they did not admit him, but they were quick to accept a new "Pledge."

The spy had searched the girl's room, discovering part of a torn photograph in the bathroom. Spring had probably tried to destroy all evidence of her destination. It was a photo of a male Veganoid, native of P#23, Paradise, one of the stops of the starship.

The spy had wired it and the information to Elton aboard the starship via photogram. He had searched the ship from top to bottom without result, but knew she had gotten off on P#23. Luck was running out for Gabriel's unfortunate daughter, Elton thought smugly.

Still, the search had not been without effort. Elton had no idea of the true identity of the plant man, and could hardly wander the sphere, searching aimlessly for him. The direct approach was sometimes the best. Therefore, when he entered the government building for his Visitor's Pass, he made other inquiries as well.

Claiming to be a business acquaintance, he said he had lost the man's name and address. It turned out that the government of Paradise kept scrupulous census records, complete with current photographs. A quick check through the Identimatch machine with his torn picture, and he learned the man's name was Herb Moss, son of a prominent local businessman. He was given an office address, but the home address was protected by the Privacy Act.

Elton had gone directly to the firm and asked to see Herb. It was his intention to say he was Spring's brother and needed to see her on urgent family business. He learned that Herb had taken the day off for illness. They would not release his home address either, but one of the secretaries he had gone out of his way to flirt with saw fit to mention that Herb's fiancée, Lily, worked at the Nursery uptown. She might be willing to pass along his message.

Naturally he could not come right out and ask Lily where Herb lived. He didn't know how much she knew. If they were in it together, she would only put him off. Yet, she was no friend to Spring. He could see that from the way she eyed the photograph.

There had been recognition, though. He was certain she knew something and he was going to find out what that certain something was. All it took was a little patience.

Fortunately for him, he did not have long to wait. Just as he had suspected, Lily was going to lead him to the elusive Herb Moss. He watched as she slipped outside the back door of the Nursery, pausing to look surreptitiously about before proceeding swiftly down the street. Elton followed at a safe distance. His trap for Spring was about to be sprung.

· 14 ·

And More Lies

$\mathcal{I}$t was sweet of you to take the day off to help me find a place to stay, Herb, but won't you get in trouble with your boss?" Spring asked.

"The boss is my father," Herb said, laughing. "Besides, I called in sick. No one should try to communicate, but just in case, I have looped the communiline. It will give off a busy signal to anyone who tries."

"What about that meeting you had this morning? Your poor secretary even made a special trip last night to bring your case," she protested.

Herb had thought it the better part of discretion not to mention his scene with Lily. It would only upset Moon, and one distraught female at a time was all he could handle. Besides that, he had also failed to mention his upcoming union in correspondence with Moon. An unfortunate oversight. How would she feel now to learn she had travelled all that way to visit a man who wasn't even free to escort her in broad daylight? Would she think him as despicable as that other man who had lied to her? Who had left her so broken and untrusting? Herb could not risk her reaction.

Lily had stormed away by the time his overnight guest had fully awakened, so she remembered only the sounds of voices and the slamming door. Herb had assured her it was nothing to worry her pretty sleepy head about, and sent her back to bed. When Moon inquired about the incident in the morning, he had contrived the secretary story to quell her curiosity.

The best thing now was to find proper lodgings for her, so she could work on that thesis for her entry to the Jupiter Institute. Herb would try to arrange his schedule so he could show her around without disturbing Lily. It was obvious what his intended believed she had seen. While he might think of some explanation she would accept, he knew she would never forgive him should she discover him in Moon's company a second time. Lily was usually a trusting woman, but there were limits to her credulity.

Much as Herb admired the pale girl, he now wished he had never answered that ad. Even an exchange of letters was more than Lily would countenance. The vine grew more tangled with each new event.

Moon, as he now called her for short, had offered no other name. She had currently disappeared into the shower room and busied herself with the items he had shopped for earlier. Herb jotted down the addresses of homes that might be willing to take her in. She returned quietly and tapped him on the shoulder. Herb turned and almost dropped his pen and lily pad.

"Lily," he exclaimed, startled to see his girlfriend.

"Who's Lily?" asked Spring. "Do I look like someone you know?"

Herb felt like a fool. Of course it wasn't Lily. "No, that is, you don't look like you, Moon."

"Good. That's the idea. So, how do you like me?" she

asked twirling around, causing the floral patterned skirt to lift, revealing slim, shapely legs.

"They're nice. That is, you look nice," Herb babbled. He could hardly ignore the well grown limbs of an attractive girl, despite having seem them before. Each time sent him into a new spin. "You look just like a Veganette."

The transformation was remarkable. The spray-on hair coloring gave her tresses a lovely dark shade of green. The makeup completely covered over her pale skin, changing it to a normal light greenish hue. The dress was typical of one a smartly dressed Veganette would choose.

The dress! Now Herb realized why he had thought Moon was Lily. Lily had a dress exactly like that one. Probably that was why it had caught his eye so quickly in the shop. He had always liked that style on Lily, and it looked just as good on Moon. In fact, Moon perhaps filled out the top a bit fuller, though it was the same size as Lily's dress.

"No one will know me from a native," Spring exclaimed, pleased with her new disguise. At least here, she could be her own sex.

"I thought you looked lovely the way you were before," Herb commented, almost too sincerely.

"Thanks, but I feel people will open up to me better if I don't look so different," Spring said. "You told me how many people are wary of strangers. I think this is best." She also thought Elton would have a tougher time tracking her down if she blended in with the locals. Her white skin made her conspicuous among all the green folk.

Herb didn't fully understand why she felt it was necessary, but if it made her happy, he had no objections. He knew how she really looked underneath. He would never forget it. But he shouldn't dwell on that. He had just decided to tell her about some of the homes on his list, when there was a knock at the door.

Both jumped, but for personal reasons unknown to the other. Herb wondered if his father had sent someone over to check on him after all. Spring feared Zygote's spies.

Herb peeked through the small viewer in the door and saw the top of a woman's head below. Then she looked up and knocked again. Lily.

Herb's heart plunged into his stomach. Why was she back? She didn't even look angry. Why couldn't she behave like a normal woman and never speak to him again? Of course he didn't mean that, but her timing was incredibly bad for him. He signaled for Moon to leave the room.

"It's my secretary again," he whispered. "Hide in the shower. If the office sent her, they might not understand why I have company if I'm sick."

Spring nodded and exited the room, pulling the wallflower partition shut after her.

Herb opened the door cautiously, not knowing what to say. "Lily. What a surprise."

"Not half the one I had last night," she said dryly, pushing past him, and looking around. "Sleep well?"

"I, uh, didn't expect to see you today," he said lamely, closing the door.

"No, I imagine not. Herb, I must know. Are you having an affair with that—that passionflower?"

Clearly Lily was upset. She never used such language. "Affair? Ha. Of course I'm not having an affair with anyone. I know what you thought. But it wasn't that way at all. It was perfectly innocent." He was dying on the vine.

"Buttercup. I knew it. I knew you had an explanation," cried Lily, throwing her arms about his neck, nearly strangling him in the process.

"You did?" he gasped, trying not to choke. "What is it?"

She released her hold, and he took a deep breath.

"I knew all along it had to be that girl's doing. She is unionized."

"What?" Herb was certain his hearing was going. He thought Lily said Spring was married.

"Yes, it's true. A unionized woman, acting that way," Lily said disapprovingly.

Herb was shocked. What nonsense was she sprouting?

"I see you are as shocked as I was," Lily said. "Her husband came to the nursery today looking for her. He showed me a photosynthegraph. It was her all right. He said they had a quarrel and she left the starship in a huff. Now he's looking for her everywhere. I didn't tell him that she was here last night. I didn't know what he might do to you."

Herb was more shocked. Moon had a husband? He sat down in the chair. "Are you absolutely sure of this?" he asked weakly.

"Yes. They were on vacation. He said she was very impulsive. I thought about it, and I knew you would never bed a unionized woman. Not intentionally." She looked at the floor forlornly.

"I didn't bed anyone. She just needed a place to spend the night. You must believe me!"

"I do. I really do," Lily said, hopping into his lap. "And I am so sorry for jumping to all the wrong conclusions. Can you ever forgive me?"

Herb cleared his throat, and spoke righteously. "Yes, I think we can let it go this time, Lily, but if we are to have a good union you must trust me in the future." He remembered an old Earth story, and wondered whether his nose would sprout a few inches.

"Yes, Herb," Lily said docilely. "She is gone now?" Her eyes darted about like an eagle's, searching for tell-tale signs of her rival.

"You can see for yourself," Herb said nervously. "Now, you run along like a good girl so I can get some rest. I had to call in sick today because I barely got a wink of sleep sitting up in that hard chair all night." That part was true.

"Oh, poor Herb," Lily said, hopping up and opening the door, pausing only to blow him a kiss. "I promise never to doubt you again."

Herb smiled and waved, and slammed the door. And locked it. He sat back down. So much to vegetate on. Could it be true? Had Moon lied to him? He had only her word for her life on New Moon. Could she be just a bored housewife looking for alien playmates for new thrills? Well, Herb Moss was nobody's joy toy.

"Moon Maiden. Come here," he called firmly. "Now."

Spring emerged from her hiding place behind the shower curtain. "What's wrong, Herb?"

"Never mind. I want the truth. Are you in Union?"

"I don't have a job," she answered, confused.

"Married. Are you married?" he shouted.

"What are you shouting about?"

"I am not shouting," he yelled. "I want to know if you are married. Are you?"

"But why ask such a thing?"

"Because Lily, that is, my secretary, told me a man claiming to be your husband asked for you at the Nursery, uh, office. Why would someone say that if it wasn't so?"

Why indeed, thought Spring. She sank down upon the bed, her sudden pallor showing through the makeup. "A man asked for me? How would he know where to find me this soon?" she asked, more to herself than Herb.

"So. You were lying to me from the start," Herb stated angrily. Never mind how he had lied to her. That was different, naturally.

"I didn't mean to mislead you, Herb. I just haven't told you everything. And I can't. I don't want to put you in danger as well. But believe this. I am not married. Whoever that man is, he is certainly not my husband."

Herb's anger left him, to be replaced by concern. "You said something about danger. Is that man trying to harm you? Please Moon, I want to help you, but you must tell me the truth."

Spring sighed. "I suppose I have to tell you now. If he saw your secretary, he must have an idea where I am." She suddenly realized what that meant. "Oh—I have to get out of here fast!" She jumped up and ran about gathering all her things from the shower and throwing them into the bag from beneath the bed.

"Wait! Are you hiding? What's going on? Tell me," Herb demanded.

"No time to explain everything. That man, or other men may be looking for me. They—they killed my father. And now they want me," she panted, trying to force the bag shut.

"Someone killed your father?" Herb knew offworlders were violent, but actually killing someone? "Why? What have you done?"

"Done? Nothing. And I don't intend to do anything," she said, thinking of the sexual requirement of the transference. "I have some information, and they want it, but to get it, they have to—oh, I don't know how you say it." She was floundering. "You know, the sex act."

"They would bed you against your will?" he breathed, shocked and amazed.

"Exactly. So you see, Herb, I can't let them find me here."

"An abomination!" Herb exclaimed. Such acts were virtually unheard of on Paradise. For one thing, it was impossible for most of the species to pollinate without cooperation. Perhaps once in many seasons, some loco weed would grow wild and attempt it, but that was a biological defect. To do such a thing on purpose was unthinkable. "Moon, I don't understand."

"Much better that you don't," Spring agreed. "This trouble is not for you." She had finished packing and tucked her small rock pouch into a pocket of her skirt. "Well, that's everything."

"But where will you go?" asked Herb. "What will you do?"

"I don't know. Maybe I'll try to get back on the starship. Or hide out here. I don't know, but for your own sake, please don't try to find me. I know it wasn't much of a visit. I wish we had more time to know each other." She smiled, fleetingly. "Who knows? We might have liked that." She stood up on tiptoes to plant a lingering kiss on his lips.

Dazed, Herb stood aside as she went to the door. Her touch had been pleasant. Very pleasant indeed. He was sorry this pale Moon Maiden had beamed into his life for so short a season. He was about to protest this mad departure—but instead stiffened along with Spring at the sudden violent banging at the door.

❧ 15 ❧

Double Trouble

Spring retrieved her case and dashed quickly into the shower closet while Herb advanced cautiously toward the door.

"Who is it?" he called, hoping he didn't sound half as scared as he felt. There was no answer. Herb pressed his ear against the frame, but could detect no sounds outside. He could see no one out the viewer, but they might be hiding at the side away from his vision. Gathering all his failing courage, he released the lock and slowly opened the door. First a crack, then all the way. There was no one there at all. Only a crumpled paper lying at the middle of the entrance where someone had hastily shoved it.

Herb picked it up and read the scrawled message: "We have your green girl, Lily. If you want to see her in one piece again, bring us Spring Gabriel. Don't call the authorities or you will regret it. We will be watching. Wait for instructions."

Herb stood in the doorway, baffled at the message. What could it all mean? Someone had taken Lily? And who was this Spring person they mentioned, and why did they think he knew anything about it? It was all some terrible mistake. He closed the door behind him in a daze.

"Herb? What is it? Who was at the door?" asked Spring, returning as soon as she heard the door shut.

Herb handed the letter to Spring. He was still too confused to speak.

As she read, dismay clouded her features. It had already begun.

"They've kidnapped your secretary? I'm so sorry, Herb."

"No. No," Herb said slowly. He was still trying to sort it all out. "I must be truthful with you now, Moon. Lily is not my secretary. She—she is my fiancée."

"Oh. I see," Spring said. Evidently she had not been the only one keeping secrets.

"I know I should have told you about this before, but it just didn't seem that important when we were only corresponding by mail. I never expected—"

"That I would end up on your doorstep."

"In my bed," Herb corrected her.

"Whatever," Spring said, dismissing the subject. "I have a confession to make, too. I haven't been completely honest with you about who I am and why I'm here either. You see—" She swallowed. "I am the Spring Gabriel in the note. I am the one they're after."

"Then, these are the same men. But what about Lily? They say they will harm her unless they get you. But I can't let you go now. They will harm you instead!"

"It's a trap. I'm convinced that once they have me, they won't let any of us go. I know that slimy little Ki behind this outrage. He has no scruples."

"We should call the Patrol," Herb said. "Ask them what we should do."

"Wait, is that the same thing as the Police? I don't think

that's a great idea, Herb. Zygote's men will be alert for any double-cross. They could disappear so fast we'd never find them again, and I hate to think of what might happen to Lily if we disobey them."

"No, nothing must happen to Lily," Herb said, blanching. He replaced the communiline speaker in its slot.

"Do you love her?" Spring asked quietly.

Herb hesitated, his eyes showing the inner turmoil.

"I'm sorry, that doesn't deserve an answer," Spring said, angry at herself for saying such a stupid thing. "You've just said you plan to be married. Of course we can't let anyone harm her. We won't," she said emphatically, trying not to let Herb see how hopeless it was to prevent it at the moment. She sank down on the bed in despair.

Spring could not deny she had been surprised by the news that Herb was engaged, but after all, it had nothing to do with her. She had come to Paradise to hide, and make plans. Certainly not for romance. Herb wasn't for her. He wasn't even human. Not that she held that against him. He was very nice, and sweet, and different from any of the boys she had met on New Landers. There was a naivete that made you trust him right away.

Well, of course that was a crock. He wasn't all that innocent. He managed to hide a fiancée well enough. What else had he been hiding behind that honest, good-looking face of his? Those big green eyes and thick lashes that any woman would envy were not going to make her forget why she was there. But, all this trouble wasn't his. It was hers. She felt bad that he and his friend had been dragged into it through no fault of their own. Herb was a nice person, and it had been nice when they kissed, too. He didn't deserve this.

Herb sat reading the note over and over again. What could they do to help Lily? Paradise was a peaceful planet. They had their share of native law breakers, but violent crimes were a rarity. It was simply not the nature of things there so he did not have the background to prepare him for something of this magnitude.

"What are you going to do?" he asked. "You might still escape if you told the Patrol. They could protect you. At least get you safely off the planet."

"You know I wouldn't," Spring said, a bit hurt. "You know I couldn't do that to your girlfriend. It's bad enough it happened. Do you think I go around leaving a trail of bodies in my wake?"

"No, but—"

"But I have a darn good track record so far?" she said sarcastically.

"I don't blame you. I just wish you had trusted me and told me about it from the beginning. We could have gone off some place where you'd be safe. And Lily would be safe."

"Ha. Don't give me that, Herb Moss. If I had said, 'Hello, I'm on the run from some powerful men who want to rule the universe. How about risking your life to help me out?' What would you have said to that, eh?"

"I—"

"I'll tell you what you'd have said. You'd have told me I was crazy. To go fly a rocket." Her defiance crumbled and she turned away to hide the tears.

Herb stood by helplessly as she cried and agreed inwardly that he probably would have thought she was unbalanced if she had told him such a story. "It's been hard for you. Alone," he said sympathetically.

"I've managed," she said briskly, in control once more. "The note said to wait for instructions. They have to tell you where to deliver me. All we can do is wait, but if we learn where she is, maybe we can think of a plan. A way to rescue her." She tried to sound encouraging.

"Yes, we can find a way," Herb agreed, grasping at hope

once more. "They won't hurt her while they still believe we will trade. We have time."

They settled down to an uneasy wait. Herb made a path to the door every few minutes to check for notes, but found nothing. Time crawled. They had a light meal which neither did more than pick at, and Herb took a short nap on the condition that Spring wake him at the first sign of contact.

The evening was interminable. It grew late and both grew tired. Herb sat nodding in the chair while Spring perched with legs drawn beneath her on the side of the bed.

"Herb, they may not even call tonight," Spring said. "They may be waiting to be sure we haven't contacted the Patrol. Why don't you come to bed? You had no sleep last night and only a nap today. Here, I'll take the chair tonight. I refuse to chase you out of your own bed another night."

"No, I don't want you to sit up," Herb protested, ever the gentleman.

"Then come over here," Spring said firmly. "We've already slept together, if that's what you're worried about," she added mischievously.

Herb's face registered confusion. He might have overlooked a lot of things about Moon, but that would not be something he would forget.

"I meant during your nap, Herb," she clarified. "When I came back from the kitchen, you were asleep and I sat down on the side of the bed. You threw your arm around me and I didn't have the heart to move and waken you." She smiled.

Now he remembered. His dream. Green hair on the pillow, and the sweet scent of honeysuckle. Moon's perfume. In the dream, it was Lily. He thought he had found her.

"Lily," he said.

"All we can do is wait, Herb. When they want us, they

will get our attention, you can be certain of that. They won't give up until they have me," Spring said.

Whether from loss of sleep, or anxiety over Lily, Herb felt incredibly tired. He looked at the beckoning bed sheets and agreed.

"You're right. We need our rest. Not that I will sleep until we know something," he added. "But it would feel good to stretch out."

He went to the opposite side and lay down stiffly at the edge, careful not to touch any part of Spring's apparel.

"Oh, for Pete's sake," exclaimed Spring, grabbing his arm and pulling him toward the center beside her.

"Who is Pete?" asked Herb. He had a cousin, Pete. Pete Moss.

"Never mind. Relax. You feel like a stick. I promise I won't break if you touch me, and I seriously doubt if either of us feels romantically inclined tonight. Try to get some rest now, okay?"

Herb recalled how different it had been when he last lay in bed with a beautiful girl. He had not been shy with Holly, his playmate on Avocado. What was it about Moon that made him so uncomfortable? True, she had not come looking for a romance, but he enjoyed her letters and thought she was very beautiful. He was strangely attracted to her, despite all the problems she represented, and despite the fact he was in no position to be. There was Lily, his fiancée. And for Moon, there was the memory of that other man who had been untrue to her. In a way, she also had ties, if only in her heart.

He stole a sideways glance in her direction and saw that she reclined on her back with an arm flung over her head. She was breathing evenly in sleep. As he lay noting the rise and fall of her breasts, he wished he could fall asleep. He never would with that distraction!

Reluctantly, Herb turned over and away from the pleasant view. Much better with his back toward her. He shut his eyes and counted pussy willows.

The shrill buzz of the communiline broke the silence. Herb awoke abruptly, realizing he had indeed fallen asleep. Groggy, he reached for the speaker, afraid of what he would hear. "Yes?" he said. His voice sounded strange and hollow in his ears. The sound of fear.

A muffled voice spoke thickly. "I won't repeat this Moss, so write it down."

Herb groped about the bed stand for a writing quill and lily pad. Spring sat alert at his side and handed him what he needed. The voice gave him an address in a seedy side of town.

"Daybreak. Got it?" the voice said.

"Got it," Herb agreed, swallowing as he replaced the communiline.

"What did they say?" Spring asked.

"We go there at daybreak," Herb said, indicating the address.

"Smart. Gives us no time to change our minds about the Patrol. But Herb, the more I think about everything, I don't see how we can do it alone. Don't you have some other private organizations, like detectives? Or—" she paused as she read the confusion on Herb's face. "No, of course not," she said in disgust. "This is such a law abiding planet."

"No, wait. I do know someone who might help us. He isn't a professional in the way you mean, but he is a friend and runs a Julep-so school."

"Julep? Like Mint Juleps?" she asked, perplexed.

"No, Julep-so. He is very proficient in that ancient art of defence. We are not a violent people, but this is a weaponless form of combat with throws and holds. It is more for exercise, and he is very fit. We've known each other since university."

"He sounds perfect. But—" She hesitated. "Do you think he would help?"

"I don't know, but I think so. He likes adventure. He is always watching Vision Plays."

"Vision Plays? Oh, yes, I know about those. Hologram tapes you play on home viewers, only in these you can enter astrally with the action and experience the story with the images. But there was a problem with addiction. An electronic drug. Many users could not tell fantasy from reality after a while. I thought they were outlawed." She raised a fine brow.

"They are," Herb agreed. "But my friend is, well, adventurous. There is not much of an outlet on this planet for that sort of nature. He knows all about offworlders, too."

"You've convinced me. Call him now."

Herb punched the communiline and was soon speaking with his friend. After Herb explained the urgency of the situation, it was agreed that his friend would assist them. Perhaps he thought it was a chance to participate in a real life adventure instead of a hologram? Herb gave him the address where they were to go. It was decided Cling Ling would go now and look it over. They would meet later and determine how to proceed from there. There was still a few hours until dawn.

"Cling Ling will help," Herb said to Spring. "He looks like the bush people you were expecting to see when you arrived here. He is a full Vinese."

Spring laughed in spite of herself. "A Vinese named Cling Ling? Do you have plant folks of Irish descent as well? Sharon Begonia? A bit of the Old Sod?"

Herb looked at her blankly. That only served to send her into additional peals of laughter. Herb decided not to comment.

"Sorry. This is no time for jokes. When I get nervous, I

get giddy. But I, more than anyone, realize the danger we face."

Herb was certain she meant no disrespect to Lily. It was a trying time for both of them. Also, the sound of her laughter had fallen pleasantly on his ears.

"I understand, Moon. We may as well return to bed. I will set the timer so we can meet Cling. It is not far from here."

Herb turned out the flowerbulb and they were left in darkness once again. He shut his eyes but all his thoughts were on the morrow and what it would bring.

Spring's voice broke the silence as he turned over. "Herb?" she whispered.

"I'm sorry. Did I wake you? I'm just so restless. I'll get up so you can sleep." He moved to rise, but her hand clutched at his arm.

"Don't be ridiculous. Do you think I could sleep any more than you? Come here." She pulled him against her breasts and cradled him in her arms.

"Spring," he protested, shocked.

"Oh, quiet. Shut your eyes. You don't have to sleep. Just shut your eyes." The fingers of one hand wandered to the back of his neck and caressed with small round strokes.

Herb basked in the warmth of the embrace. It did help to be with someone. Perhaps she was just afraid as he was. She always seemed so independent that he took her strength for granted. She really was a caring girl.

He adjusted to put his arms around her as well, but he didn't feel the way he usually did in a similar situation. It was just a contented feeling. Just to lie there and nothing more. It was complete the way it was. He sighed deeply and slept.

The next thing he knew the timer rang. The quiet moment had ended. Spring was already up, bustling about, putting on her Veganette disguise. She did it very well. Even though Herb knew what she really looked like underneath—did he ever!—he would not have known the difference seeing her with the eyes of a stranger.

Herb splashed water on his face, and drank a hot cup of coffee beans that Spring had brewed for them. She was becoming quite handy in his little kitchenette. In a few minutes they were ready to leave the safety of the apartment and venture into the darkness toward their rendezvous with Cling Ling.

The address turned out to be an old deserted greenhouse. The glass was cracked and dirty, and it had not been used for many a season by the look of it. It was a setting tailor-made for kidnappers.

As agreed, they met Cling Ling a short way down the street. He had scouted the area and climbed onto the roof of the fragile structure to look for signs of Lily. He reported that there was only one guard attending her, and that the other parts of the building appeared empty for the present. If they could entice the guard outside for a minute, someone could sneak in through the back way and free Lily.

Their loosely conceived plan was to have Spring bait the guard. Herb would then go to get Lily, while Cling Ling covered him in case of trouble. In her Veganette disguise it was unlikely anyone would recognize Spring as the girl they were seeking. She would simply knock at the front door and pretend to be lost.

The plan would fail if the guard decided not to answer the door, but they were betting he wouldn't want undue attention called to the hideout, and would attempt to quiet whoever was there.

They guessed correctly. The Vinese signaled from his

post on the roof to let her know the goon was approaching the door. As agreed, Spring removed a shoe and used it to bash in some of the glass, covering the noise of Herb breaking in from the opposite direction in back.

The guard opened the door and glared out. He looked about eight feet tall.

Spring tried to act innocent and smiled up at him sweetly. "Oops. Guess I knocked too hard," she laughed nervously. "Is this the residence of Mr. Smith?"

The guard stared at her in disbelief. "How did you get out?" he growled, reaching for her with his hairy arms.

"Hey. What are you doing?" she gasped as he pulled her inside and slammed the door behind them. That wasn't part of the plan. How could he have possibly recognized her? She was totally green. Struggling in vain to escape his grip, she saw Herb making good his escape with Lily out the back. And now she understood.

For some reason, she and Lily were dressed exactly the same. No wonder this idiot had grabbed her. He thought she was Lily. Damn that Herb Moss. He had dressed her up like his girlfriend. She should have known the outfit showed too much taste for a man to have selected on such short notice. Just her bad luck that Lily had chosen to wear it that day.

The goon thrust Spring down in the chair Lily had just vacated and began binding her wrists. At least Lily was free and Spring took satisfaction from that. The plan had worked like a charm except for that one little flaw.

"Looks like our day for unexpected company, Trog."

Spring looked up as a well-dressed woman entered, herding Lily and Herb ahead of her with the deadly vapor gun pointed at their backs.

"Miss Eloise," Trog said. "You're back."

Eloise? Spring looked directly into Elton's steely eyes.

The Ki was dressed like a female now, but she would know "him" anywhere.

"Elton," she corrected for the others present. Make that two little flaws.

❧ 16 ❧

Lady Be Cool

E lton had great timing and a big gun. It was hard to argue with a winning combination. Spring and Lily looked each other over with cool appraisal. Herb looked upward to the heavens, but no miracle was forthcoming.

"Don't bother with the rope, Trog. Throw them in the cage," Elton ordered, "her" manicured hand motioning with the slim handle of the vapor gun.

"Uh-huh," answered Trog, typical of Elton's intellectual hirelings of late. He yanked Spring up roughly and pushed the others ahead of him. They were quickly routed out into a small room at the back of the greenhouse. It really was a cage.

Herb explained to Spring that it was where the wild flowers had been kept at one time; they tended to wander about unless confined. Then the goon locked them inside and positioned himself on an old crate nearby. Elton stood gazing at the two identical green ladies.

"Twins. How very original. But your warpaint is wearing a bit thin, my dear," he sneered to Spring.

It was true. There were long smears of white skin show-ing through the makeup where his goon had grappled with her. The stain she'd used for the lightship trip had been much more reliable. It seemed the masquerade was over. Not to mention the party.

Lily had begun to realize who her look-alike was, as well.

"The foreigner," she exclaimed, looking nettles at Herb.

"I'll explain later," Herb said miserably. If there was a later, he thought.

The shock of capture had worn off at last and Spring spoke up now. "Let the others go, Elton. I'm the only one you need. They don't know anything about all this."

"How noble," Elton said sarcastically. "But you should have thought of that before you chose to involve inno-cents. Master Zygote has plans for you, so I can't take the chance. You could be right about the little flower there, but you've been cozied up with your boyfriend for several hours now. I'm sure he knows the score, right hero?"

Herb only glared.

"You're wrong. I didn't tell him anything," Spring protested.

"Perhaps. But Master Zygote wants that secret kept a secret."

"Zygote. He killed my father. He'll get nothing from me," Spring spat.

"I fear you've little choice in the matter. Better get used to the idea, my girl. After all, he will soon be your first love," Elton laughed.

"That bag of bones touch me? I'd rather die. Why, I would as soon sleep with you—Eloise," she said with loathing. The remark was meant as the ultimate put down, but caused a surprising reaction.

The Ki stood pondering, a strange look coming over

"her" face. "Would you really?" said the Ki thoughtfully. "Now, what an interesting notion."

"What?" Spring said with disgust. What kind of game was the Ki playing with her now?

"Yes, indeed," said the Ki, warming to the possibilities. "Why should Zygote be the one to gain all the riches and power? Why not—me? Haven't I always done his dirty work? Where is my compensation?" The Ki smiled meanly to itself, lost in thought.

"You can't," Spring exclaimed in horror.

Herb began to catch his drift and was appalled. "You can't," he repeated. "You're a—a woman."

"At the moment. But we Kis are adaptable. I just need a little time to change into someone more comfortable. Trog!" he called out impatiently. "Where did he go?"

"Here," called the goon, emerging from another room. "Have message from Master."

"Give me that," Elton said, snatching it from the goon. His face registered annoyance and fear. The message was definitely not to his liking. "Trog, bring the girl in to me when I call."

"Girl? Which girl?" the creature asked dumbly.

"Look at the arms, man. Bring the one with the white on her arms. That's easy to remember, isn't it?"

Trog looked at the girls' arms. "Easy," he answered.

Elton exited into the other room adjoining them. Trog returned to his packing crate and sat down to wait. The troubled captives huddled at the far corner of the small cell. Lily looked from Herb to Spring, from Spring back to Herb.

"All right," she said, "Who wants to go first?"

Herb didn't want to, but knew he could no longer avoid an explanation. He began by revealing his connection to Spring, how they had become pen pals before she came to their planet to work on her school thesis. He finished with the account of how the strange, dangerous aliens began chasing her and how they plotted the ill-fated rescue.

Spring in turn, had to explain that was what Herb had believed since it was what she had told him, but that she had never been married to Elton. That the Ki had been searching for her ever since her father's death, so she had sought to hide on P#23 until devising a plan to bring Zygote to justice for his crimes. She assured Lily that there was nothing between her and Herb but friendship and that he had behaved as a perfect gentleman throughout their time together.

Lily had remained silent through the alternate explanations, and listened compassionately at the events surrounding Spring's father's death, and how the evil magician, Zygote, wanted the secret that would pass to him when Spring lost her virginity. At last she spoke.

"There's only one solution," she said.

"One? I can't think of any," said an amazed Herb.

"As I see it," continued Lily, "the most important thing for us to do now is prevent anyone from, uh, molesting Spring."

"Yes," agreed Herb emphatically, "No one must touch her."

Lily looked at him sharply, but said nothing.

"I don't see how we can stop them," Spring said, despondently. "That disgusting weasel is determined to have the secret. It's in there now, preparing."

"It is terrible for you," Lily said, "but it will affect all of us in the long run. If what you say of these men is true, I do not think they will confine their greed to one planet. What could such men do with unlimited power?"

"She's right, Herb. Both Elton and Zygote are power hungry. They won't stop at anything less than ruling the universe."

"The secret you possess? It is that powerful?" Herb said in awe.

"In evil hands, yes, I think it could be," Spring said. "Don't forget that Zygote is no ordinary man, but a magician. With those additional powers there would be no stopping him."

"This Zygote, is he truly that evil?" asked Lily.

"Yes. He killed my father. He's heartless. Old. A conniver. A thief and a murderer. Does that answer your question?"

"I am sorry. Of course you would hate him. I only wanted to understand what we were up against. This Elton?"

"Two peas in a pod," Herb said. The idea of these aliens wanting to place their nasty hands on Spring was more than he could tolerate. "We have to stop them."

He shook the bars of the cage in futile anger. The goon reached out and shoved him backward. He went flying and slammed against the window behind them. It also had bars.

Lily reached into her pocket and took out a small object. It resembled an eye shadow case, but Spring recognized it as the makeup kit used by the green-skinned women of the planet. Lily edged behind Herb and passed it across to Spring.

"Repair the smears on your arms," she whispered.

"What for?" asked Spring. It hardly mattered what she looked like now. The disguise had failed.

"Just do it," Lily hissed.

Spring did it, but she was still perplexed. In a few moments, she was as green as Lily again. She returned the case and Lily opened another section, smearing her own arms with some white cream. Suddenly, Spring understood.

"No. You can't," Spring whispered.

"I must. I wanted to have a union with Herb and raise

our family more than anything else, but I don't know if that will be possible. They won't let us go. I know that now."

"But you can't fool Elton. He'll know you're not me. If not before, then—afterward."

"But we have to try. We need time. Don't forget Cling Ling. He probably went for the Patrol. They may be surrounding this greenhouse right now," Lily said hopefully.

"That's right," Herb said. He had been listening to the confusing conversation about makeup. He never realized what a good mind Lily had before. Perhaps because he had never given her a chance. No wonder she had become so passive. She thought that was what he wanted from a wife. They had both made so many mistakes!

"The Patrol? I doubt that," Spring said. "Remember Herb, you told me the story of how the offworlders were never punished for murdering your children. Elton has immunity. More than likely the Patrol would be only too glad to help Elton claim his wayward 'wife' and vacate the planet. They would hasten the process just to get rid of undesirable elements as soon as possible."

Herb realized she was probably correct, but he had difficulty in thinking of Spring as undesirable.

Herb sighed. "Yes, I suppose the Patrol would be no help after all. But Cling Ling may realize that. I know he wouldn't desert us now."

"Then I must buy that time. I must make Elton believe I am Spring," Lily said firmly.

Herb couldn't believe his ears. Lily was actually volunteering to bed with Elton in place of Spring? In all the years he had known her, she would never let him near her that way. A strong social conscience was one thing, but surely there were limits.

"Lily, you can't actually—" he began.

"Try to understand, Herb. I wanted the first time to be

with you, naturally. I see now how foolish I have been, denying our pleasure until it's too late. If we get out of this, I will understand if you no longer wish union with me. I will be—soiled."

"Don't say that. Cling Ling will help us before that happens," Herb exclaimed, hoping it would be true.

"Trosh," Elton's slurred voice called from beyond the door. "Bring Sping, uh, Spern, ah, bring the girl in."

"Too late," sighed Lily.

"Wait. He's sloshed," exclaimed Spring.

"What?" asked Herb.

"Drunk. Maybe he was looking for some manhood in the bottle."

"Oh, you mean he drank distilled water?" Herb asked.

"Yes, and too much of it from the sound of him. This could be a lucky break for us. Maybe Lily can fool him, after all."

Trog had moved to the cage and was looking over the two girls to see which was which. Lily stepped forward to keep him from examining them too closely and discovering the deception.

"I'm ready," she said to Trog, exiting before him. Trog slammed the door shut again, and Lily was ushered off to the room where Elton awaited her.

Meanwhile, Spring was pacing up and down in the cage, consumed with guilt. The notion that Lily should submit to that evil little twerp was more than she could bear. They could hear loud voices issuing from behind the door, mainly Elton's. Why was he shouting? Poor Lily, she must be terrified. If only they could understand what they were yelling, but the walls were too thick.

Herb had retreated to the cell window, overlooking an alley. He assumed it was an alley; they were on a split-level at the back of the building, but the window was so caked with dirt, it was impossible to see.

Then, as he watched, some of the dirt began to flake away from the outside glass. A small circle appeared and the pointed tip of a leaf. It was Cling Ling! At last!

His vine pointed to the guard, then beckoned to the window as he made a striking gesture with his leaf. Herb understood.

Moving slowly so as not to attract attention, Herb leaned against Spring and whispered for her to stand away from the window. She didn't know what he had in mind, but at that point, any kind of plan was welcome. She obeyed without hesitation and watched to see what would happen next. With a sudden motion, Herb beat his fists against the bars of the window, the vibration causing the glass to break and fall down to the street below.

As expected, the goon unlocked the door and rushed to silence Herb. As he entered, Herb grabbed for his huge, hairy arm, pulling him toward the window. Caught by surprise, the guard fell back exactly as Herb hoped he would.

Cling Ling was waiting. Quick as a flash, his strong vines shot out and flew through the bars to wrap around the guard's thick neck. They tightened and jerked. Trog groaned and fell in a slump to the floor of the cage. He did not get up.

Spring gasped at the sudden altercation. "Is he dead?" she whispered.

"No, merely out," answered the Vinese. He had used a paralyzing grip that worked on the nerves in the neck region. "It should keep him out of our foliage for now, however."

Herb and Spring dashed from the cage and slammed the door, locking the lummox inside. That would slow him down if he came to. Then Spring ran to the front and opened the door so Cling Ling could enter. He rolled along behind as they stormed the door where Elton had taken Lily. It was not even locked.

The room was totally dark. Spring fumbled for a switch and soon the room was flooded with a bright light. The three stood staring at the scene on the broken down old sofa. Only Elton lay sprawled out, clutching an empty bottle in his hand. He looked up with swimming vision at Spring and sputtered in confusion.

"You? You're gone. Zygote sent the Freesher," he babbled.

"Freezer, you mean?" asked Spring.

"He thinks you are Lily," Herb said.

"You are Lily. Spring is gone. She's on ice," he giggled foolishly.

"You vile excuse for a man. You've raped her," yelled Herb, reaching for him.

"Rape?" snorted Elton. "Did you hear any screams?"

"Only yours," admitted Herb, "But I know she didn't want to be with you, so it was still rape even if she submitted." He tried to yank Elton to his feet, but the Ki fell down again; the drink had taken its toll.

"Stop," pleaded the Ki. "It wasn't that way. I tried to change before Zygote's men came for her, but there wasn't enough time."

"The message Trog gave him. They were coming to make the pickup!" Spring said.

"Yessh. I tried. I tried. But it takes time to change sex. I took this stimulant to help accelerate the process, but too late. They came before it was completed."

Herb let go of Elton's hair and allowed him to fall back on the sofa again. "Are you saying you never touched her? Why should I believe you? You'd say anything to save your miserable skin."

"Ish true. That privilish has been saved for Master Zygote after aaall." The sentence trailed away as Elton passed out cold. He had overdone the stimulant. Herb tried to shake him awake but it was no use.

"Herb, forget about Elton," Spring said. "It just registered with me what he said about Lily. He put her on a Freezer."

"So? They're taking her to Zygote."

"You don't understand. It wouldn't harm me, but Lily isn't me. She's part plant. Extreme cold doesn't preserve plant life in the same way it does with flesh. She'll wither. It's like frost falling on a fragile blossom."

"She's right, Herb," Cling Ling spoke up. "If she isn't put at the proper setting, she could die."

"But, they think Lily is you, a human!" Herb cried. "We have to stop them!"

"The ship port," Cling Ling said. "They may not have gotten clearance to take off yet. We must get there immediately, or—"

He didn't have to finish the sentence. Herb knew they had to get to the nearest transport trolley leaving for the ship port, but that was blocks away. By the time they reached it and the trolley shuttled them the few miles to the port, the ship could be light years away.

Herb had always liked the natural pace of life on P#23, free from the combustible engine transports of other planets whose residents choked on the fumes from their filthy exhausts. Now, he cursed the environmentalists who controlled the number of vehicles a city could support. Certainly neither Herb nor Cling Ling owned a private transport. Spring looked at Herb in despair, knowing what they both were thinking. It was absolutely hopeless.

❧ 17 ❧

Fast Friends

Cling Ling had rushed them out the door and across the street where they stood by watching as he spoke to a shady looking Treeple. He accepted some merrygolds from the Vinese and motioned them to an old warehouse. The Treeple raised up the wide door and pointed inside.

Spring gasped in surprise. "A Turbocar. I didn't think any of those still existed!" She hurriedly explained to Herb that they were an outlawed conveyance used on hers and some other planets until recently. They were practically indestructible. It was their passengers that met early demise. A quirk of construction that enabled their great speed also crushed the inhabitants on impact since there was no safety device in the universe able to protect them in a crash at that speed.

They had all been recalled, but only speed reduction would correct the problem. Unfortunately, that was what had made the Turbos popular in the first place. Special destruction plants had been set up for the demolition. Evidently not all had met that fate.

"You are familiar with the operation of this machine?" Herb asked.

"Well, yes, but—" She hesitated. She did not like to drive a recalled vehicle. She looked around but saw the Treeple had already disappeared with his merrygolds.

"I think it wise to depart now, Miss Moon," Cling Ling said. "You see," he confessed, "this vehicle is not the property of the seller."

"A hot car," exclaimed Spring. That made sense because no one could legally own a Turbo.

"I arranged for transportation before we arrived. I felt we might require a fast means of escape with Lily. I did not know the nature of the vehicle, but it was all our friend could do on short notice. You are an offworlder. I thought you would be able to operate it." He climbed inside.

Herb had already taken the back seat. It was a four seater, one directly behind the other for the sleek line the fast Turbo was known for. It resembled a small rocket in more ways than one, as Spring demonstrated by turning the car about and shooting out onto the road toward the ship port.

The ship port was next door to the commercial lightport, so she needed only minimal directions. They careened down the narrow byways at breakneck velocity. She had succeeded in reaching the outskirts of the community when they heard a high pitched hum coming from a bright green vehicle she passed.

"That's the Patrol," cried Herb. "Slow down."

"This is no time to worry about speeding tickets. Hang on," Spring said, accelerating and pulling back all the way on the throttle. "I'm taking her out of second."

Herb shut his eyes. He had never ridden in anything so fast. The small vehicle seemed to almost glide on air. He opened his eyes cautiously and decided to peek back to see if the Patrol car was still there. It was. About thirty feet below them. And they were still climbing.

"Spring," Herb gasped. "We're flying."

Spring pressed a little harder on the pedal and suppressed a smile. "Didn't you know, Herb? Second gear is for ground travel, first is for flight." She looked below to spot the Patrol car swerving wildly, barely missing a tree in the center of the road. Obviously, they didn't expect their speeder to take to the sky. The tree was shaking his branches angrily as the official car screeched to a stop. It would take some explaining. The Patrol was supposed to protect pedestrians, not run over them.

"That should keep them busy for a while," Spring laughed, looking back to Herb. He was sitting very still, and had turned an unhealthy shade. Spring sympathized. Flying must be unnerving on a species bred for rooting in the earth. "Cheer up, Herb," she encouraged him, "I think that's the ship port just below us."

Making a wide circle, she brought the car down for a landing. Sparks flew as she switched gears and drove into the port on firm ground again. The Vinese rolled out of the car and into the terminal like a ball of green lightning, and returned a short while later.

"Too late," he reported. "There was only one Freezer in port today, and it left just minutes before we arrived."

"Oh no!" Herb groaned. "Lily."

"I have taken the liberty to inquire about private transport, Herb, and I should have my answer in a moment," said Cling Ling, dashing back toward the terminal.

"Then we still have hope, Herb," Spring said. "It will be cutting it close, but with a fast ship—we could still revive her. I assisted my father in his practice and I know a lot about plant life. I'm certain I can help."

"Then I will not give up," Herb said gratefully.

Cling Ling was motioning for them from the entrance. They abandoned the Turbo where it stood and ran toward the terminal where Cling Ling hurried them through the big dome toward a dilapidated Txnghc ship.

Spring's eyes widened. "Uh, Cling."

"I know, Mistress Moon, but it was the only ship available, and they are very fast, once launched. They have light propulsion and limited timewarp. We could do worse."

That was hard to believe on the face of it, but what choice did they have? The Txnghc pilot looked like a giant larva; clear goo oozed from his upside down eyelids, his six hands waved frantically in the air as he spoke gruffly with the Vinese. Neither Herb nor Spring spoke Txnghcian, but it sounded none too friendly.

"What's he saying?" Spring whispered.

"He has another passenger," Cling Ling said, "that must be delivered first. I could not convince him that we require priority delivery."

"But we'll be too late again," despaired Herb.

"Perhaps not. He thinks we can make the time window for entry to Kamalot. The Freezer had a head start, but this ship is faster, and it is, after all, all we have."

The Txnghc spoke harshly again.

"He says we must leave now or stay behind," Cling Ling said. He looked questioningly at the other two.

Herb surveyed the pile of strange pipes and knobs with dismay. The thought of going up into space in that curled his tendrils.

"I'm not sure," he said, fighting the cowardly urge to scream "No!"

"Yes. Tell him yes," Spring said, looking over Herb's shoulder into the terminal behind them. "We'll go now." She shoved Herb ahead of her and up the boarding ramp, never pausing until they had slipped down into the hatch with Cling Ling close behind.

"Hey. Wait," Herb protested as he was propelled forward. He looked up as the heavy hatch door slammed shut like the lid of a coffin. "Spring!"

"We have no choice, Herb," she said breathlessly. "I saw the Patrol coming, and you get one guess who they're looking for. Maybe we should have hidden the Turbo. If we get tied up with them, we'll never reach Lily in time."

Herb sighed with resignation. She was right, of course. They had to go. Two days ago he had been a simple workaday Veganoid, dating a normal girl, heading for a normal future. Now he was in a garbage can with a grub worm at the controls, preparing to hurl his body into outer space to the castle of some mad magician to try saving his fiancée who would probably freeze to death if they didn't find her in time. Under the circumstances, it seemed appropriate that the Patrol should be after him as well.

Herb seemed to step outside himself. Now he could really see who he was—a pervert. "Yes, you can't deny it, Herb Moss. All of this happened because you wanted to write a couple of innocent letters? Don't give me that, Moss. They weren't all that innocent. A nice girl wasn't good enough for you. No, you had to go looking around for some exotic little blossom with a foreign fragrance to spice up your ho-hum life.

"Well, congratulations. It's spicy now, old man. Lily may die, killers are after you, you have one girl too many, and your face will probably end up on the wall of the Paradise Post Office. There goes your promotion. So what if you feel guilty about kissing Spring? You liked it. You liked it a lot."

Spring shook him. "Are you all right? Snap out of it, Herb. We're outside the hanger and ready for blast off. We have to strap in."

Herb stepped back into his body. His sleazy, pervert body. Ah well, it was the only one he had and he would have to learn to live with it, he thought, as Spring's touch sent tingles down his thighs. Pervert.

Cling Ling translated the take-off procedures, which involved lying down and inserting themselves into long sacks like cocoons. This seemed a trifle extreme at first, but when the ship suddenly lurched upward and began its jerky roll and thrust into the atmosphere, accelerating as it twisted like a snake in a cactus patch, they reconsidered. Perhaps, just perhaps, the precautions were warranted. They slunk deeply into their sacks, glad they could not see what their stomachs were feeling.

Herb had thought nothing could be worse than the Turbocar ride, but quickly retracted that premature assumption. He felt like a tossed salad. No wonder Paradise natives had chosen not to be space travellers. If he lived to plant his feet on solid earth, he would dig in roots and never dream of such adventure again. He wondered how his companions were faring, and dared to crack open one eye.

The Vinese seemed to be taking it in his usual leafy stride, eyes closed in peaceful vegetation. But then, Cling Ling had taken many journeys in Vision Plays. Perhaps this was not that different? Herb envied such composure. He took comfort from the thought that at least poor Lily did not have to endure such a harrowing trip. Freezers did not use such energetic contortions to propel themselves. The Txnghc engineers must be mad. He shut his eyes tight and tried not thinking at all until jolted awake with the tremendous sound of crushing metal, and another body slamming into his.

Spring lay squashed against Herb with Cling Ling's sack pressing her from the other side. She wiggled up and out of the bag. "I think we've landed," she said.

Herb and Cling Ling extricated themselves from their

own sacks. Herb leaned against the still rocking walls, trying to steady himself. He had not yet acquired his space legs.

The Vinese stretched out his long vines tautly, a lengthy process. Herb's eyes popped as Spring reached her arms above her head to stretch, causing her top portion to lift and expand. He ripped his attention from that view and shifted it to the porthole where all he saw was lots of red, sandy dirt. It was a considerable letdown.

"I don't think this is Kamalot," he said.

"Of course not. The pilot had to deliver his other passenger first, remember?" Spring said.

"Oh. Yes, now I do," Herb groaned inwardly. That meant they would have to go through another mad takeoff and landing.

The inner hatch to their compartment popped open. "Everybody out," came the voice from the cockpit.

"Well, why not? Let's go outside and stretch our limbs," Herb said, standing aside for Spring to climb up first. Maybe she would do that interesting gesture again.

"Wait," Cling Ling said. "He was speaking Unispeech, not Txnghcian."

"That's right," Spring said, puzzled. "Why didn't he use it before so we could understand him instead of having to translate through you?"

"Because I think that is not our pilot," Cling Ling said.

"Then, where is our pilot?" Herb said.

The Txnghc's head poked through the hatch door and was followed swiftly by the long body. He plopped face first to the floor below and lay there, very still, looking very dead. Spring screamed.

❧ 18 ❧

Ant We Got Fun

Herb listened to Spring's scream, wanting to join her but knowing it would hardly be the manly thing to do. Plantly, either. Cling Ling wasn't falling apart. He was putting his vine against the alien's midsection. Was he listening for a heartbeat or pulse? Did a Txnghc have either? Cling Ling withdrew his tendrils and stood vegetating in silence.

The voice boomed again. "Passengers will vacate this ship at once." This time there was heavy emphasis on the "will" and "at once." Whoever it was, was short of patience.

"I think we should obey for the present," Cling Ling said, mounting the ladder.

Spring looked around anxiously to Herb, who offered her his arm and guided her up and out onto the outer hull. He was climbing out behind her when a small voice called from inside the cockpit.

"Hey. Wait for me."

"Is that a child?" Spring said in astonishment. "The other passenger!"

"I'll get him," Herb said, backing down into the ship again. He emerged a moment later holding a small boy of perhaps six years, and lowered him down to Cling Ling. Then Herb slid down to join the others.

"Halt," came the command. It was the same voice they'd heard earlier. It came from a huge red creature at the back of their ship. It looked like a giant ant. The ant stood upright; it wore a helmet and carried a pipe-like weapon slung about its upper section. It stood wiggling its antennae and moving its mandibles.

Herb gave an involuntary shudder. There were no harmful insects on P#23 but he knew something of the species. Most of them ate plants. Of course, so did Herb, but he doubted creatures of that size worried about a little thing like sapience and nonsapience. He also noted that Cling Ling appeared nervous for the first time. That was not comforting.

Spring had taken charge of the child and held him by the hand as she advanced on the big bug with a bravery born of the maternal instinct.

"Just what is the meaning of this outrage?" she exploded. "What have you done to our pilot? How dare you terrorize women and children."

The ant was momentarily cowed by her verbal bombardment, but quickly recovered. "We know nothing of your pilot. As for terrorist action, it is you who have invaded our territory," he counter attacked.

Snapping out orders to the others of his kind in his own chirping language, they came forward to escort them from the ship across the soft, shifting red dirt. It was a strange landscape, with the same reddish covering as far as they could see.

"What is this place? Where are you taking us?" Herb demanded despite his fear.

"To the Commander. It is he who shall decide your fate, Invaders," the head ant answered.

"We aren't invaders," Spring protested. "Let us go and we will gladly depart this planet."

"Quiet, spy!" barked the ant, clicking his mandibles loudly. "March."

They marched. Eventually, they came to a small opening in the dirt and were pushed through the entrance down long, winding tunnels to a small cell of a room.

It was dark and cool like a cave. The only light came through a ceiling opening where thin rays of sun beamed through. They were alone except for one guard at the doorway. The other had left, to report to this Commander, no doubt. Army ants. Where in the universe were they?

"Intolerable," the young boy said. "It will not bode well for them when word of this reaches the High Council, you can bank on that, my friends."

They all stared at him.

"Oh. Allow me to introduce myself. I am High Commissioner Pat Tikakes of the planet Tetrahedron, at your service." He clicked his little heels together and kissed the hand that had been holding his for so long.

"Patty Cakes?" Herb asked, astonished at the small child's manner.

The smile faded from his little face. "That's Pat Tikakes. And may I inquire of the rest of you?"

"Oh. Uh, we are your fellow passengers, on our way to Kamalot on a mission of mercy," Spring said, coming out of her trance. "Do you mean to imply by what you said earlier, that you know where we are?" she asked.

"I do so imply, for I know only too well. This is Formicidae, a primitive planet under military law. The whole planet is one giant anthill. They are presently engaged in warfare with the Cracks, another species of mutant ants inhabiting this dreary world. They have been in conflict for eons over racial superiority. The Cracks are more Beetle than Ant, and the Army ants more so than Beetle. Both have a slight touch of Arachnoid—notice the mouth?—but both tend to ignore that. They have obviously mistaken us for spies of their enemy."

"But we don't look anything like ants," Herb said.

"Ah, but they'd be expecting that, wouldn't they? In any case, I hope to dissuade them from this regrettable misapprehension."

"You know a lot for such a young man," Spring remarked, smiling.

"I am a duly appointed diplomat," he sniffed. "I am returning home from an important mission. It would be unfortunate if I did not know my job, young lady."

"Children can be diplomats?" Herb exclaimed in disbelief.

"Naturally not. I was a grown man then," he returned impatiently. "No doubt you are from one of those backward planets where time moves forward. Try to comprehend. We of Tetrahedron live our physical lives in the opposite direction from most of the universe. It does make travel difficult, but such is the price of an advanced culture."

Cling Ling took a sudden interest in the conversation. "Are you saying you possess the body of an adult when a child, and vice versa?" he asked.

"As you put it, yes. It is quite a bit more complicated than that, however. I am now in the advanced period. I reached puberty yesterday. I am on my way home to my parents to experience birth, so you can see it is imperative that I return at once."

"Ah," Cling Ling said. He had much to ponder.

"Do you mean you were a teenager yesterday and now you are a child? Isn't your life span exceedingly short?" Herb asked tactlessly.

"Quite long enough," snapped the boy indignantly. "I have completed a lifetime of achievement in this cycle. In previous ones I have been a warrior, a politician, and wealthy businessman. I expect to experience many more cycles if I do not miss my birthday."

"Why, that's instant reincarnation," Spring said in amazement. "But what about your families? Do any of them still live? Doesn't it cause confusion?"

"That is a personal question, but I will answer it in the interest of coexistence. The birth party returns in differing bodies from his former cycles. Such members would not recognize him. There is an emotional death as well. No attachment remains. It would be an impossible situation to cope with were that not so."

"Yes, I see that it would be. Still, it seems sad," Spring said, thinking of her father. "There is pain in losing a loved one, but so many precious memories as well." Memories were all that sustained her at times, Spring thought. She would never want to forget her father.

"Our society is so interwoven that any missing piece could cause untold chaos. It is almost time for my birth and I must be there. If not, events leading to that birth would be altered, causing unknown repercussions. Perhaps even the end of civilization."

He considered himself pretty important, Herb thought. "Surely," he said, "there have been other times, accidents, unforeseen circumstances that prevented births."

The diplomat glared at him. "Never. We live our lives reversed so what happens had already occurred. We know how it is to be. We have—" he paused, groping for the right word.

"Hindsight?" suggested Spring.

"Just so. Ordinarily, I would never have left my planet during such a critical period of the cycle, but I am a diplomat and the mission was essential. It was all proceeding on schedule until the pilot timewarped and went into—"

He was interrupted by the arrival of the helmeted guard.

"The Commander will speak with you now, Spies. Choose your spokesman."

"We aren't an army. We aren't spying. We aren't even ants," protested Herb.

"Never mind. I will handle this," said the diplomat, toddling across the floor. He seemed to have grown a bit younger during their confinement.

The guard looked down dubiously at the small figure, then shrugged. The ways of aliens were unfathomable. He gestured for the child to precede him, but the diplomat held up his little arms and asked to be carried. As it was the most expedient means of transport, the guard complied, hurrying away with the little child in his first set of arms.

"It's all grown wild," moaned Herb. "Lily is freezing to death and we are trapped in some alien ant farm."

Spring put her hand on his shoulder to comfort him. He always felt more than comfort when she touched him, but he appreciated the gesture. He placed his hand over hers and would have left it there, but she stiffened and removed hers. Herb could not fail to note the reaction. Of course she had only meant to give him sympathy; he was a fool to think she felt anything more.

For that matter, what did he feel about her? He didn't even want to think about it, since he had no right. What must she think of him now? He was a pledged man and she respected that kind of commitment. Lily was the hapless victim of his long-distance flirting. He had deceived both women, and they were being remarkably decent about it. The least he could do was behave himself. He touched the place on his shoulder that she had touched. It was still warm.

"I recall this planet from Vision Plays," Cling Ling said. "It is not that far from our destination. If we could return to the ship now—"

"What good would that do?" Herb asked despondently. "We can't fly it. The pilot is dead."

"I wonder," said Cling Ling, stroking his stiff leaves like whiskers.

The other two gave him looks of surprise.

"But we saw him. He fell down lifeless," Spring said.

"If you recall the words of our young diplomat just before he was interrupted, he mentioned that the Txnghc timewarped. I think he did it to allow all of us to reach our destinations on time. In doing so, he unavoidably moved the diplomat's cycle ahead, but he still should have sufficient time to make the birth."

"He moved ahead? But shouldn't he have gone back instead?" asked Herb.

"I expect he would have, once he had gotten closer to the planet. That way, he could skip this part of the flight by moving ahead of it; that is, it would have already taken place. Then before landing, he could move back and arrive before the birth. At least, that is my theory," explained Cling Ling.

"I see. I think," Herb said.

"Then what went wrong?" Spring asked.

"I believe for some reason, the pilot did not take his own problem into account. Thus, this unexpected detour."

Herb frowned. "What problem?"

"The pilot had a transformation of his own pending. Probably he had no way of knowing it would be that soon, for like us, he does not live backward and cannot read the future."

"So he changed, too. He's not dead, just in metamorphosis, like a caterpillar," Spring said excitedly.

"If my suspicion is correct, yes. Theoretically, we could remain here for a year, yet go back in time and still arrive to connect with the landing of the Freezer," Cling Ling said.

"Do you think that's possible?" Herb asked doubtfully.

"What about in between? Wouldn't other events cancel out our attempt?"

"It depends on the events, but we should be able to override. Naturally, the sooner we get on our way, the better," he agreed.

"Then we do have a chance," breathed Herb. "We have to go. Attack them. Escape." He started for the door.

"Herb, slow down," Spring said restraining him. "There's a whole army out there. I haven't wanted to mention this, but you may have noticed that they are insects and they could, well, hurt you badly," she finished lamely.

"Eat us, you mean," retorted Herb. He certainly had noticed, and had no desire to be masticated to death by some overgrown ant.

"Not just you and Cling," Spring said. "Some insects like ants are scavengers. They wouldn't turn up their noses at a little protein either." She pinched her arm.

"She's right, Herb," Cling Ling said. "Besides, we can't leave without the diplomat. And who knows? Perhaps they will listen to him. This sort of thing is his forte after all."

"Sure, Herb. He's a diplomat. They know all about wars and incidents and stuff like that. They'll listen to him, I'm certain of it," Spring said, attempting to bolster Herb's spirits and keep him from doing something foolish they might all regret.

A guard stalked through the entrance at that moment, thrusting a small bundle into Spring's arms. It looked up at her and said "Goo." It was the diplomat.

❧ 19 ❧

Time and Again

Spring cradled the infant in her arms. The ants had provided some make-shift diapers and a baby bottle. She was not experienced with small children, but had figured out the basics well enough.

It was unnerving to realize that intellectually it was a grown man she was dandling on her knee. Perhaps he gave it no thought or simply accepted it as the way of his kind?

She looked into his pudgy little face, seeking some answer to their dilemma there.

"Were you able to speak with them at all?" she asked. The baby only gooed and smiled. Probably gas. Spring sighed. "I'm sorry. I know you understand me, but I can't speak baby talk." She tilted him onto her shoulder and patted. The diplomat burped.

Herb watched Spring with her small charge. It was a pretty enough picture, young mother and child. If she were his wife but of course she wasn't, and never would be. If by some miracle they survived the fix they were in, Lily would become his life mate. Lily was a fine woman and would be a wonderful mother, he was positive.

Lily had grown up quite a bit from the silly hot house blossom he had known. The trials they had all gone through had changed them, making them somehow stronger. He saw Lily in a new light, and felt more confident about their union. He only hoped they would have that chance.

"He is regressing swiftly," Cling Ling commented. "Soon, he will disappear altogether if we do not get him to his planet."

"Shhh, Cling," Spring chastised him. "Not in front of the B-A-B-Y," she spelled.

"Spring, he can spell, too," Herb said, amused.

"Oh. I keep forgetting he's not a real baby. But we have to do something. We can't just sit here and let him vanish. Oops. Sorry, Diplomat," she apologized.

Before they had time to worry further, an escort of Army ants entered, commanding their party to accompany them immediately. Spring hastily gathered her baby paraphernalia and trotted along beside Herb. Cling Ling rolled behind them, followed by more ants.

The strange group trekked down one long passage after another, around and through the deep labyrinth beneath the hill, stopping at last in a large cavernous room.

There was an odor in the air of cooking vegetables originating from a huge iron pot in one corner with hot coals beneath. The cook stood stirring the steaming soup with a long ladle. He looked up and smiled, which was hard to decipher with a sideways mouth, while the guards indicated a long bench where the group was to sit.

It had been some time since they had eaten, and Herb found his mouth beginning to water in spite of his fear. Perhaps it was a new type of torture.

Spring leaned close to Herb and whispered, "Now what?"

Cling Ling answered. "It appears to be the mess hall for this camp."

A guard addressed the cook in Universal so they all understood him. "Do you need anything else before you serve?"

"Not anymore," the cook replied, smiling. "All I needed was a nice green herb—"

"Oh no you don't," Herb shouted, rushing across the floor before the guards could stop him. "You won't put me in any pot."

He gave a kick and the huge kettle overturned. Hot soup and veggies flooded the hard dirt floor in every direction. Those nearest yelped in pain and jumped quickly away. Cling Ling had already gone into action, thrusting and twining his vines in a fine exhibition of Julep-so, clearing a path to the exit.

"Run," he yelled to the others, but they were already heading out the tunnel as the burned ants fell over each other in confusion.

"Halt! Halt!" one cried out as they raced for topside and freedom.

"Which way?" Spring panted at the junction of tunnels.

"Any," Herb yelled.

"That one has light at the end," Cling Ling said, pointing with a small branch.

They could hear the shouts and cries of ants as they got organized behind them. They ran faster until at last they spotted the opening to the outside. It was good to see daylight again.

"This way," Cling Ling called out, rolling ahead. "We must get to the safety of the ship."

Herb looked back and saw that several ants were close behind them, and more were crawling out of the tunnel. It was hard to run in the loose, sandy dirt, and Spring couldn't navigate too well holding the baby. Herb took the child from her and made her run ahead.

The ants were gaining fast. This was their element and they could revert to all six legs for speed. Cling Ling reached the ship first, stretching down his vines to pull Spring aboard. Herb slammed against the side and held up the baby for his friend to take, then climbed in after. He managed to slam the hatch closed just as the first ant crawled up the side of the ship behind him. They couldn't have cut it any closer.

Inside, they heard a steady pitty patting sound against the portholes.

"Rain?" Spring asked, frowning.

They descended the ladder into their compartment and looked out. The ants covered the sides of the ship and were tapping furiously against the windows with their feelers.

Cling Ling quickly lowered the covers so they couldn't look in. "I think we are safe for the moment" he said.

Spring let out a blood curdling scream. Everyone looked to see what the new crisis was. She had spotted their pilot in the corner, but now he was covered with a thick, squishy substance that seemed to be slowly hardening. Cling Ling poked at it with a leafy finger. A small bit came off like cold batter.

"It's only his cocoon," Cling Ling explained. "It is as it should be. I must locate the ship's flight manual if we are to escape." He climbed topside, and returned a short time later with an octagon shaped object. It had numbers and symbols engraved on all sides and looked like translucent plastic.

"It looks like a giant dice. Can you actually translate that thing?" asked Spring.

"It has diagrams. I need a minute to absorb it," he said, rolling to the side to study his find.

The steady rapping continued, and the baby awakened, adding his voice to the melee. He had slept all through the mad race out the tunnels, unbelievable as it seemed. He was so tiny now, he looked like a newborn.

"Oh. He's shrinking again," cried Spring. "Please hurry and get us out of here, Cling."

Abruptly, the rapping noise ceased, and the silence was deafening.

"I wonder what they're doing out there now?" whispered Spring.

Herb climbed to the upper hatch and listened, but there was no sound. "Maybe they're gone?" he said, climbing back down the ladder and lifting the cover from one of the portholes. "Uh-oh!"

"What?" Spring asked, pushing close to peep out. Her breasts jammed against Herb's side. He moved away so she could have the view to herself. Close proximity was too much to bear. It seemed even at a time like this he was susceptible to her feminine charm. He cursed his male weakness and deliberately forced thoughts of Lily to the fore. How she would despise him if she knew. How both of them would despise him!

"We're surrounded," Spring wailed, as she observed the circle of ants, each holding one of the long, tubular weapons. Who knew what damage those things could do to the ship? At one side of the circle stood a large one, resembling a cannon. Primitive it might be, but surely effective at that range. It could probably rip a hole in the side wide enough to walk a whalephant through. "Cling," she called nervously.

"Yes, I am aware of developments, Mistress Moon." He had been watching from his porthole. "I think I can manage the ship now, but we can't achieve take-off before they could fire upon us. It is a dilemma." He returned topside with the flight manual.

"Now what are we going to do?" she cried, clutching the tiny baby to her breast.

"What else can we do," Herb said in disgust, "except surrender?"

"We can't do that either," Spring said.

"No. Not all of us. But, if one went out and distracted them, perhaps drawing their fire away from the ship, the others might have a chance to escape," he said.

"But Herb, who?" she asked.

He pushed her aside and bounded up to the cockpit, unfastening the hatch.

"No," she screamed, realizing his intent, and quickly scrambled up the ladder to stop him.

"Get her out of here, Cling," Herb ordered, crawling outside and slamming the hatch shut beneath him.

Spring tried to follow, but Cling Ling quickly fastened the latch and gently pulled her away from the door. "It is best," he said, and began to man the controls, pulling levers and pushing buttons. The Txnghc ship jarred to life.

"But you can't leave him," Spring said in disbelief. She raced back down to the compartment and tucked the baby into one of the sacks, then pressed her nose to the nearest porthole.

There was Herb, out in the dirt now, and walking purposefully to the Commander. He was saying something she couldn't hear, then two of the guards came forward and escorted him to one side of the circle. The ants began to form two lines behind each other, raising their weapons.

"Cling. It's a firing squad. No! Not Herb!" she sobbed.

A sudden lurch of the ship sent her reeling backward, falling to the floor just as the thunderous sound of the weapons exploded in her ears.

"No," she screamed. Hot tears burst forth to stream down her face. The rocking of the ship made standing up impossible. She crawled on hands and knees to the ladder to pull herself up, then began to climb up it.

She had to get off the ship and see about Herb. Another lurch dislodged her hold from the railing and she fell back to the second level, striking her head against one of the metal rungs. She was out before she hit the deck.

When she awoke, they were in deep space and she was tucked neatly into her sack. Slowly, memory returned, and with it, more tears.

Herb, brave, good, kind, innocent Herb. He deserved much better than that ending. Now Spring had two deaths on her conscience because of Zygote. Perhaps three if they couldn't reach Lily in time. Poor Lily. She would have to be told about Herb. So many victims in this trail of terror. She had to find a way to stop it.

A small hand wiped away the moisture from her cheek. She opened her eyes and saw the young diplomat. He wasn't an infant anymore. The timewarp must have worked. Cling Ling must have taken them backward again. That was good. The baby had almost shrunk into nothingness before she passed out. Spring put a hand to her forehead and felt a big goose egg. "Ouch."

"Excellent. You have returned to us," said the young diplomat. "How do you feel?"

"Miserable," she answered, remembering Herb. "But I'm relieved to see you are well. That was a close call for you, Diplomat."

"Thanks to your excellent care and our bush pilot, I have survived. Soon we will be warping forward and I will regress once more. I may need to impose one more time."

"I am glad to help. I know this has been hard for you," she said.

"Actually, it has been rather exhilarating. I think in my next cycle, I must consider becoming a space pilot," he said, smiling.

"Our pilot," Spring said, looking around. The Txnghc was gone.

"Yes, he is functional now. It happened as surmised by your Vinese friend. Going back reversed his metamorphosis as well."

"And we will go forward to deliver you?"

"The pilot will go into his cycle, but now we have Cling Ling to take over, so it should be safe this time."

"Yes, it's all working out just wonderfully—" Her composure suddenly crumbled. Spring pulled herself from the sack and walked to the porthole, stopping to hold the ladder for support.

"Are you unwell?" asked the diplomat solicitously. "Your injury?"

"It's not that. It's just a bump. I just can't believe Herb is gone. I didn't even get to say goodbye to him." The tears began to flow again and she hid her face behind her hands. "Oh, Herb!" she cried.

"Yes?" he answered, coming down the ladder.

Shocked, she turned, hardly believing her eyes. She launched herself at him, kissing him and hugging tightly as if she would never let him go.

Herb returned her embrace and they stood entwined for a long, wonderful moment. Suddenly, Spring pulled away and punched him in the stomach with her fist.

"Ouch," Herb said. "What's that for?"

"For lying to me. I thought you were shot."

"I never told you I was dead," he protested.

"But, I don't understand," she said, walking to the porthole and gazing out into the darkness. "The last time I saw you, the ants were preparing an execution. I heard the gunfire."

Herb looked sheepish. "Well, things are not always as they seem," he said with embarrassment. "The diplomat had already reaped the harvest."

"My talk with the Commander went very well," the diplomat interpreted. "I reminded them of their trade agreement with my planet. It is one they would not wish to disrupt. They agreed to release us with all proper respect due a personage of my rank. That went for my companions as well, naturally."

"Then you were able to speak with them before you regressed to an infant," exclaimed Spring.

"Yes indeed. Previous to our, ahem, 'escape,' we were being ushered to the banquet hall for a proper feast. The ants are not used to feeding humanoid guests so it took them some time to gather what they needed. We were about to be treated to the first course when our friend, Herb, panicked. And, as you humans say, the rest is history." He smiled.

"Then we weren't going to land in the soup, after all," Spring said.

"No. It was just that I had heard so many frightening rumors about insects and when I heard what I thought was my name as an ingredient—" Herb shrugged.

"At least you didn't spill the beans," Spring laughed.

"What?"

"Nothing. But what about those guns? I know I heard them fire."

"They fired all right," Herb said, "but not at me. The ants were really upset when I dumped their soup. You see, they thought I was rejecting their pact with the diplomat. They had no way of knowing we could no longer communicate. When they ran after us and banged on the ship, they just wanted us to come out so they could make it up by the honor of a twenty-two gun salute. By the time I returned to the ship with the good news, you had injured yourself. So you see, I am no hero."

Spring turned and faced him squarely. "Herb, when you left the ship, you didn't know you would return. That was quite a sacrifice. If that's not a hero, then I've never seen one."

She threw her arms around him once again and this time did not let go until Herb broke the embrace. He knew she was grateful to him, but he was not going to take advantage of that gratitude this time. He changed the subject.

"We will go forward soon. Right now we're in Drift and that's why we can walk about. It's necessary to give the propulsion units a chance to cool. Timewarping takes its toll on these old ships. We better strap in, though," he warned.

All passengers except for Cling Ling battened down for the rough ride. Herb glanced over to Spring, but she had her eyes shut. He thought her cheek was damp. He worried that her head hurt more than she had let on.

The noise began like someone shaking broken glass in a tin can. A two ton can. Over they rolled, shaking and rattling, gathering speed until the ship was a streak in the empty space of time. A last huge vibration rocked the ship as they crashed down for a landing.

Cling Ling climbed down the ladder to help the others out of their sacks. Spring took the diplomat, now a baby, in her arms and they all exited past the Txnghc who was tucked into his cocoon once more.

An impressive assembly was on hand outside the ship to greet them. The diplomat had given Cling coordinates where to land before he was reduced to baby talk, and Cling Ling had hit the mark squarely.

The dignitaries were dressed in formal tie and tails with tall, black silk hats. Red sashes and ribbons adorned the vests of the men, and women were in long gowns, decked in heavy jewelry. One couple moved forward to receive their group, a distinguished looking man, and striking woman. Spring thought she detected something familiar about them. Of course: they were the child's parents!

Following proper welcomes, handshakes, and introductions all around, Spring presented the mother with her child. As she lifted the blanket of the bundle away from her breast, it fell empty to the ground. She gave an involuntary scream of horror. He had disappeared.

The mother's eyes widened momentarily as she gave a slight gasp.

"I'm so sorry," Spring said. "I thought we were in time."

A slow smile began to break across the mother's face. She placed both hands upon her stomach and gave a small exclamation of joy as it expanded.

"All is well, my dear," she assured Spring, opening her cape to expose her bulging form.

"That's him," Spring exclaimed happily.

"We've always wanted a boy," said his father proudly.

❧ 20 ❧

Snow Job

Once the elation of the family reunion had worn off, the group settled back soberly in their sacks, battened down for their original destination. Although Cling Ling assured Herb no time had been lost which could not be regained, it was difficult for Herb to grasp emotionally. With each minsec that passed, he envisioned Lily withering away, calling his name in hopeless sobs.

He knew that was ridiculous, since if she really were to expire on the Freezer, she would feel no pain, and certainly not be aware of her plight. It would be rather like dying peacefully in sleep. If it had to happen—

"Herb, nothing will happen to Lily," Spring said, from her sack next to him. "We won't let it."

Herb smiled at her gratefully. The Founder. Could she read his mind now? No, of course not. She was simply a sensitive, kind person. Simply Spring.

The warning light for warp-out blinked. It was time. The Txnghc pilot touched the control.

The group stood in the huge ship port terminal looking at each other in shocked astonishment.

"What happened?" Herb asked, surveying the familiar surroundings in confusion. "Why did we return here? We should be in Kamalot."

"Wait. Wait a moment," Spring said. "I don't remember landing, do you?" She put her hand to her head. "I feel odd. Dizzy."

"I believe I see what has happened," Cling Ling said with a concerned look overtaking his foliage. "We have returned to Paradise."

"We know that," Herb snapped in annoyance. "That idiotic pilot—"

"No, you misunderstand," Cling Ling said patiently. "Not by flight, by time. This is our past. The ship must have malfunctioned at a critical moment."

Spring looked across the terminal, her eyes widening as Patrol officers entered, running toward them. "He's right, Herb. We're back where we started. Quick. Into the ship before those cops get here," she said, pushing him forward.

"Halt in the name of PPA," came the stern warning from behind them. It was clearly too late to run any place. They halted.

"Cling," Spring whispered, "If this is our past, why didn't we escape?"

"We must have arrived a minsec or so off. Time has not changed. We are the ones out of step," he explained.

"If I'm not interrupting," said the ranking officer, none too patiently, "there is the small matter of an arrest here?"

"Of course, officer," Spring said sweetly. "You go right ahead."

He gave her a withering look and her smile shrank. She bit her lip and zipped it as well. Police or Patrol, whatever they were called on whatever planet, were famous for their lack of humor. To tell the truth, she didn't much feel like a bundle of giggles herself.

"We haven't done anything wrong, officer," Herb interjected. "We are trying to stop a crime."

The patroller looked at him as if inspecting an aphid. "And what crime might that be, sprout?"

Sprout. Herb colored in anger. That was typical. Give some small town cop with an over grown ego a uniform and he turns into an aster. Cling Ling answered for him before he had a chance to protest.

"My friend is telling the truth, officer. A young lady has been abducted from our planet."

"Uh-huh. Why hasn't the Patrol been informed of this?" the patroller inquired skeptically.

"Uh, well, that's a long story," Spring said, impatiently.

"Aren't you lucky? We'll have all the time in the universe to discuss it where you're going. Charges," he bellowed to his fellow officer.

The uniformed Treeple pulled out a small lily pad and read aloud. "Receiving stolen property."

"We didn't steal anything," Herb said.

"He means the Turbo," whispered Spring.

"Possession of an unlawful vehicle," he continued, "consorting with known offenders, speeding, flying without a license, contributing to an accident—"

"Wait a minute," cried Spring. "What about our rights? Don't we get a chance to defend ourselves?"

"Naturally, you will be met by your defendant upon arrival at the Tribunal. You know that," the officer said with irritation.

"No, she doesn't," Herb said. "She's not a real Veganette. Let her go back to her own planet."

"Herb." Spring elbowed him. True, he was only trying

to help, but it looked as if he had just added fuel to the inferno of troubles they were already roasting in.

The officer's face lit up with undisguised glee.

"Impersonating a native? Entering the planet without a pass? I haven't seen such a variety of charges since—never. I may be up for promotion for this one!" He sneered.

"Oh really? Well, what about Intergalactic Immunity?" Spring challenged. He didn't look so smug now.

The smile faded from the officer's face to be replaced with his usual look of hostility. "That's for the Tribunal to decide. I just bring 'em in. Move out," he barked briskly, as they were escorted to a Patrol car, and transported to a waiting booth at Tribunal Hall.

The three sat alone in the small room debating their fate.

"Cling, what do you think they will do with us?" Herb asked. "We don't have time to be prisoners. We have to get to Lily."

"Yes, it is essential for us to return to the Txnghc ship and reverse this timewarp," Cling Ling agreed.

"We must have hit a bump and been sent back too far by mistake," Spring said.

"A bump?" Herb yelled. "There aren't any bumps in space. I may not be a hot shot space traveller like you, Spring, but even I know that."

"I was speaking metaphorically. Calm down, Herb," she said defensively. "We all want out of this as badly as you do."

"I agree. We must not rustle our leaves needlessly. In a way Mistress Moon is correct. I believe the timewarp was properly executed. Yet, some physical interference such as a magnetic storm may have thrown us off course for a moment. A moment is quite a lot when time is to be overlapped. This is a slightly altered history. If we could but return to the exact point we erred, this would be cancelled out. But if we must go on from here—" Cling Ling trailed off, looking very unhappy about the prospect.

Spring completed the miserable thought. "We cancel out the other. I'm beginning to catch on. We can remember the other future because it has actually become a part of our past? This is too confusing. Let's go."

"We can't just walk out," Herb snorted. "We've been arrested, remember?" He lowered his voice. "Besides, even if we tried, what about the patrollers?"

"Spring has the right idea, Herb. If we don't return within the hour, it will be too late. The Txnghc will leave with his other fare, minus us," Cling Ling said.

"He may be gone already," Herb said in dismay.

"No, while you two were bantering with the patrollers, I asked the Txnghc to give us an hour to return and he agreed. Since he was with us, he shares our memory," Cling Ling explained. "He isn't anxious to repeat the entire journey. Even without us, he could still end up with the ants, and who would fly him out of there? But there are limits to the time window, so we cannot delay."

"You mean, we have to do everything all over again?" Herb asked in amazement.

"Not if we get back on track and find our former notch in time. We can then proceed as planned."

"Then we have no choice. We have to escape," Herb said with calm new determination. "Any suggestions as how?"

Just then their counselor entered and introduced himself. He was a thin Vinese with waxed leaves. As he saw it, they could not be held over until the Tribunal met, and Spring could not be held at all. Intergalactic Immunity did indeed cover all charges against her. She would be deported as quickly as the arrangements could be made.

As for Herb and Cling Ling, since the main onus fell

upon Spring as the driver of the outlawed vehicle, they could be charged only as accessories. With their clean records, however, and in Herb's case, prominent family, their dismissal was all but assured.

"Then, we are free to leave?" Herb asked, considerably perked by the news.

The counselor confirmed that was so. All they had to do was pay the routine Assurance fee that they would appear for the next Tribunal and they would be out on their own recognizance.

"You mean bail?" Spring asked.

The counselor handed Herb the appearance ticket with a schedule date and the fee amount. Herb blanched white. "That much?" He passed it over to Cling Ling. "I have enough to cover our expenses, Cling, but I can't meet this."

Cling Ling shook his foliage. "I regret I cannot find sufficient funds to cover it either." They looked at Spring.

"Well, don't look at me," Spring said. "It took everything I had to pay my fare on the lightship. I have reserves on New Landers, but that would mean going back in person. I'm sure Zygote has a watch there. Anyway, most of it is tied up in legalities since Father's death. It would take time."

Herb frowned. "We don't have that either."

"If I may suggest?" said the counselor, handing them a small card. It read: THORN AND THISTLE—PERSONAL LOANS.

"A loan. That's what we need," Herb agreed. "Quick. We need a communiline to call them."

"Would they lend us that much?" asked Spring, doubtfully.

"Ahem." The counselor cleared his throat for attention. "Mr. Moss's father is not unknown in this community. I feel confident his name would suffice to secure your fee payment." He smiled ingratiatingly.

"That's right. Your father. He's rich, isn't he? Why don't you just call him?" Spring asked.

"Because I don't care to explain how I landed in jail for stealing hot cars," he snapped. "Not to mention what's happened to Lily."

"Oh. Yes. I see your point," Spring said, biting her lip.

"I agree for other reasons," Cling Ling said. "The fewer others we involve in this hopefully temporary history, the fewer loose ends we have to contend with upon return. However—"

"Then get the loan quick," Spring interrupted.

"Mistress Moon—" Cling Ling said.

"Please, Cling. We have no more time to waste," Herb agreed.

"I shall be honored to handle the transaction for you, Mr. Moss," the counselor said, smiling his oily smile and rolling out of the room.

"I can't believe it's that simple," Spring said with a sigh of relief. "We're actually getting out of here."

"Yes, and I won't even have to pay back the loan when we return because all of this will be erased," Herb said.

"Herb, I must speak with—" Cling Ling began.

But before he could finish, the door opened and the counselor returned in the company of a shady looking Treeple. Perhaps that wasn't a fair assessment, Spring thought, considering most Treeple's natural appearance. She was later to have more faith in first impressions.

"This is Mr. Thorn," their counselor said. "Because of the considerable amount of the loan involved, he wishes to consult with you in person. If you will excuse me?" He rolled out, securing the door behind him.

The Treeple leaned across the desk and spoke in a raspy voice. It could have been natural, or it could have come from an addiction to raspberries. Herb frowned and began to wonder what sort of company they were dealing with.

"Why should I fork over three G's on a bunch that's going to skip planet?" he asked.

They all looked at him in surprise. How could he possibly know they were planning to leave?

Spring asked, "How did you know that?"

The Treeple snorted coarsely. "One of my boys did a deal with the bush face, over there." He jerked a branch toward Cling Ling. "Got him a unique vehicle, you might say."

"I thought you looked familiar," Herb said, remembering the Treeple from the garage.

"My cousin, Leafty. There's a slight family resemblance. But I digress. You're on the wind—you're blowing planet. I can't hand out three goldenrods when I may never see them again. Mr. Thistle wouldn't like that."

"But we'll repay you. We're good for it. We just don't have it at the present time," Spring pleaded.

"I know. Herb's old man is goldleaf. Why not ask him for it?" Thorn asked.

"I have my reasons," Herb answered, avoiding eye contact.

"And goodies they are, no doubt. So it's like this. You need G's, and you need them fast."

"Right," Herb and Spring said together. Cling Ling said nothing.

"I know you're good for it. But who says you'll return?"

Spring opened her mouth to protest, but the Treeple held up a branch.

"No offence, Little Blossom. In space, there's no guarantee. Ah shucks. Maybe I have soft roots, but there might be one way we can deal. Something that wouldn't upset Mr. Thistle. You wouldn't even have to pay us back."

Herb and Spring looked at each other in amazement. It

was too good to be true. There was a Founder looking out for them.

"That is, you wouldn't pay in goldenrods. Our firm would accept a small service for the fee."

"Service?" Spring said, wrinkling her forehead. "I don't know. What sort of service?"

"Do we have a deal?" he pressed.

"First, tell us what the service would involve," Herb said.

"Deal or no deal?" he repeated as if Herb hadn't spoken. "My final offer."

"Deal," Herb said, quickly.

"Herb!" Spring and Cling Ling chorused together.

"What choice do we have? We have to get to the space port. Whatever it is, it can't be worse than losing Lily," he blurted in anguish.

"True," Spring agreed. "I'm not sure I like this, but what else can we do?" She looked at Cling Ling.

Cling Ling only shrugged, being outnumbered. He had tried to warn them about these Loan Barks, but they wouldn't listen. Now, the decision had been made.

"You've done the smart thing," Thorn said with a prickly pear smile. "I'll pay your fee and take you straight to the space port in my Traveller. We can discuss everything on the way," he continued jovially, slapping Herb on the back with a hearty branch. Spring shrank back from his grasp, but went along meekly. Cling Ling rolled glumly behind them.

It went like clockwork. Thorn's fast transport took them straight to the waiting Txnghc's ship with a minute to spare. The pilot was clearly relieved to see them. They were aboard in no time, sacked up and cringing for take-off.

It was another gut wrencher. Several woozy stomachs later, they were idling in Drift, getting set for the time warp to the future they had left behind earlier. Cling Ling and the Txnghc were in conference, calculating their destination to the nth degree. No one wanted a repeat of the last fiasco!

Everything had moved so fast, they hardly had time to discuss their bargain with Mr. Thorn, but it seemed simple enough. All they had to do was deliver a small package to planet Snowball. So called, because the temperature never rose above zero, and the entire surface suffered constant blizzards.

Herb wasn't thrilled about going there, but it turned out to be only a hop and jump from Kamalot, so distance shouldn't present a problem. Indeed, the Txnghc ship seemed at its most adept when flying in hops and jumps. Herb's stomach was still doing somersaults.

He knew Cling Ling had not approved of the transaction, but it seemed a small enough task in exchange for their huge Assurance fee. The package was actually a small, thick, metallic container like a square bucket, which felt rather warm to the touch.

When Spring inquired the nature of the package, Thorn had only replied that it was a valuable shipment of perishable goods. That was why it was necessary to find a quick means of delivery and why he was willing to take their service for the fee. The goods had been prepaid so all they needed to do was deliver it.

Perhaps it was a gourmet feast for some rich snowman, Herb mused. He hoped it was nothing illegal, but asked no more questions lest he discover it was. It was none of their business, and in any case, the deal had been made and they were stuck for it. Herb secured it at the bottom of his sack to keep it from careening about the ship during take-off.

Spring sat at the side, talking to the diplomat. He had returned in this time frame, although they had already delivered him to his home to be, uh, delivered. Some birthday.

But that would be corrected as soon as they timewarped properly this time. She knew Herb had no desire to see those ants again, even though he had come to no harm. Reasonable or not, insects bugged him.

Cling Ling stuck his leafy face down the hatch from above. "Sorry to delay, but we had to be certain of our co-ordinates this time," he explained.

"Here, here," concurred the diplomat. "Popping in and out of my mother's womb is an unnatural act, to say the least. Hopefully, this will be my last attempt."

"Warp out in ten minsecs," Cling Ling said, shutting the hatch.

Everyone sacked up. Spring helped the child into his, and then slid inside her own. Herb checked them both before climbing into his, scooting well down to the bottom.

"Yeow," he yelped, leaping back out and grabbing for his burning feet.

Spring watched as Herb hopped ludicrously around the small room.

"Hot foot," he yelled in explanation, flopping down upon the floor to peel off his smoking socks.

Spring was already out of her sack, looking to see what had caused his sudden leap. A smoldering hole was burned through the end of his sack, and there across the way where it had slid, was the container with its lid ajar. It must have popped open. She bent over it to peep inside, then let out a piercing scream.

The top hatch was flung open immediately, and Cling Ling slung himself down the short ladder. "What's wrong? It's almost time for warp-out."

"Look," Spring cried, pointing a shaky finger toward the glowing container. "Squiggly things." Herb had limped over beside her at the scream, and held her protectively in his arms.

The young diplomat was at their side now, peering down into the open box. His eyes opened wide as he looked back to Herb. "My stars," he cried. "You've got a bad case of the HOTS."

Herb stumbled as he released Spring and backed away, coloring deeply.

"Yes, it's HOTS, all right," he said to Cling Ling. "I have seen these once before on a dead planet."

Cling Ling looked closely. "Yes. I agree. They are Hybrid Oxalic Taproots," he said in horror.

"Hybrid Oxalic—Oh. HOTS," Herb said, realizing the diplomat had not been commenting on his behavior with Spring after all.

"I've read about those in some of the material Herb sent me about plant life on P#23. Aren't they extremely dangerous?" Spring asked.

"Dangerous hardly describes them. What do you suppose killed that dead planet where I saw them?" he asked. "They must be properly contained or they will burn right through this ship. There is hardly a more acidic substance in the universe than HOTS."

Herb could vouch for that. He had touched it for only a second and his scorched feet were barely cooling off.

Cling Ling raced back up to consult with the Txnghc pilot who had been busy with the final machinations of the controls. He rolled back, slinging a thin metallic sheet over the HOTS box. It was a sheet from their Cold storage, he explained, and should help to cool the box until they reached their destination. Once there, it should be safe enough, since the freezing temperatures would be in their favor.

"No wonder Thorn was willing to take this delivery in lieu of our debt," Spring said, looking aghast at the smoke curling up from beneath the sheet.

"He did say it was perishable," Herb said.

"Not as perishable as us," Cling Ling said. The ship gave a preliminary shudder. "Hurry and sack up. The warp-out's beginning," he shouted, flinging himself back through the upper hatch and slamming it tight.

Everyone was inside sacks, waiting. Herb's sockless foot stuck through the hole at the end. Luckily, he had removed his shoes or he would have no footwear at all.

He should have known there would be a catch to it for that much money, and he had literally put his foot into it this time.

They warped. The noise was deafening, the speed incredible. It was indescribable. The nearest analogy Herb could find was a vision of ten nets balls banging inside an ancient washing unit at translight speed. The group of them, of course, were the ten nets balls. As suddenly as it began, the ship was spit out and splashed down into an icy sea. They had arrived on Snowball.

Cling Ling quickly joined the others in inspecting the shipment of HOTS. They had ceased smoking, and that was encouraging. Using the end of the Cold sheet, Cling Ling secured the lid and lifted it by the handle, carrying it out through the hatch.

The Txnghc was topside breaking out Snuggies for them. The garments were paper thin and looked like shiny pink foil, but once on they proved toasty warm.

Before emerging into the raging snow storm outside, they fortified themselves with nutrition pellets from the Txnghc's larder. Not too tasty, but surprisingly filling. Herb stuck a few extra in his pockets.

The pilot had also dropped a dinghy outside into the choppy waters and helped lower Cling and Herb down the side. Spring slid down last with Herb's help. He caught her at the sides of her waist as she landed, and felt his breath intake as her breasts pressed up against him. Even through the foil material, she was soft and warm. Spring returned his gaze as he looked helplessly into her eyes.

"Please to sit," Cling Ling instructed. "We must not rock this craft. The water is frozen."

It certainly was. It was practically a sheet of ice, with only a few cracks here and there of dark, churning water.

"How did he ever find a space safe enough to land?" gasped Spring in awe of the surroundings.

"He didn't. Heat jets. They melted a place as we landed. Now we need to hurry to shore before the water freezes over again," Cling Ling said. "We wouldn't wish to be caught inside this glacier."

"No, I have no desire to turn into a Burr Sicle," Spring said. "That's a frozen sweet," she explained to Herb.

He smiled. It was an apt analogy.

"Our pilot landed close to the delivery point," Cling Ling informed them, as he consulted a screen on the dinghy control panel. He pointed out a red blip. "If I am not mistaken, that is our destination."

"How can we see? This snow storm is getting worse," Herb complained, as Spring snuggled closer. Well, it was an ill wind that boded no one any good.

"I will home in with this instrument," Cling Ling said, guiding the small vessel with his covered vines. After a bit, they saw the faint glow from buildings ahead. The storm had let up in intensity and Herb gaped in disbelief. Buildings made from ice? But why not? There was certainly plenty of it available, and no danger of melting in this frozen world. A sensible use of a natural resource.

Cling Ling had run their craft as far as the crack in the ice extended. They pulled it ashore and pressed forward on foot. Fortunately, as they reached the "road" to the buildings, they discovered the walk way was heated. Only a bit of stubborn ice melted and refroze here and there as they approached the entrance of the main building.

Herb's foot found a slick piece and he slid through the door on one foot, dragging Spring with him. It was an outer portico, with a large door at the side. Cling Ling pressed the bright red lever and it opened to reveal an efficient, official looking business office waiting room.

"It looks so normal," Spring said.

"I know what you mean," Herb agreed. "After seeing an ice building, I thought we might be greeted by Polaris bears or snowmen."

"Good day," said a voice as soft as drifted snow. "I'm Miss Frosty, Mr. Zeroid's secretary. So sorry to keep you waiting."

Herb's eyes bulged. That was no snowman. Snow bunny, perhaps. He ogled the tall, statuesque, platinum haired, incredibly well-grown female with skin so white it was lustrous. This ice maiden was definitely hot.

"We just arrived," he squeaked.

Spring's eyes narrowed as she pushed ahead of Herb to speak, since for reasons she didn't care to think about, he seemed to have lost his voice. "We have a delivery from Mr. Thorn," she said coldly.

"You are most welcome. We have been expecting you," the vision beamed.

"You have?" Herb croaked.

"Oh yes. Mr. Zeroid has been most anxious. I will let him know you have arrived safely. Please make yourselves comfortable, and if you should need anything before I return, just press this button," she said, indicating its location, "and call me." She smiled at Herb. "I am Frigidda."

"I don't believe that," Herb said under his breath.

"What?" Spring asked as the icy beauty departed through another door.

"Uh, nothing. I just wondered how they knew we were the ones delivering their package," he said stupidly.

"I imagine the Txnghc has been in communication from the ship, and even had he not been, just how many green snowmen do you think they see around here?" she said testily.

Herb decided to remain quiet. For some reason he didn't understand Spring had lost her usual good nature. He heard her make a barely audible snorting sound. Women could be so moody.

The three of them sat in strained silence until Miss Frosty returned to smilingly announce that Mr. Zeroid would see them now, indicating the doorway.

"Why, thank you, Miss ah, ah—" Herb stammered, awed for the moment by the brilliance of her sparkling white teeth.

Spring sprang to the rescue, taking his arm and tugging him along. "We mustn't keep Mr. Zeroid waiting, Herb. Besides, I'm sure Miss Frostbite has work to do."

They entered with Cling Ling moving ahead of them with his burden of HOTS. Mr. Zeroid rose from behind his desk to greet them. He was a large, rounded gentleman with the same snow-white coloring as his secretary. He did indeed resemble a jolly, plump snowman.

"I'll relieve you of those," he said to Cling Ling, placing the box on his desk. "You've arrived just in time, too. Our power is nearly exhausted. I've already notified our engineers. They'll be right up for those." He sat back down after indicating chairs for the trio. He seemed clearly relieved that the shipment had arrived safely.

"What were you saying about your power?" Spring asked politely.

He looked surprised. "You don't know what they're for?

They are the only power source feasible for our planet. Even they don't last forever. The extreme cold, you see. Our sector had only a few more hours' heat and then, well, we are certainly glad to see you." He laughed nervously.

"But why did you wait so long to get replacements?" asked Herb.

"You really aren't aware of our situation here, are you?" asked Mr. Zeroid, amazed.

"Please be most kind to explain," Cling Ling said.

"Certainly. Hybrid Oxalic Taproots are only grown on P#23 under certain specialized conditions. They are not only rare and expensive, they are difficult to ship because they—"

"I think we already know why," Spring interrupted wryly.

"Yes," he continued. "We do order them well in advance, but variables such as bad crops, budget problems, or transportation can always cause hazardous delays."

"One must ask. Why rely on such questionable sources of energy?" Cling Ling asked.

"Because Hybrid, er, HOTS, are virtually the only heat and power source that won't freeze up on our world. Before they were available, we were more or less an isolated chunk of ice. They have enabled our civilization not only to interact with our own kind, but to open communication with the outside universe. Without them, we'd lose everything."

"Ah, indeed," Cling Ling agreed.

"I'm afraid persons such as Mr. Thorn realize our desperation and it's become tougher to meet his price. Oh, not that we don't want to do business," he quickly added, obviously fearing he had said too much.

"That is terrible," Spring exclaimed, outraged. "We have no loyalty to Thorn, Mr. Zeroid. This is a one time job. So don't worry, you may speak freely. There must be something we could do to help, Cling? This is a matter of survival."

"You see the situation exactly," agreed Mr. Zeroid, relieved he had not spoken out of turn.

"We must bring this to the attention of the diplomatic services," said Cling Ling.

"Yes, Patty Cakes will know what to do," joined in Herb.

"Rest assured we shall apprise the proper officials, Mr. Zeroid. I know Paradise would not wish your planet to be exploited in this manner. There will be an inquiry, and no doubt, new regulations will follow," Cling Ling said.

"Well, that is just wonderful. Thank you all," Mr. Zeroid said, gratefully reaching out to shake hands all around. "It was our lucky day when you folks arrived on the scene."

"And a very bad day for one Mr. Thorn," grinned Herb.

"And Thistle," added Spring, giggling. "Serves him right for trying to trick us."

A short time later, they were aboard the dinghy and safely away from the dazzling Miss Frosty. They had wrapped up tightly in their Snuggies and braced against the storm as Cling Ling headed back to the ship. Their passage route was showing signs of icing despite the heat jets from the Txnghc craft. The snow had become so heavy no one could see anything. Cling Ling had to rely solely on the dinghy's instruments to guide them back.

Suddenly, the vessel came to a dead stop. "Why are we stopping here, Cling?" Spring called from beneath her hood. The snow was almost blinding.

"We have not stopped. It has stopped us. The heat jet must have dislodged some larger ice fragments and one is blocking our path through the glacier."

"Great. Could we get out and slide the boat over it?" Herb asked.

"Not advisable. This vessel has a heated flooring. The

temperature of this ice and water are far below anything we could survive. One step outside and you would surely lose a limb," Cling Ling warned.

"We can't just sit here. Heated bottom or not, we'd freeze to death soon."

"I must agree with you, Mistress Moon," Cling Ling said.

"We have to do something," Herb said. "Call the Txnghc. Maybe he can help us."

"Regretfully, I have tried to alert the ship of our predicament without success. I fear the instruments have frozen."

"Wait," Spring said. "I hear something. Maybe he's seen us anyway. Maybe he's coming out to get us."

"I hear it, too," Herb said. "Funny, it doesn't sound like another dinghy motor. It's more of a—crunching sound."

"You're right. Like something breaking off chunks of ice. Crunch—crunch," Spring said puzzled.

The snow fall had noticeably abated while they discussed the mystery sound, which was getting considerably closer. Spring turned to look out the back of the small craft and screamed.

It was definitely a screaming situation, Herb agreed as he saw the source of the loud noise.

"Ice Eater," Cling Ling gasped. "Hit the deck," he yelled, as the gigantic jaws of the huge monster loomed above them.

Herb pulled Spring down and fell prone across her. If they were doomed to be eaten by the horrific beast, at least they would meet their fate together. He felt the small craft rise up on a giant wave and then plunge flatly down into the water, splashing them with liquid so cold, it seemed to burn through their foil clothing. Then, all was calm.

"We're alive," breathed Herb through chattering teeth,

as he helped Spring up from the floor of the dinghy. Cling Ling was working the controls and announced they were moving again. As they watched, the monster ploughed straight ahead. If he kept to his course, he would pass directly by the ship. Cling guided the dinghy straight down the wide path made by the monster. They would soon be safely aboard.

"But why didn't he eat us?" asked Spring, basking in the warmth of the ship's compartment. Herb basked in the warmth of Spring. He was still shaking inside from their close call.

"It was an Ice Eater," Cling Ling explained. "There was never any danger of its devouring us intentionally, as its sole diet is ice. But if it had capsized our craft, which it nearly did by swimming so close, we would now be resting in an icy grave. Fortunately, that did not happen."

Cling Ling had given the information about Snowball's HOTS situation to the Txnghc pilot to relay to the authorities. It was useless to tell their diplomat friend since he would soon become a new person, returning to his proper place in time with the next warp. As would they all, it was to be devoutly hoped.

Herb could hardly believe it, but the warp was successful and they had connected with the elusive point which restored all to a present reality. They had reached Kamalot, Zygote's private moon.

Per instructions, the Txnghc pilot navigated to a secluded spot near a dense forest for touch down. The Vinese had been correct. The ship was fast, the pilot proficient. The only real danger was that the ship might have fallen apart. It had certainly been through a rough time lately. The Txnghc seemed unconcerned, however, and bidding them a fond farewell—for doubtless he was used to far more peaceful flights—he lifted off in a red blur toward the distant stars.

Herb had mixed feelings. While he didn't relish being stranded on some alien, artificial planet, neither had he the stomach for stepping foot in that rattle trap ship again. He stood staring forlornly into the silent forest. He was so tired. How could he go on? Spring joined him and took his hand in hers. Suddenly, he knew he would, even if he didn't know how.

❧ 21 ❧

Inner Struggle/
Outward Bruises

"$\mathcal{T}$he magician undoubtedly has some transportation at his disposal. For all his power, I doubt he can jump from planet to planet on his own," Cling Ling said.

"Don't ever underestimate him," Spring warned. "He's an unscrupulous viper, but a fair magician. This whole world is his handiwork, remember."

"In any case, our Txnghc friend could not wait. He had to return home to complete his transformation in safety. Mistress Moon, you are the most familiar with this world. Where do you think Zygote would take Miss Lily to—to interrogate her?"

"Cling, I've heard only secondhand stories. Zygote spoke more to my father than me, and I avoided him whenever possible. I only know he lives in a huge castle, but as to where it's located—" She shrugged. "But I would assume he would take her there."

"But, we'll still be too late!" Herb cried. "If we don't even know where she is, how can we possibly save her now?"

"Because we shall find this castle," Cling Ling said calmly, "and be there when she arrives."

"When?" both Spring and Herb asked in astonished confusion.

"But—but—I thought she was here," Herb exclaimed.

"You forget the last timewarp. Due to our pilot's own personal problem, he had to back up, so we are here earlier than we would originally have landed," Cling Ling explained. "He needs the time to complete his journey home. This is to our advantage. It gives us needed time to locate Zygote and plan our rescue." While Herb and Spring were left to mull these things over, he decided to scout the area.

The two found a hidden spot at the edge of the forest to wait for Cling Ling. They both had so much to think about now that they were actually here. Herb leaned against the wide trunk of a huge oak, while Spring sat cross legged on the ground upon a bed of colored leaves, examining some tiny purple flowers peeping through.

Herb felt at a disadvantage. Cling Ling knew so much more of the ways of the universe than Herb did from his studies and his Vision Plays. Even Spring was a seasoned space traveller. Right now, the ordinary family life of an ivy covered cottage sounded wonderful to him.

Lily was the obvious choice. They were the same kind, they shared a common culture and outlook, and they had grown up from the same roots. It was a natural union.

Spring, on the other hand, was a woman of the universe. She could never thrive in the quiet surroundings of Paradise while the grass grew greener elsewhere. They were from two different worlds: his a peaceful, green, pastoral one; hers a teeming city life, full of magicians, fast cars, and scientific wonders. With her botanical background, she would plant a name for herself, of that he was certain.

"Why are you staring at me that way?" Spring asked, perplexed by his intense gaze.

"What? I must have been lost in thought. About Lily," he lied.

"I understand," Spring said quietly. "I was thinking about my father. And Zygote," she added with hatred. "Now that I'm here, there are so many plans to make, and—" There was a loud rustling sound from the bushes behind them. "Oh, here comes Cling."

"That was a short trip," Herb said as he turned expectantly to see his Vinese friend. "Find anything?"

"Yeah. We found us two little green men from Mars. Right, Charlie?"

That was spoken by one of two rough looking characters seated on horseback. Herb stared up in surprise while Spring recoiled from their unsavory appearance. She could be mistaken, but they looked like trouble. Maybe more than the two of them could handle.

"You apologize to that there lady, Samuel," laughed the other one. "She might be green, but she sure ain't no man." His eyes crawled across her body like lice. There was no misunderstanding that evil look.

"Herb," Spring said nervously, moving close beside him, "I—"

"You her man?" Samuel asked, and snorted derisively. He had discolored teeth and scraggly whiskers.

"We are—together. What do you want from us?" Herb asked with more bravado than he felt. He hoped Cling Ling would be back soon.

"What do I want?" Samuel said with a dreamy look. "Oh, just what every man wants. A big, fine, castle with lots of buxom wenches to pass my time 'o day. And gold. Lots and lots of gold. You can't keep fancy ladies without the gold, my friend. And, say. That brings us to the business at hand betwixt you and me, lad. Hand over 'yer booty."

"Booty?" Herb asked, swallowing.

"He means money. Valuables. They're outlaws." Spring

glared. "And I don't think they're part of Robin Hood's merry band."

Charlie gave a hoot and slapped his knee. "Robin Hood? Why, that's just what we are. We take from the rich and give to poor us." He laughed at his own joke, drool oozing from one side of his mouth.

Spring wrinkled her nose in disgust. These oafs stank, too.

"But we have no merrygolds," Herb protested.

"Guess that means he don't have no money, Sam," Charlie said in mock surprise.

"Well," Samuel said, scratching his filthy beard, "if they don't have it, we can't get it."

"What we going to do now, Samuel?" Charlie asked with exaggerated earnestness.

"If they don't have money, guess we just have to take something else," Samuel answered brightly, leering at Spring.

"That is a sure 'nuff fine idea," Charlie agreed, dismounting and moving toward her with undisguised lust.

"No!" Herb said, angrily, suddenly understanding their confusing conversation. Were all offworlders animals? No one was going to molest Spring. Leaping for Charlie, he took him off guard and wrestled him to the dirt.

The larger Charlie recovered quickly, and slammed a fist through Herb's middle, sending him rolling to the side in pain. But it didn't matter; he had to protect Spring.

Before Herb had reached his feet, Charlie grabbed him at the collar and followed with a right cross to his chin. Herb went down in a sprawling heap, head reeling from the explosion.

Spring flew to his side, cautiously examining his jaw. It was bloody, but no teeth were lost. He would surely have a fat lip for several days to come, though.

Charlie looked up at his companion who hadn't stirred

an inch from his saddle during the fight. "You didn't help me a bit, Sam," he said in a hurt tone, rubbing his fist. "Just look how he got my duds all dusty, too." He made a big display of brushing himself off.

"Never mind. You're a working gentleman. And still a handsome fellow, ain't he, gal? That little greenie was spunkier than he looked," he said to Spring, as if paying her a compliment.

Charlie grunted. "I don't like spunk." He lifted his boot and shoved Herb over.

"Leave him alone," Spring snapped, finding her courage. "Haven't you done enough to him? Go away. We don't have anything for you." She cradled Herb in her arms.

"Aw, I can't agree with that. You're a fine looking filly," Charlie said. "We goin' to have us a good time." He grabbed her and dragged her squirming and kicking back to his mount.

Herb's dizziness was finally subsiding. Looking through aching eyes, he spied one of the bandits manhandling Spring, to get her onto his horse. He felt desperately about in the dirt and finally found his weapon, a large jagged rock.

Herb drew back and aimed, but something shoved at him just as he let the missile fly, causing it to fall short. Sam had run his horse against him, spoiling the throw.

Now Charlie was angry. The rock had missed his head, true, but ploughed cruelly into his shoulder blade. He released Spring and turned for Herb, his whole arm swinging to connect for a sound blow to the belly. Herb went down, tried to rise, then collapsed face first in the dirt.

Charlie reached down and shoved Herb's face into the soil, cursing.

"Stop it, you slime," Spring screamed, leaping on his

back to beat fruitlessly. It was like pounding steel with a feather. She couldn't make a dent.

Samuel rode over to peel her off Charlie and held her at arm's length, where she struggled helplessly. He called to Charlie. "No sense beating a dead horse," he said, giving Spring a shake.

"He ain't dead. Yet," Charlie growled.

"We better make tracks out of here. All this ruckus might have roused some of their friends. They thought we was somebody else when we found them," Samuel reminded him.

"Well, I ain't goin' empty handed," Charlie said, looking at Spring. He was beginning to drool again.

"Never said we was. Here, strap this wildcat to your saddle. My arm's gettin' tired from tusslin' with her."

Charlie hauled Spring up and flopped her onto her stomach. Her head was facing downward, and her legs dangled off the other side. After tying her wrists together, he mounted behind her and slapped her bottom. The final indignity! When Spring tried to bite Charlie's leg, he pulled off his dirty bandanna and crammed it into her mouth. She gagged, but ceased struggling. They were just too strong for her.

Satisfied, Samuel kicked his mount and galloped off. Charlie and Spring trotted close behind.

Herb came to just as the cloud of dust was settling around him. His eyes were dull with despair. They had taken Spring! He had let her down when she needed him most.

"Spring," he called weakly, falling back to his knees. He had to find her! His head flashed with yellow pain, and then the darkness came again.

"Herb?" Cling Ling said. "Can you hear me?"

Herb felt the cool wetness run over his face, his tongue

hungrily swallowing the water. He opened his eyes. Oh, they hurt. He looked into the concerned foliage of Cling Ling's bushy face, and took more water. Now he remembered.

"Cling," he said thickly through swollen lips. "They took her. Spring."

"I saw them riding away just as I came back, but I had to attend you first. I don't think any limbs are broken. How do you feel?"

"Like I've been run through a lawn mower. But forget about me. Go after them, Cling! Find Spring!"

"They cannot get far," Cling Ling said confidently. "At the risk of immodesty, I remind you it is doubtful a mere horse could outdistance a Vinese at full roll. They shall not harm our Mistress Moon." He rolled off with all the speed a Vinese could muster, which was considerable.

Herb pulled himself up against a tree trunk and gulped down a few more swallows of the water Cling Ling had brought him. Luckily, they had taken canteens and rations from the Txnghc's ship. Herb washed down a nutrition pellet from his pocket. He had to recover his strength and follow Cling.

For now, all he could do was wait. His head was too unsteady to allow him to stand. He had to believe Cling Ling would find them, and stop them from—

The Founder! he swore mentally. Could they have been sent by Zygote? Somehow, he didn't think so. Zygote might lose his precious Secret after all. Herb wouldn't cry about that, but about Spring. To have to submit to those filthy—At least Zygote was only interested in her from a scientific viewpoint, but who knew what those two might do!

This could never happen on P#23. Maybe he could persuade her to come back with him, just as a friend, and stay for a while. Surely Lily wouldn't mind that. Not after all that had happened. No. That was crazy. After all this was over, he would never see Spring again, and that was for the best. For everyone.

Meanwhile, the horsemen had not gone far before they came to the stream where Cling Ling had filled their canteens earlier. Samuel set up camp while Charlie watered the horses. Spring was tied to a tree limb at the edge of a wooded area. Every now and then, Charlie would call back to her, describing what he intended to do with her after he had some "grub."

One sleeve of the floral dress had been torn off her shoulder, revealing the true pale color of the skin beneath. Charlie was fascinated by the discovery, and promised to "take her skinny dipping to see what else was under all that green paint."

Cling Ling's vines reached from behind the tree trunk and began meticulously undoing the ropes that bound her. Spring gasped and looked back with her frightened eyes. A hopeful smile briefly creased her lips when she saw Cling, but she did not dare to move or speak.

Charlie looked toward her once, but she remained stiff as if still bound. He looked right past Cling Ling without seeing him. If he had noticed anything, he must have thought him part of the shrubbery.

Having freed Spring, Cling Ling took full advantage of his natural camouflage, and flattening out his vines, inched forward toward the two men seated at the campfire.

Sam glanced over his shoulder toward Spring. She held her breath, certain he would spot Cling Ling, but he didn't notice anything out of the ordinary. She breathed again as he turned back and reached down for the coffee pot, first filling his own tin mug, then offering some to Charlie. Charlie held out his cup, then yowled in pain as the hot liquid sloshed over him.

One of Cling Ling's vines had tripped up Sam just as he lifted the pot. For a brief moment they all stood comically suspended, the two men trying to figure out what was going on. Then Cling Ling pressed a nerve on the injured Charlie's spine, sending him crumbling into the ashes of the fire.

Samuel reached for his knife. "An enchanted weed," he bellowed, wielding the weapon at Cling's foliage. Unfortunately for him, he hesitated, trying to find where the bush was vulnerable. It was a split second too long. One of Cling's vines shot out to snatch away the blade, sending it sailing off into the creek. It sank with a small splash.

"My father's silver handled stabber," Samuel cried. "Why you bloody bush! I'll break you to kindling!" He reached wildly, picking Cling Ling up and squeezing him in a tight bear hug against his chest.

It was probably the worst possible move he could have made. Cling's vines wrapped around the man's bull neck and contracted. Sam let go to clutch at his throat. He tried to speak, but the air was gone. He turned a motley shade of blue and dropped to the ground, taking Cling Ling with him. The man was done for.

Slowly, Cling unwound his vines and rolled back to Spring. She was up and watching the struggle from a distance. When Cling brought the last man down, she had untied the horses and given them a sound smack on the backsides, smiling with satisfaction as they galloped away down the stream.

Cling nodded approval. "By the time they recover and round up their horses, we shall be long departed."

"Herb?" she whispered. She knew he would have come with Cling Ling were he able, so she was almost afraid to ask.

"Roughed up, but he will recover," Cling Ling said. "He put up a valiant fight for your honor, Mistress Moon."

"I have no honor left," she scoffed, thinking of all the trouble she had brought down on them. "Please, let's hurry, Cling Ling! I want to tell him how much—how much I appreciate what he did for me," she finished quietly.

Without another word, the Vinese led her back through the woods to the place where Herb lay, hardly moving since his friend had left. His head still throbbed, and his lips felt the size of Freezer wheels.

"Herb," Spring gasped, shocked at his appearance now that the bruises were in full color. Even on green skin, they were beauties.

"Spring," he said weakly, trying to smile and wincing at the attempt. "Are you well? They didn't—they didn't harm you?" he asked fearfully.

"How could anyone harm me with you and Cling to protect me?" she asked in return, smiling. "Oh, Herb. You were wonderful!" Then she hugged him soundly.

"Ouch," he yelped.

Spring quickly released him. "Sorry. Is there any place it doesn't hurt?" She leaned forward and cautiously, carefully placed a kiss on an unbruised spot of forehead. "There," she said. "That's for defending me."

"They beat me to a pulp!" Herb snorted.

"Well, yes. But you were outnumbered," she reminded him.

"I suppose I didn't do too badly under the circumstances," Herb agreed, grinning through his pain. "But I couldn't let anything happen to—to the Secret." He caught himself. Damn the damn Secret! It was Spring. She was all that mattered, but she certainly didn't want to hear that kind of crazy talk from him.

"I see," Spring said, some of the enthusiasm fading. "Well, just so you know. I am very grateful."

"Where are the bandits?" asked Herb, trying to sound matter-of-fact.

"Oh, dreaming sweet dreams," she answered. "Cling Ling took care of them."

"Speaking of Cling, where is he?" he asked.

"I don't know. Around, I imagine. You know Cling Ling. He doesn't leave much to chance."

"Yes. Yes, we are fortunate to have him with us," Herb agreed, wondering why suddenly all they could talk about was Cling Ling. Why did a barrier always pop up just when they were getting–close?

Why? He knew very well. Lily. Zygote. Spring's long lost lover. If those weren't reasons enough, he was sure he could find plenty more.

Cling Ling returned shortly bearing news. He had rolled some distance earlier that day searching for any sign of Zygote's castle. The area they had landed in was mainly forest and largely uninhabited. This time out, however, he had met up with a hunter. The man could not, or did not want to give him any information about Zygote, but he did let slip that they were not far from a castle. Cling had continued to search until he made a discovery.

"I found the castle not far from here, but I suggest we proceed with caution," he said. "We will be no assistance to Miss Lily if we become prisoners as well."

Lily, Herb thought. How long ago and far away the two of them seemed now. Just a memory, like a picture on a postcard.

Only none of them "wished they were here."

❀ 22 ❀

Jasmine's Castle

They waited as long as they could before starting out.
Cling Ling needed a breather after his workout with
the bandits, and hike through the woods. Herb was still re-
cuperating, but it was vital to press onward if they hoped
to reach the castle Cling Ling had found, before nightfall.

They moved quietly through the woods, as the dusk
turned too soon into darkness. It was not the wisest course
to wander about at night in a possibly enchanted wood.
They proceeded with caution, but the only sounds came
from the dry leaves cracking beneath their feet, and the occasional rustle as small woodland creatures scurried from
the trespassers. The stillness itself was eerie, and as they
came to a clearing, it was with relief that they spied the tall,
dark walls of the castle looming ahead of them.

Just then, a dark shape swooped down, causing Spring
to give a muffled cry, but it was only a night owl. It flew
away as suddenly as it had appeared.

They followed Cling, who guided them to a pathway
leading close to the castle. The tall peaks of the towers

gleamed in the moonlight, making dark blue and purple shadows along the path. It was beautiful and frightening at once, like a child's dream. As they drew nearer, entering through garden gates, lights from the tall windows above gave off a soft, golden glow.

"There seem to be an uncommon number of statues in this garden," Herb commented. "Is your friend Zygote a patron of the arts?" He gazed at the form of a muscular young soldier, sword raised high above his head as if to strike.

"I don't know," Spring answered. "But you're right, it is a bit busy." She looked across the ornate lawn at the profusion of sculptures. There seemed no pattern to their placement, and they appeared to be all male likenesses, as well. She advanced to the nearest and stroked the smooth surface, giving a small cry at the touch.

"What's wrong?" Herb asked anxiously.

"I can't believe it. I wish I could see better, but Herb, I think all of these statues are carved from gemstones."

"Crystals? The sort of stones your father used for healing?" he asked.

"Some crystal, probably, but others too," she said excitedly, examining another. "Emeralds, and diamonds, and rubies. Incredible. How could stones of this size exist?"

"They are very valuable, then?"

"Yes, depending on the kind they are, of course." She looked with a trained eye to another beside them, and drew in her breath. "If this really is one emerald, I couldn't begin to calculate its worth."

"But if this Zygote is so wealthy, why would he care about your secret? He could have whatever he wants anyway," Herb said.

"Power, Herb. Riches are nothing to some men compared with that."

Cling Ling had left them momentarily to roll about the

grounds. He had just returned when a brilliant light suddenly lit up the garden, bright as day. The scene was breathtaking. Statuary of every kind of stone stood glistening like giant jewels. They were all colors, emerald green, ruby red, sapphire blue, and delicate shades in between. It was like standing in the center of a rainbow. The light seemed to come from no specific area, but magical or scientific, it provided a beautiful spectacle.

It did mean, however, that someone knew they were in the garden. There was nowhere to run, so they tried concealing themselves behind the statues. But as it turned out, they were too late.

Through the center of the stones glided a lovely young woman who called out sweetly to them: "Please Travellers. Be not afraid. Welcome. Enter and rest within. The nights be not safe to fare abroad."

The girl's hair was long, full, and jet black, set with a circlet of gold. Her color was deep olive, her form fair and slender. She was attired in a flowing gown of rich, dark red, with midnight lace at the sleeves and low bodice, and golden ornaments encircled her wrists. A single, perfect crystal hung from the delicate chain at her neck, nestled in the V of her breasts.

"Fear not, strangers," she entreated kindly, her arms opened wide in welcome. "You are safe here."

They stood in silence. Even Spring had been struck by the strange girl's beauty. "What do you think?" she whispered to the others.

"Does Zygote have a daughter?" asked Herb.

Spring gave a snort. "Who would marry Zygote? Either it's a trick to lure us in, or—this isn't his castle."

They looked to Cling. "It could be a trap, but I must agree with Spring's supposition. I have seen no signs of the magician here. There may be more than one castle in Kamalot. Given a choice between staying the night here and venturing through the dark to an unknown destination, I believe I would select the lesser of risks."

The others saw his point. They stepped forward into the light.

"Why bid strangers such a warm welcome?" Spring asked suspiciously.

"I have no reason to fear," answered the girl, "but certain strange creatures walk the night. 'Tis no place for the innocent." She smiled, her beauty intensifying.

And perhaps you are not as innocent as you seem, Spring thought.

"We thank you and accept your hospitality," Cling Ling said. "We seek the castle of Zygote."

"The magician? Nay, his abode be much too far to journey this night. I am Jasmine, and this is my castle. Please follow me." She led them inside through a corridor lined with marble pedestals, which held small statues of animals and flowers, carved of the same precious materials as the statues outside.

Spring was enthralled. Never had she seen such a grand display of gems. "Jasmine, if I may ask, how can such large pieces of precious stone exist? The artistry is fantastic." She paused to examine a small rabbit of sapphire, and pyrite flowers. "They are even cut to scale."

Jasmine glowed with pleasure. "This is a magical world; many facets of natural law do not apply here."

That was the only explanation, Spring agreed.

Jasmine showed them to a group of rooms along another long hallway, inviting them to take their choice. The castle was so large, a few overnight guests could hardly burden their hostess. She then bid them goodnight with a promise to send refreshments to their quarters, and departed.

The guest rooms were sumptuous. As Herb lay on his comfortable bed, he reflected how good it felt to be resting on something that wasn't hurtling though outer space.

True to the lady of the castle's word, a tray of wine, fruit and rolls was delivered to each of their rooms. Herb was too restless to eat very much, and soon found he was more than a bit lonely for company. He wandered out into the hallway, intending to see if Spring was still awake.

The swish of a feminine skirt sounded behind him. He turned to find Jasmine at his side, smiling sweetly. She had lovely features, no doubt of that, and her dark coloring was closer to that of his own Veganoid race.

Before he could speak, she placed a well-manicured fingertip to her lips, motioning him away from the other doorways.

"My servant says the lady was fatigued and requested an herb tea to help her sleep. Needs must you disturb her rest? May I be of assistance?"

"Oh, I was just looking for company, nothing important. Of course, she needs her rest and I won't bother her. I apologize for keeping you up as well. I will return to my room."

"Thou art restless. That is understandable after a long journey. Why not join me for a walk in the garden? 'Tis a fine warm night with a full moon."

"But I thought you said it wasn't safe to go out at night here," Herb reminded her.

"My grounds be secure. None would dare to trespass the garden now. It is protected," she assured him.

"Oh, do you have guard dogs?" asked Herb.

"Dragon. But thou needst not fear him. We shall be together," she said, taking his arm and guiding him down the hall.

Herb knew he should decline and return to his room. What if Spring should awake and need him? She might be afraid all alone. It was out of the question.

"Yes, a walk would be pleasant," he said. Wait, was that what he had intended to say? He couldn't seem to recall now, but no matter. There was no reason not to go. None at all.

Such a lovely night. The sky was a deep velvet blue with distant stars twinkling like diamonds. A full moon hung suspended just above the tops of the trees. A moon orbiting a moon? How could that happen? He asked Jasmine. She seemed amused and explained that magic indeed had its uses, and could produce beautiful results. Herb couldn't argue with that. The garden reminded him of his own world, fresh and green, filled with the sweet scents of night bloomers.

Herb was glad to answer all of Jasmine's questions about who they all were and the purpose of their journey. He trusted her completely. He could not believe such a beauty would be aligned with Zygote to do them harm.

They drifted past several of the fine statues to a low, rocky fence surrounding a fountain where they paused to rest. Herb put the fingers of one hand down into the trickling water, letting the peace and serenity of the night wash over him as well. How relaxed he felt!

Jasmine's soft hair brushed against his arm as she moved closer, looking deeply into his eyes, capturing them in her spell. Her eyes seemed to glint like the crystal around them. The reflection of the moon, Herb imagined, but beautiful. Something deep inside tugged at him to look away, but he ignored it. Such a vision of loveliness! Why should he not drink it in?

Her full red lips parted slightly as she looked deeper into his eyes. She had said nothing, yet he interpreted the message. She was no stranger to the silent language of love between woman and man.

Meanwhile, Spring paced fretfully in her room. She had napped and eaten a bite of the repast, but remained keyed up. Thinking she had heard voices, she'd gone to Herb's room, but gotten no answer to her knock. Possibly he was a sound sleeper. She had returned to her room and tried to do the same, but to no avail. She needed to talk. And the truth was, she had grown accustomed to Herb always being there. She missed him.

The soft knock at her door caused her to jump. She hastily opened it, expecting Herb, but it was only a servant inquiring if she needed anything more before retiring.

Spring replied in the negative, but asked if the servant knew whether Herb was asleep. The servant informed her he was not in his room a few moments before as she made the rounds of their guests.

Spring waited until the servant disappeared down the corridor and ran to Herb's room. Still no answer. It occurred to her he might be in with Cling, discussing plans for tomorrow, so she knocked at his door as well. Also no answer. That settled it. They were together.

But where? They wouldn't depart without her, unless— unless there was trouble. She turned and ran along the hall and down the steps to the outside. She paused at the entrance and looked out into the darkness. She began to have second thoughts. They might be only stretching their legs, with nothing amiss. They would think her foolish to come crying after them in that case.

The garden. That was the logical place to look first. She slipped quietly out, and headed for the moonlit garden gates.

It was a bright night, so there was no problem in finding the way. The statues sparkled in the distance like a gathering of fireflies. Herb and Cling might be standing among them. It was difficult to tell which was stone and which flesh from a distance. They were all so lifelike.

At last Spring saw Herb, seated near the fountain ahead. He was closely examining a statue. No. That was no statue, it was Jasmine. Why had they come to the garden together? Why were they bending so close?

Oh, why indeed? Spring turned and ran back toward the castle blindly, for unreasoning tears had begun to blur her vision. How could he do it? What about Lily? What about—she didn't want to finish the thought. Oh, Herb!

Something grasped her wrist at the garden gate, halting her flight from the shattering scene. She gasped in fear and surprise, starting to cry out.

A soft leaf clamped across her mouth. "Shh. Mistress Moon, it is I, Cling Ling."

"You frightened me," she whispered, trying to compose herself, wiping a stray tear from her cheek.

"I must speak with you and Herb. It is a matter of some urgency, for you see, I have discovered the secret of the crystal statues," he stated ominously.

That hardly seemed important to Spring at the moment in face of recent events. "Oh?" she said with disinterest.

"Yes. It is sometimes an advantage to possess this form," he said, indicating his leafy visage. "I positioned myself outside the servant's quarters near the potted plants. It was most interesting. Most interesting," he repeated.

Spring sighed inwardly. All she wanted to do was find her room and throw herself across the bed and cry. She had thought Herb truly cared about Lily, and maybe even her, as a friend. That they would confront Zygote together. Now she was alone again.

"Very well," she said, since Cling Ling seemed determined to tell her anyway. Let him get it over with, and then she could go. "What did you find out?"

"They are not crystal," he said.

"Of course they are," she said a bit too sharply. "If there's one thing I know about, it's precious stones. So, take my word, they are crystal, and fine works of art as well."

"Yes. Very realistic. Very lifelike."

"Incredibly so," she agreed, wondering why Jasmine's statues had so fascinated him.

"Because they are alive."

"What are you trying to say?" Spring asked. Really. Would this inane conversation never end?

"That is, they were. They are all human victims of our lovely hostess. She is a beautiful version of the legendary Gorgon creature."

"Gorgon? Medusa? I always get my myths mixed up. You mean, the ugly, snake-haired sisters who turned men into stone?"

Cling Ling was nodding in the affirmative. "It is not just her look, for the servants were saying she had the kiss of death. So, it is different, but—"

"You're serious, aren't you?" Suddenly, it all became so clear to her. "Oh, no," she exclaimed. "Herb is out there, in the garden with her. I thought—Oh! What an idiot I am. If she kisses him—We have to stop her!" She turned and ran toward the spot where she had last seen them. Cling Ling rolled after, and passed her by with no time to spare.

At the other side of the garden Herb stood gazing helplessly into the deadly Jasmine's eyes. They swirled with the depths of a maelstrom, drawing him in, deeper and deeper. And why should he fight it?

She was a beautiful woman. He could see she wanted him to kiss her as much as he wanted to do it. As much as he ached to kiss her. His desire burned like a torch in his center, now. It had to end, he had to touch her. Inclining his head toward hers, he saw her moist, red lips tilt upward, awaiting his caress.

Spring reached them first. She grasped Herb by the shoulders and spun him around, intercepting his kiss on her own lips. The spell was momentarily broken.

"Spring?" he asked, still dazed.

"You foolish female," screamed Jasmine, advancing on Spring. "You dare oppose my will?" Her lovely features were twisted with the rage within her, and Spring knew the meaning of fear as the being held up one hand from which a brilliant light glowed. It leaped from her fingertips to Spring, and a strange sensation rushed down her body. She stood as if frozen. Try as she would, she could not move so much as an eyelash. She stood in helpless horror, watching as Jasmine turned to Herb once more. He was still beneath her evil spell. Unresisting, his lips sought hers.

Suddenly, Jasmine screamed, and stood unmoving. Spring felt life course back into her body. Something had happened to remove the spell, but what?

Cling Ling stood between Herb and Jasmine, holding a smooth piece of crystal in his vines; it was the shield from the soldier statue. It now caught the full light of the moon which reflected brightly into the face of the evil sorceress.

"I don't understand. What's happening?" Spring cried.

Herb shook his head at the sound of her voice. He was still confused, but unharmed. Jasmine had not budged an inch. Nor was she ever likely to. Spring put out a hand and touched the smooth surface of Jasmine's face. She was a perfect statue of priceless ruby.

"Regrets for the delay," Cling Ling apologized. "I had difficulty removing the shield, but needed it to imitate the myth. The crystal surface acted as our mirror. I thrust it in her line of vision just as she prepared to kiss Herb, so she kissed her own reflection instead. It worked in much the same manner as the legend. That was only a story, while this was reality, but I counted on the same result. Fortunately, Zygote stuck to the basics. She was one of his magical creations, you see."

How like Zygote to create monsters to do his dirty work! But right now, Spring was more concerned about Herb. She rubbed his hands in hers. He seemed to be coming out of it at last, and was looking at his surroundings in bewilderment.

"Why are we all in the garden?" he asked.

"Don't you remember?" Spring asked.

"Yes—I think so. Yes. I wanted to see you, Spring." He turned to her. "But Jasmine said you were sleeping. She invited me to come with her, but I didn't want to at first, and then she looked and—" He blushed furiously, remembering.

"And she led you down the garden path," Spring quipped.

"Yes. Is that her?" Herb asked, noticing the statue for the first time.

"Yes," Spring said with the satisfaction of a job well done. "And may I say she never looked lovelier."

The three decided to remain at the castle for the night, and though there was no longer anything to fear from their hostess, they took the precaution of sharing one chamber. The night passed uneventfully, but as they prepared to depart the next morning, they heard a commotion taking place in the garden. They had hoped to slip away unnoticed, but as they paused by the gateway, that was not to be. Several of the servants surrounded Jasmine's statue. It was obvious they were in an emotional state. One of them spotted their small group by the gate and alerted the others.

"The strangers," another cried. "This must be their doing."

"Uh-oh," Spring said.

The way out lay through the garden where the servants now gathered, blocking their exit. Spring recognized two of the women who had attended them the evening before. They had been joined by three more strong men. Would they attempt to exact vengeance for their Mistress' demise?

"Good morning. We'll be on our way now. Appreciate your help," Spring said, smiling, trying to bluff their way past. No one moved.

"You did this?" asked the youngest servant girl. "It was your magic which turned her to stone?"

"It was unavoidable," Herb said, putting a protective arm around Spring. "Jasmine tried to turn me into one of those things. We had to protect ourselves. Surely, you can understand? We had no choice."

"She's dead," said one of the men, stepping forward. "She is cold and lifeless like the stones of the earth."

Cling Ling moved in, assuming a defensive stance. "I must warn you. I am expert at the art of Julep-so."

The older woman turned to the others. "We be free," she cried. "Slaves no longer. Free!"

"Yes! Yes!" the others joined in.

The young girl made a deep curtsey to Spring. "We be forever in thy debt, Mistress."

"You aren't—angry?" Spring breathed, relieved.

"We be glad. Yet, 'tis so hard to believe. We never thought ever to be free."

"We must repay the great magicians," agreed one of the men.

"You owe us nothing," Herb said. He was just happy not to have to force their way out. The memory of his last fight still lingered heavily on his mind, and in his sore limbs.

"If I may ask one favor?" Cling Ling interjected. "Please to tell. Where is the castle of Zygote?"

A hushed silence fell upon the group, then the young girl spoke. "Ye be friends of the magician?" she asked hesitantly.

Spring wasn't sure what they should say to that. If these people were loyal to Zygote, they would be foolish to trust them. Trust had proven folly the night before. Yet, it went against her grain to lie again, especially to feign friendship with that monster, Zygote. She looked to the others, but it was plain they were leaving it up to her.

"He has something," she said, swallowing, "that belongs to us. We've come to take it back." That was no lie, but even though the servants seemed grateful for their new freedom, she was not certain where their allegiance lay.

"Ah," answered the girl, relaxing once more. "Jasmine was a conjuration of the magician. She paid him service. He be not pleased to lose her, methinks."

"We must be wary," Cling Ling agreed. "Zygote has peopled his domain with many such creatures as Jasmine. We may not have encountered the last of his magical traps, I fear."

"Wait," Herb said, intrigued. "You said something about Jasmine doing 'service' for Zygote. Are you saying they were, uh, lovers?"

"Oh, no!" laughed the girl, finding that idea most amusing. "He be old and not interested in such diversion. Besides, one kiss of Jasmine and he be stoned. She entertained many guests at the castle. All sent by Zygote, and all remain. Her kiss be forever binding." She indicated the garden.

"Horrible," Spring shivered. Herb had almost joined their ranks, and as for her? Who could say? Perhaps it would have worn off. There were no females in the garden. Jasmine would have had to dispose of her by other means, but that was not any more appealing.

"Zygote be not generous with his enemies. Be therefore careful if thou goest to the castle. Mayhap thy loss be not now so dear that thou knowest now the nature of the magician?" asked the girl.

"I know his nature only too well," Spring said coldly.

"It is more important than you can imagine," Herb said, grimly, thinking of Lily. A man who could sanction turning flesh to stone would hardly be kind to a strange, alien girl, masquerading as his prey. Herb feared for her now more than ever. And for Spring.

"Zygote. Hie we must away from this place," said one of the men, fearfully.

Most of the group seemed to agree, and scurried off leaving only the young servant girl. The older woman waited at a distance.

"My sister," she explained. "But truly, Zygote will not look kindly upon us now. We must depart also. First, needs must I direct thee to thy heinous destination. Methinks it poor thanks for thy deed." With that, she scratched a map in the dirt with a stick, and hurried to catch up with her sister.

The directions were simple, and they made swift progress until they came upon a narrow swinging bridge stretched across a wide chasm with a small stream below. It did not look dangerous since it hung only a few feet above the water, but such bridges were difficult to navigate if a person wasn't accustomed to them, and one could find oneself tumbling off the side into the wet.

"I suggest we proceed one at a time," Cling Ling said, testing the ropes. "More risks upsetting the balance, though I think it is strong enough to bear the weight of two."

"Why take chances?" Herb said. "Ladies first," he added, sadistically. But he had trouble suppressing his smile; he intended to take the first risk himself.

"Thanks." Spring smiled wryly. She suspected he would enjoy seeing her swaying hips as she progressed over the bridge. Yet, that thought was not too unpleasant. She made a playful face at him, and stepped on, gripping tightly to both sides of the rope handles. They felt firm.

"Wait—I didn't mean—" he protested, too late.

"I know," she said.

She walked forward at a steady pace, neither fast nor slow, lest she bounce or swing. She had just passed the midway point above the deepest part of the stream when the ropes jerked sideways. Spring cried out as she lost her balance and stumbled toward the edge.

❦ 23 ❦

Child's Play

Spring had good reflexes, so was not thrown. She steadied herself, then looked to see what could have caused the action, but could see nothing. How mysterious! And then again, maybe not. If Herb Moss thought dunking her in the water was a joke, she would soon fix him. It would be just like him to jerk on the ropes once her back was turned.

Spring continued across, planning her revenge. Perhaps a good tickling. It would be an excuse to get really close to him, and—and what? What was she really thinking of?

Suddenly, a horrible hairy monster arm appeared at the side of the bridge. It could easily pull her into the chasm with him if it tried.

Herb and Cling Ling could see the scene from where they stood. Herb started to run for the bridge, but Cling Ling restrained him. The monster was in charge of the bridge now, and could shake Spring off into his clutches before they could ever reach her. Yet he had made no other move, so they should plan how to help her.

Herb might wade out as close as he dared and attract the monster's attention, while Cling Ling scurried onto the bridge and caught Spring before she fell. It was not far, but there could be unknown dangers, jagged rocks, and so forth.

But now the monster was actually speaking.

"Who is crossing over my bridge?" growled the gruff voice. "I must teach you a lesson by eating you up."

A talking monster? Why not, thought Spring. This was a fairy tale world created by Zygote, so—

Of course. No wonder the lines sounded familiar. This was a child's story. Another myth like the Gorgon incident. If she played along correctly, she might escape unharmed after all.

"Oh, please, please, Mr. Monster, please don't eat me," she begged, speaking loudly so both Herb and Cling Ling could hear. "I am so small. But my friend Herb, who is to follow soon," she almost shouted, "is much larger and meatier. Don't spoil your appetite on me. He's a real meal," she concluded, warming to the part.

"What?" Herb blinked. He knew she was afraid of the monster, but to throw him to it seemed a bit unkind.

Cling Ling noted his expression in amusement, chuckling through his leaves.

"Really, Cling Ling. I see nothing humorous in this situation. We have to do something."

"So sorry. It is but another legend. A story for children. An Old Earth nursery tale of three goats who must cross a bridge to eat grass, and how they tricked the Troll, another monster, to achieve their goal. Mistress Moon is aware of this story. She is trying to tell us."

"Oh," Herb said, abashed. He should have remembered that story, himself. Paradise was derived from New Earth and had the dubious benefit of much human culture. His personal favorite had been "Jack and the Beanstalk." He hoped they wouldn't encounter any giants here.

Spring had made it safely to the other side of the chasm and stood waving to them from the bank. Cling Ling gestured for Herb to go next. "You are the middle goat, my friend. I fear the Troll and I may have to wrestle, but I feel I am a match for him," he said confidently.

Coached in his part by Cling Ling, Herb stepped onto the bridge and proceeded dubiously toward the center. The monster appeared as if on cue.

"Who's that tromping over my bridge?" he growled.

Though shaking within, Herb followed through with his lines and was soon stepping off the other side to join Spring. They watched as Cling Ling approached the center. This time the monster leaped upon the bridge and engaged the traveller in combat.

First, he attempted throwing the Vinese off balance into the water, but Cling Ling clung on with several of his tendrils, countering the lashes and swipes of the monster with his Julep-so holds and thrusts. He gave a fine account of himself, and in the end, it was the monster who tumbled into the water.

Cling Ling raced quickly across with a combination of rolling and swinging his vines. He was on the other side before the monster could swim up again.

"I congratulate you on your perceptiveness, Mistress Moon," Cling Ling said. "It was a simple problem to overcome once we knew the rules."

"Easy for you," Spring laughed. "I don't know how Herb or I would have defeated him alone."

Herb blushed with shame, realizing that was probably true, but no man liked to feel a woman had so little confidence in his abilities, especially a woman whose admiration he valued.

Spring couldn't help noticing Herb's color transformation, and saw she had erred. In trying to praise Cling Ling, she had inadvertently insulted Herb. Oh, men and their stupid egos! He should know how much she thought of him by now.

"Of course, I was only speaking for myself," she quickly added. "I know Herb would have thought of something."

That made it a little better. Herb said nothing, but Spring could tell it had taken the sting off. When she reached for his hand to help her over a large branch that blocked their path, he kept holding it as they continued on their way to Zygote's castle. Spring smiled with relief, for now she knew all was forgiven.

In the deceptively idyllic setting, it was almost possible to forget why they had come there. Herb felt Spring's hand in his, realizing he had been holding it longer than necessary. She hadn't objected. Could it be she enjoyed his company as much as he did hers?

Stealing a glance at her face, he saw she was deep in thought, walking along automatically as he guided her. That explained it. She probably wasn't even aware of their contact. He, however, was only too aware.

A part of him wished that time could stand still, so he wouldn't have to relinquish the moment. Yet time could not, and he felt guilty for even thinking about it. Lily needed him more than ever. There was no place for dalliance while her life remained in peril. Or, thereafter, he reminded himself, sharply. It was this place that sent his notions wandering. So unreal. Things would be right when he was back on Paradise where he belonged. He was sure of it.

Cling Ling left them alone again, while he forged ahead. Because of his leafy camouflage, it was easier for him to scout unnoticed. After the bridge incident, he wanted to check out the route, so as to be apprised of any more potential dangers.

Now they sat waiting for his return in a small clearing. Spring surveyed the pleasant surroundings. The morning walk through the forest had been delightful, once the Troll was behind them. Golden beams of sunlight pierced through the tree tops, sprinkles of colorful wild flowers and mushrooms dotted the lush carpet of grass, and butterflies fluttered and honeybees buzzed. The serenity of nature confronted them at every turn. Too bad it had to end.

"This is lovely," Spring said.

"Maybe," Herb said.

"Why? What are you saying?" she asked, puzzled.

"Only that Cling Ling is right. After that ugly bridge monster, we have to stay alert for others. I recall many an Old Earth fairy tale took place deep in forests just like this one."

"Um. The cookie children and the old witch woman. The little blonde girl and the bears," she agreed.

"Bears? Let's see, aren't those fur-bearing animals, like—like chippermunks?"

Spring laughed. "Herb, it would take about a hundred of your chippermunks to make up one small bear. If you see one, you'll recognize it. But I hope not. I've had enough monsters for one day."

"Yes, me too. I hope Cling Ling hasn't run into any ogres or giants out there. He should be back soon."

"Does my company bore you?" Spring asked teasingly.

"No. I mean, I just wish we could get there. To the castle. To Lily, I mean."

"Yes, I know exactly what you mean," she said soberly. Fairy tale it might be, but would there be a happy ending? Soon, they would know. Was Lily alive? Could they defeat Zygote? Reality would come crashing down all too soon.

"Sit back, Herb, and I'll tell you a tale," she said grimly.

"A fairy tale?" Herb smiled, not noticing her change of mood.

"Of course, a fairy tale. I'll tell you 'The Dragon's Bride.'"

THE DRAGON'S BRIDE
As told by Spring Gabriel

A dragon's breath can melt a good knight's armor at twenty paces. Is it any wonder many a fair damsel has grown to old age awaiting rescue by a handsome hero? Princess Qwendell did not intend to be counted among their number.

In case of a dragon attack, she had sewn two small vials in the bodice of her royal gown within her royal cleavage. It had cost several pieces of gold, not to mention a questionable reputation, but she finally managed to persuade the wretched Wizard Supreme to part with a magical potion to disguise herself.

One drop on the tongue would instantly transform her into the very likeness of a large beastly dragon. In such way, she fully expected to escape by posing as a dragon herself.

Sure enough, one fine day, a wandering dragon stumbled upon the princess's castle and left it a fine pile of rubble. As he searched amongst the debris for the princess, she swallowed the potion and turned into the most ravishing female dragon the other had ever beheld. The dragon forgot all about searching for a mere princess, and proposed marriage to her upon the spot.

Life was not working out the way she'd planned. "Ick," said the princess.

"You are no ordinary dragon, Lady," her suitor said, so excited that he blew smoke rings.

"Quite correct, tall and scaly," she said, trying to leave for a safe spot to turn back into her royal form.

"I shall woo you," said the dragon, and pounced to woo in the forthright way that dragons do.

"Woo. Woo," said the dragon.

"Woah," said the princess, quickly thinking of a way to rid herself of the creature long enough to drink her antidote from the second vial and return as a princess. Many the times as a princess, she had demanded a knight slay a dragon to prove his worthiness. That was it.

"No, no, no," she said. "First you must slay a knight. No slay, no play!"

Now this particular dragon had kidnapped many a princess, but he had never slain a knight. It simply had not come up. He decided to secure his lady in a cave while he went off to consult his best friend, another tall, green, scaly dragon. He rolled a big rock across the entrance and left his lady love to breathe fire in anger. But, huff and puff as she might, the rock would not roll.

The dragon's friend listened carefully and decided what with the recent shortage of available knights, they might have to resort to sorcery to win the fair dragon lady's claws in marriage.

It so happened that he also knew of the same Wizard Supreme and demanded a disguise potion to turn a dragon into a knight. Taking the potion, he returned to his lovesick friend, and they set out to the cave to perform a play in which the dragon suitor would pretend to slay the dragon now disguised as a knight.

When the rock was rolled away, the princess saw what she believed to be a real knight, drank down the antidote, and reverted to her own regal form. She raced to the knight and promised her hand in marriage if he would but slay the ugly old dragon.

Enraged with jealousy, the dragon slew his friend, and stole the potion from him. Even though the princess was no longer a dragon, she had stolen his heart.

Quickly gulping down the potion, he became a knight and returned to the princess. She had been fooled the first time, but had since wised up.

As he approached, she took the remaining disguise potion and became a dragon, whereupon she slew him with one blast of her hot breath. Then she took the antidote, and became a princess. A handsome prince found her and fell madly in love, and they lived happily ever after.

The End

"But, that's a terrible story," Herb said. He felt sorry for the dragon. "How like a woman. And after he had turned himself inside out to please her."

"That's the whole point, Herb. No matter how much you may wish it to be otherwise, some loves were never meant to be," Spring said.

Herb decided to change the subject. "It's hard to comprehend that the man who created this world with all its beauty, could at the same time be so evil."

"You'd better believe it," Spring snapped. Her disposition had deteriorated considerably during the telling of the story.

"Sorry," Herb said. "I know how you feel about Zygote. With good reason."

"No, I'm the one who's sorry," she apologized. "It's just that I know how horrid he is. You and Cling have had but a very small taste of his cruelty. Kidnapping Lily was all in a day's work. A man who could sanction the death of a wonderful, brilliant person like my father—is beyond words," she finished, as her voice failed. Sometimes the pain came rushing back at unexpected moments. This was one of them.

Herb pretended not to see the tears. It was so hard to keep from hugging her in his arms, but he knew there was no place for him in her life. It would be wrong to encourage feelings that could not, and should not, be returned.

Even so, his heart went out to her, and his arms would surely have followed, had not Cling Ling returned soon.

Spring hastily wiped her face and went behind Herb to meet the Vinese. "There is a fresh water well not far from here," he announced. They had exhausted most of their supply, so this was good news. They still had several of the Txnghc's nutrition pills, so food was not a problem.

They had not gone far until they came upon a small pathway leading to the well. It was a covered redwood one with ivy growing up the sides and smooth decorative stones around the base.

"It's just like a picture card, or a wishing well," Spring said.

"Well, I wish only to drink," Herb said. "I just hope the water tastes as good as the well looks." He lowered the wooden bucket until it splashed down, sinking beneath the surface. He turned the crank to draw it back and tied off the rope.

Spring handed him the pewter dipper that hung from a peg at the side of one post. He plunged the dipper into the water and offered the first drink to Spring. She tipped it and drank deeply, spilling a little from the sides.

"Umm, cool." She dipped it again and held it up for Herb this time. "For my Knight in Shining Armor," she teased.

"From the loveliest princess in the land? How can I refuse?" he replied, drinking with relish. He hadn't realized how thirsty he was. Much better than the tepid water left in the canteen.

Spring reached for the dipper to serve Cling Ling next. "Cling–" She felt strangely disoriented and blinked her eyes. The dipper seemed to slip from her hand.

Everything around her was swimming together, her vision was so blurred. She closed her eyes and when she opened them again, she looked for Herb and Cling Ling, but all she saw were walls. Walls? Where did the others go? Where was the forest and the well? And most of all, where was she?

Spring climbed out of the huge four poster bed and ran to the single window in the small, round room. She looked out and down. She was up in a castle. Leaning out as far as she dared, she looked across the tree tops. There was no castle. Just a high tower, like a rook, the chess piece.

A spectacular view of the forest was spread before her. Perhaps she could spot Herb or Cling out there somewhere. But it was no use; there was just the wide expanse of green, and both Herb and Cling were green. It would be impossible to spy them from this height. She would have to go down and look for them.

Spying the small door, she ran to it and pulled hard on the knob, but it wouldn't open. Locked! Someone had locked her in! Rummaging about the room, she searched for a key, but found none. If only she still had her things, with the magical key of her father's. She looked beneath the bed, but there was no sign of her belongings. Mysterious. How could she have gotten here without knowing it?

Sitting down on the bed, she went over everything that had happened before she appeared here. They were walking through the forest on the way to Zygote's castle. Cling Ling had found the well. They drank, and then—this. Nothing else had happened. So there had to be a connection.

Had they evoked some spell without being aware of it? What had they said? Now she remembered. They had been talking about fairy tales while waiting for Cling. She had told him her story about the Knight and Dragon and Princess, and then they had been joking about it at the well. They—of course. That was it. It really was a wishing well.

And if it was active? Probably so. Even if it was artificial, it was still Zygote's magic realm. If they had only thought, they could have simply wished themselves to Zygote's castle then.

No, wait. They hadn't been making wishes, exactly. Yet maybe the well was set up to take wishes with a drink, so anything a person thought about while drinking was considered a wish? The well couldn't tell the difference.

But what had they been saying? She had been teasing Herb. Calling him her Knight in Shining Armor. But it didn't make sense. Herb wasn't there.

Herb wished he wasn't there. He stood cowering at the back of a narrow ravine, his gauntlets held firmly over the mouth of the horse, trying to keep him quiet. There was a dragon out there.

Herb had no idea just how he had gotten to wherever he was, but he sure wished he could leave. Where were the others? He had awakened as if from a dream to find himself in the strange setting. More of Zygote's evil doings, no doubt, but what was he to do?

He had been standing with Spring and Cling Ling at the well talking, and the next thing he knew, galloping full tilt across a grassy plain toward a fire breathing dragon. That had limited appeal.

Herb had pulled on the reins and turned the charger in the opposite direction. You would think a dragon would be happy to be rid of him, but oh, no. It had to pursue him. Herb had plunged his steed down into the maze of ravines in hopes of losing his fiery friend. It could still work if the annoying nag would only be still.

He had handled the horse amazingly well for someone who had never sat upon horseflesh in his life. If this was some sort of story scenario, such as the Troll at the Bridge incident, he would probably be equipped to enter into whatever plot it foretold. And if it was only a story, perhaps he had nothing to fear, after all. That is, if he could avoid becoming a one man feast until discovering the plot line.

The horse pulled away, reared up and whinnied, giving Herb a look of stern disapproval. No doubt it was used to jousts, and dragons, and bold goings on, and Herb had somehow offended its sense of valor. Well, tough grass. He was no Knight of Olde and he wanted to grow older.

Suddenly, the horse broke free and scrambled back up the side of the ravine. Herb rushed up after it. The last thing he needed was to be caught out in the open without a steed. He wasn't quite sure how he knew that, but he was certain it would be the end of him if he was.

Puffing up after the wandering mount, that was now standing still, naturally, since it was in full view of the dragon, he put his foot in the stirrup and tried to hoist himself up. It wasn't so simple in armor.

How did those Knights do it? Now he remembered. They had help. It was bad news for any Knight who fell off his steed during battle. A full suit of armor was hard to get up in.

Herb looked around the landscape and got inspired. He led the animal over to a large clump of rocks and climbed up to mount. The dragon was there, but seemed occupied in thought. Maybe it had found someone else to eat while he had been in the ravine.

If Spring could only see him now, he thought, as he mounted. Only today she had called him her Knight in Shining Armor. Herb looked down at the shine on his armor. He could comb his hair in its reflection.

Spring. Somehow, she had done this to him. Oh, would he love to get his hands on her. And this time, for a very different reason.

* * *

Spring had put two and two together at last. Their "wishes" had worked on each other. Right now, Herb was probably in some King Arthur tale, while she was, where? What would Herb have thought about? He called her a Princess, but fairy tales were full of princesses trapped in towers. That was it. Trapped. A Prisoner.

She turned quickly to the window, and tripped. Her foot had caught on something. Looking down to see what it was, she gasped to discover it was her own hair. But that was impossible. Her hair was not that long. Until now.

She reached back and pulled, watching the braid uncoil like a rope. Well, one mystery solved. She was Rapunzel, the girl with the long golden hair!

It figured. If any story would have appeal for Herb, it was one centered on a woman's lengthy tresses. Hadn't he always managed to put his hands on hers whenever the occasion presented itself? And the story of a beautiful girl, held captive in a tall tower for his exclusive pleasure was just the sort of thing he would conjure up. Based on a child's story perhaps, but many a grown man's fantasy.

Spring made another search of the room, this time for scissors or a knife; anything to cut with. If she could whack off the thick braid, she would try tying it to the window and climbing down. Even as a child, this possibility had occurred to her and she wondered why the silly Princess had never thought of it.

Well, she wasn't vain, and this hair wasn't really hers. In fact, it was a rather brassy shade of blonde. So much for Herb's taste. Freedom was of higher priority than sex appeal at the moment. She kept on searching.

"Rapunzel, Rapunzel, let down your long, lovely hair," came a call from below. Who could it be? It didn't sound like either Herb or Cling.

She leaned out and looked down. Oh no. She had forgotten about the other part of the Rapunzel story. A bent old hag in a long, black cloak stood gazing up at her. A witch.

What to do? If she didn't go along, the witch could suspect something. She couldn't afford to distort this reality yet. Best to play along and see. Spring gathered up the long rope of hair and tossed it out, taking a firm grip from her side. There was a slight tug, but nothing as uncomfortable as she'd expected. Thank goodness this witch was skinny.

Suddenly, the witch's ugly face was at the window, her long nose twitching over toothless lips. Her eyes were cruel and beady.

"Who's been here since I've been gone?" she hissed.

"No-no one," stammered Spring, jumping back. That was true. Or, was it? Now she remembered. Rapunzel had a boyfriend. He had been climbing in to romance her. And if she could see him when he came again, he might help her escape.

"That's my good girl," cooed the witch. "Come. Sit with me, and I'll comb out your hair."

What was there to do but go along with it? Worse could happen than getting her hair done.

The witch combed and rebraided the long length of silken hair while giving Spring sage advice on men. The funny part was, it was actually good advice. She remembered to behave like a docile doe and say "Yes, Mother" a lot. Satisfied, the witch climbed back down and left Spring alone again.

She was still hunting for a cutter when the call came again, this time from a male voice. Herb? She rushed to the window and looked out. There was a man, but not Herb. He was dressed in a pastel pink tunic over lavender tights and had a pointy feathered cap on his head. Rapunzel's guy.

Quickly she threw down her hair and he climbed up,

reaching through the window for her. She backed away, tripping again.

"Wait. I'm not who you think I am," she exclaimed.

"What game be this, lass?" he laughed, chasing her around the small room.

"But I'm not Rapunzel. It's all a mistake," she gasped, dodging his hands. "We have to get out of here before the witch returns. Do you have a knife? Cut off my hair and we can climb down it together."

He stopped dead in his boots. "Cut your wondrous hair, my beauty?" He looked aghast. "Better to ask me to cut out my heart."

"But, it's the only way. I don't have a key."

"The witch has done this. She has spun some evil spell to make you speak such words, my dove."

"Okay, okay, forget I mentioned it," she said, holding a chair in front of her. This man was beyond it. Obviously, these characters went by only one story line and could not be deviated. She would have to try another tack.

"My hero!" she emoted. "You slay the witch for me. You can hide and attack her when she returns. Save me, you—" she paused, gazing at his pastel outfit, "you, big strong man."

"Yes," he agreed. "I shall free you and we will live happily ever after." He seemed elated at the prospect.

"Yeah, I thought you'd go for it. I mean, yes, my hero! The witch probably has the key on her. Good. Now all we have to do is wait," she said, sitting down on the side of the bed to rest.

"Nay, not all, my lovely," the Prince said suggestively, approaching with outstretched arms. This time he was too quick, and caught her fast.

"Prince. Down, Prince," she panted. "This is a bad idea. While the witch is loose, I mean. She might come any moment."

The Prince was busy kissing upwards on her arm, stopping at the shoulder. "Don't be coy with me, you saucy wench. Many the time we have lain together. I know thee too well." He leered.

Oops. She hadn't thought of that part of it when reading Rapunzel's story as a child. What did she think they were doing up there on those visits? Playing pat-a-cake?

"Oh. You weren't playing checkers, were you?" she cried, trying to free herself from his grasp.

"Thou speech be strange, but thy lips sweet. I must taste their nectar," he proclaimed as his lips crushed hers.

She pulled away and ran to the opposite side of the bed.

"No! No!" she cried, exactly like a Damsel in Distress.

"But, yes, yes," he said, ripping off his garments and flinging them to the floor. As Spring had suspected, he'd nothing to hide.

"This new game doth please me. Thou hast spirit, wench," he said, his eyes attempting to do to her clothing what his hands had done to his own.

"But I don't want to play anymore," Spring wailed.

He lunged across the small bed and caught her at the waist, ripping open the lacy bodice of her gown. It came loose with dismaying ease and she tumbled out. Spring looked down in amazement.

"Where did those come from?" Of course, they weren't hers, they were Herb's idea of Rapunzel's. There wasn't a mirror, so she had just assumed she looked like herself, but she must have looked like the Rapunzel the witch was used to, or she would have been discovered. She looked down again. How did the girl tie her shoes? No wonder the Prince was so determined!

"Help! Help!" she screamed, back in Damsel in Distress mode. D&D for short. But who would hear?

A big black bird landed on the window ledge and flew into the room. It disappeared in a puff of smoke and became the witch.

"Swine," she screamed at the Prince.

"Yeah. Swine," agreed Spring, beating him off.

The witch pointed a long dirty fingernail, and the Prince was turned into a lizard. He went scrambling across the room and out the window. Spring could not feel too sorry for him under the circumstances.

"You nasty little girl," the witch said, turning on Spring now.

"Hey, wait a minute, here. He attacked me," she protested. "I'm the injured party. He's not even my type."

But the witch was not listening, she was conjuring up a terrible spell, if Spring knew her kind. Quickly, she lunged and pushed the witch through the open window. Instead of falling, the hag turned back into the bird and flew off, cawing. Spring wasn't about to wait for her to return.

A shiny object had caught her eye when the Prince was disrobing. It was still there among his rumpled clothing. Quickly, she pulled the knife from the scabbard and slashed it through her braid.

The room bent in half and began to swirl around, faster and faster. Was she going to faint? Ridiculous. She had never fainted in her life. She fainted.

"Idiot horse," Herb yelled. But to no avail. They were right back where they started from, the horse's hooves beating a tattoo back toward the waiting dragon. It was as if he had been waiting, knowing Herb would return to his proper role. If this were one of Zygote's preordained tales, there was no escaping the inevitable.

Herb raised his sword and prepared for the conflict. The dragon reared upon his back haunches, fire issuing in a roaring inferno toward him. Herb knew he would be fried before he could get in one good swipe.

How did Knights beat that problem? A lucky thrust? Herb knew his luck had just run out. As the charger closed in, he lashed out, and missed by a mile. Worse than that, the force of his thrust threw him off balance and sent the sword flying from his hand. Herb shut his eyes to wait for the end to come as he fell from the horse.

Herb waited. He felt odd, but not scorched. He opened his eyes to see Spring and Cling Ling standing over him next to the well. How had he returned?

"Oh Herb," Spring cried, throwing her arms about him. "You're back."

He was back. He wasn't going to be a dragon barbecue. But he was less than grateful. "You and your Knight in Shining Armor! I was almost devoured by a dragon!" he shouted, looking daggers at Spring.

"Oh excuse me, but that was no vacation you sent me on, either, Herb Moss! I was Rapunzel, locked in with a witch and a rampaging Romeo. It's tough all over, okay?" She glared at him.

"Oh," Herb said, remembering his own fantasy. "We must be more careful. How did we escape?"

Spring was still pouting, so Cling Ling had to answer. "When you two vanished, I surmised what the properties of this water must be. It was a simple matter of drinking and wishing for your safe return."

"I apologize, Herb," Spring said, having calmed down in that mercurial way she had. "I'll bet you were handsome in your armor!" she giggled.

"I cut quite a figure," Herb said grudgingly. But her change of mood was contagious. "How did you like yourself as Rapunzel?"

"Well, I was a lot of woman, Herb. A lot of woman." She smiled as she looked down at herself, seeing much less.

Cling Ling would have raised his eyebrows, had he had them.

"Shall we continue our journey?" he asked.

"Wait, I thought of something while I was in the tower.

Why can't we use the well and just wish ourselves there?" Spring asked.

"Oh no! That thing is too dangerous," Herb said.

"A moot point," Cling Ling explained, "since we only get one wish."

"Stingy old Zygote. Anybody knows it's supposed to be three," Spring said.

"Three between us. Must suggest we continue without further delay."

Herb and Spring grinned at each other like two naughty children. They had been very fortunate to have Cling Ling along to keep them in line. As they followed through the forest, the memory of the frivolous moment slipped away to be replaced by the seriousness of the task at hand. They had not really forgotten, but sometimes, it was just too painful to remember.

❦ 24 ❦

Zygote

The top of the towers peeped over the tree tops ahead. The castle was set upon a rise surrounded by dense woods and a protective moat.

Herb and Spring stayed out of sight at the edge of the woods while Cling Ling elected to scout the area. Certainly, he would be the least noticeable. Even if he were spotted, he would likely be taken for just another magical conjuration of the Master's.

Spring had heard that Zygote had done extensive experimentation upon both plant and animal life to create his mythical creatures. He had done well creating the illusion of a storybook world, and she had to admit it was impressive.

White, fleecy clouds positioned themselves next to the perfect points of the high towers. A perpetual rainbow hung across a vibrantly blue sky, and the beautiful backdrop of the distant, hazy mountains and green forest completed the idyllic scene.

"How ironic that this monster should reside in such an innocent setting," she commented. "Perhaps that is why true evil is so seductive."

"Yes," Herb agreed, "the most beautiful of flowers may conceal the stinging bee."

Spring smiled ruefully. "Guess I opened a hornet's nest for you, Herb. I am truly sorry that I ever involved you or poor Lily in my troubles. I know you wish you'd never answered that ad."

Herb realized she had taken his analogy personally. That wasn't the intention, but he could see it did apply. There was a time not long ago he had wished exactly that. Life had grown in a straight row then.

By this time, he and Lily might have formed their union, for the seeds had been sown for their well-arranged life together. His father was considering him for a promotion, so pleased was he with the way Herb had conformed to the work of the firm.

"A man has nothing, if he doesn't have roots." That was his father's motto. He was gratified that his only son had at last planted his feet firmly in the ground.

Yet, had Herb not answered the ad, he wouldn't have met Spring, the Moon Maiden. He still recalled the first time he saw her. Her surprise at finding him at home, and how she had dropped her towel. Herb sighed. As he pondered upon these things he knew that in spite of it all, he could never regret meeting Spring.

Then there was Lily. Naturally, he would not have her harmed for the universe. She had been the true innocent party in all this madness. She must not be made to suffer for his indiscretions. Aside from her innocence, she had shown herself to be a strong, brave woman, revealing a side to her nature he had scarcely known existed.

Because she was strong, he knew she would understand.

When all this was over, Founder willing, he would have to explain why they could not proceed with their union. He knew now that Lily deserved a better man than he. One who truly loved her in a way he never could.

Herb knew that he had fallen in love with Spring, and that could never have happened if he loved Lily in the way he should have. It was not her fault. He would always care for Lily in a special way, as a dear friend, and yes, more than a friend. But his heart belonged to Spring.

Spring, Moon, by whatever name she chose, filled his very veins with their life's blood. Before her, he had merely existed. Now, he lived. It was awkward not only because of Lily, but because of the way Spring felt. There was that other man. The one who had betrayed her. Would she ever get over him sufficiently to love again?

There was the loss of Spring's father, and the hatred she felt toward this magician Zygote. Even if they somehow rescued Lily, Herb knew that was not the end of it for Spring. She would not rest until the evil magician was brought to justice, and how could they accomplish that as well?

He could not be so brutal as to force his attentions upon her at this trying time. Perhaps the time would never come. But he had to hope.

Spring mistook his prolonged silence for agreement. "I don't blame you for feeling as you do, Herb," she said.

Feeling as he did? If only he could tell her! But before he could gather his courage, Cling Ling was rolling back to them.

"The cooling unit is there. It means the Freezer made its delivery," he reported. "Our misadventures on this planet have delayed us more than I anticipated."

"And Lily?" asked Herb, fearing the worst.

"Alive. I am certain of it. I overheard a maid mention the 'Master's patient' in the kitchen. It must be she."

Both Spring and Herb were heartened by the news. Lily alive! Then there was hope.

Cling Ling believed Lily was being held in one of the tower rooms, possibly a medical laboratory. He had observed the maid coming from there with her tray. She did not appear to be guarded, but in her condition, it would hardly be necessary. And besides, where could she go?

He had seen only one grounds patrolman, but he was a giant of a man. If they timed it correctly, however, they might invade the castle before his round was completed, and then escape the same way. It was decided Herb and Spring would enter the castle alone, and Cling would remain close by to watch and act as backup as he had at the greenhouse, though they hoped with more success. They had learned from that fiasco not to take chances. This rescue had to succeed.

Herb realized his declaration to Spring would have to wait, and perhaps that was best, after all. They followed closely behind Cling Ling as he led them over the lowered moat bridge, inside the castle walls. The imposing front gate had two huge eyes painted at the top. It gave the otherwise lovely castle an eerie look. So much for good taste, Spring thought.

Cling Ling pointed out a small window that was unlatched, and took up his own vigil as look-out near the entrance. Herb boosted Spring up and through the window by clasping her waist and lifting, while she caught the ledge and pulled up. His heart quickened at the movement of her hips as she gained entry and dropped to the other side. He gave a jump and caught onto the ledge, following after her.

Fortunately, they found themselves alone in the big hall. It was typically medieval in decor, with much armor and woven tapestries around the walls. They crept stealthily down the side, into a narrow passageway.

"Which way now?" whispered Spring.

"The tower's on the left, so that way and any stairs, I guess."

They opened several doors, but none seemed to lead upstairs. The first floor was strangely deserted, a fact which began to disturb Herb, but he didn't want to upset Spring. So far, they had met no opposition, but how long could their luck hold?

"Herb?" Spring asked, gesturing to a couple more doors at the side.

"Just keep looking until we find Lily, or get caught trying," Herb said.

"That's what I'm afraid of. One session with Elton was enough."

"I agree. And I had a bad thought. If the Freezer has arrived, it's possible Elton isn't far behind. He could be here now, for all we know."

"We'll just have to chance it," Spring said, spotting one last door, and cautiously opening it. At last! It was a winding stair. "This has to lead to the tower."

Herb nodded agreement, and closed the door quietly behind them. Small torches lit the way up the treacherous steps.

They climbed cautiously and carefully to the top, stopping outside on the landing. Spring edged the door slowly open. Seeing no one inside, she nodded to Herb, and they rushed inside, latching the door behind them.

It wasn't a torture chamber, at least. In fact, it was more like a ritzy hospital room, Spring observed. There were cabinets with all sorts of medications and bookshelves, and there at the corner was a built-up bed of medieval fashion with thick curtains draped along the sides, obscuring the view of whoever was inside. Could it really be?

"Lily!" Herb cried.

"Herb!" she answered. "Is it you?"

Herb pushed aside the curtains as Spring stood beside him. Lily! She was alive! Herb sank beside her on the edge of the bed, taking her hand. It felt so cool.

Spring reached for her bag of stones and selected a large, violet piece, placing it upon the vital center chakra.

"How do you feel, Lily?" she asked.

"That feels nice. Like energy going into me. Is it magic?"

"Magical science. I'll be glad to explain it to you in detail if we manage to escape from here. Do you feel strong enough to walk yet?"

"I don't know. I'm so confused. I was much better, and then when I heard you call, I awoke here—I—it doesn't make any sense."

"Don't worry. It's probably just the effects of the medicines Zygote has given you. I have to admit, he's worked a miracle! Try to stand," Spring urged.

"I'll try," Lily said.

"Zygote helped her?" Herb asked.

"He must have. Look at her," Spring said.

"Yes, the Freezer," Lily said. "Now I remember. The units have built in alarms. When my demise grew imminent, the attendants were alerted. They transplanted me to another unit more suited to my needs. I was wilted, however, and am still very weak. I would not have survived if not for Zygote's magic. But—"

"I don't know why he helped you, Lily. Probably to hold you as a hostage as Elton did before, but in any case we can't lose any more time. We have to get you out of here. Cling Ling is waiting for us outside."

"She's right, Lily. Here, lean against me." Herb put a supporting arm around her waist and guided her as Spring led the way to the door, opening it. She jumped back with a small cry, gasping "Zygote!"

The tall, wizened magician entered and closed the door

behind him, a benevolent smile playing at the sides of his mouth. "Yes, my dear Spring. We meet at last. But then, I have been expecting you for some time," he said.

"No one saw us enter," Herb said.

"No? It is said the walls have ears. Here, they have eyes as well." He smiled.

"The front gate! Those ugly, painted eyes! It was one of your tricks," Spring said.

"Yes, they are a bit unsettling, but what they lack in beauty, they compensate well in usefulness. I observed your every move from the moment you entered these walls."

"Then, you knew from the start that Lily wasn't me?" Spring asked.

"Oh, yes dear. I was quite aware we had received a substitute in your stead. You are forgetting, I too, am a physician. I know nonhuman physiognomy when I perceive it, and the Freezer ride did little to aid her disguise." He observed Spring's green makeup. "But you look charming."

Anger surged up in Herb. He released Lily and rushed Zygote. He bounced off harmlessly into the wall, a foolish surprised expression on his face. Spring went to his aid.

Zygote looked on patiently. "As a magician I have a multitude of defences at my disposal much less pleasant than that, young man. You would do well to remember it."

Herb got to his feet scowling. Only his pride was injured, however.

"Be careful, Herb," Lily cautioned, leaning against a shelf for support, since Herb had left her.

"She's right, Herb," Spring agreed. "He's dangerous as a scorpion. Don't provoke him."

Herb had no notion what a scorpion was, but he had some ideas of the powers magicians possessed. Of course Zygote would be protected. Herb had acted by reflex, allowing his emotions to rule over judgment. It was clear they could not win by force alone. He stood sulking, but said nothing more.

"A wise attitude," Zygote commended Spring. "My powers have served me well in the past, and with your added knowledge, I doubt there is a force in the known universe that could successfully oppose me."

"Then—Lily—you haven't?" Herb ventured, knowing Zygote fully understood his meaning.

"Molested this charming young woman? Hardly." He turned a paternal eye to Lily. "But this is an outrage. You should not be allowed to stand like that." He led her to a nearby chair and saw her seated. "Forgive my neglect, but as you see, pressing matters required my attention. Your well-meaning friends may have cost you the strength we have worked so hard to regain."

Lily accepted the chair quietly, leaning back with obvious exhaustion. Herb felt guilty for taxing her strength in the weakened state, but there was no avoiding it if they were to escape. She probably would not have made it outside the castle even if Zygote hadn't intercepted them. Her infirmity was an element they had not fully anticipated. Their mission had been doomed from the beginning.

Zygote returned his gaze to them now. "As I was saying, I realized you had slipped from my trap when I first saw Lily. But I have great respect for all types of life forms, as you would know if permitted the run of my extensive grounds. Alas, it is not possible to extend such courtesy. I admit realizing you would probably come to retrieve her, but I have no desire to harm such a lovely creature."

"We met one of your creations, Zygote," Spring interjected. "Sorry to inform you, but your friend Jasmine, is now just another lawn decoration."

The magician's brow went up in genuine surprise. "You nulled Jasmine? Truly, I have underestimated you."

"Well, don't get all broken up about it," Spring said, sarcastically. "I suppose you can just conjure up a replacement." She did not bother to conceal her disgust.

"Hardly. No, I'm afraid the lovely Jasmine was one of my failures. We all make mistakes, you know. Once she had her full powers, she was quite uncontrollable. We had an uneasy truce between us, but I never turned my back. She did so enjoy practicing her talent."

"But all those statues. People. The servants said she silenced them by your command," insisted Herb.

"My command? She would take no order from me, dear boy," Zygote scoffed. "It would be just like Jasmine to place the blame elsewhere, and perpetuate her innocent act. I suppose it helped keep the servants in line."

Herb reluctantly agreed with the line of reasoning. She did seem innocent. It was not likely she would worry about using Zygote for an excuse. Herb knew only too well how she enjoyed her power for its own sake. The memory of his close call brought on an involuntary shudder.

"I would believe him, Spring," Lily said, revived by her brief rest. "He has treated me well, except for my confinement." She looked around the small room.

"To keep you from harming yourself, only, dear Lily," Zygote answered. "I assure you, you are still too weak to wander very far. It was best you not try."

"I'm glad you've been less the monster than we supposed, Zygote," Spring said. "But the fact remains that you caused my father's death."

"That," Zygote said grimly, "was an unfortunate affair, which I deeply regret. The overly zealous bitch I hired to induce your father to cooperate became carried away by blood lust. Yet, I believe he would have survived had not young Elton lost his temper." He looked genuinely chagrined. "I needed your father's help to implement the information you store. If only he had been more reasonable, he would be yet with us. I had great respect for him, whether or not you believe that."

Fury swept over Spring's face. "So it was Elton! But it was your fault. If you had left my father alone, it would never have happened!" Her rage turned to despair as she remembered.

"Yes. I concede that much. Still, however I regret the means, there remains the end to accomplish," Zygote said meaningfully. "Else, all has been for naught, and that would be hideous, considering the price."

"I won't let you touch her," Herb exclaimed angrily. He grabbed up a glass container and threw it at the tall magician's face. It, too, hit against the invisible barrier, shattering to the floor as the others dodged the sharp, flying bits.

"Really, Herb," Zygote sighed. "This becomes tiresome. I can see if you keep this up, you'll succeed only in harming the ladies, and probably yourself." He snapped his fingers and the door clicked behind him. He moved aside to admit a fierce giant of a man. Probably the guard Cling Ling mentioned roaming the grounds earlier.

Herb was thankful Cling Ling retained his freedom. Perhaps even now he had conceived some plan to set them free. The last time they had tried to rescue Lily, they had met with the same lack of success. History had a way of repeating itself in discouraging ways.

"Show our friends to one of the guest rooms downstairs, Larg," Zygote ordered.

Large? That was an apt name for the monster. They were hassled back down the narrow stairway, but did not emerge on the first floor. Instead, they continued on through a different door leading farther down. This time they ended up deep beneath the castle walls in a section of dungeons.

Lily was not among their number. Zygote evidently still

considered her as a patient under his protection. Though they had to be separated, Herb was thankful that Zygote seemed to bear her no ill will for her part in the deception.

They were abruptly thrust into separate cells in the darkness. The closing doors clanged loudly behind them.

❀ 25 ❀

Truths

Spring screamed. Herb pressed against the adjoining bars of their cells, extending his arms and reaching frantically in the darkness for her.

"Spring, where are you? What's wrong?!" he called out. Then his hand made contact with her body. She was soft and warm there. She grasped his hand in hers and moved it.

"I'm all right. Something ran over my foot. I think it was a smouse. It frightened me! I'm not fond of smouses," she said, remembering the ones back on the lightship.

"Smouses? Oh, yes. We have a kind of smouse on P#23. They are partially plant, green, and resemble pine cones."

"How funny."

"Not to Veganettes. They are harmless pests, really, but the feminine gender seems to get overly excited whenever they see one." He laughed softly.

"Oh really? What about men? No one likes smice. Admit it!"

Herb smiled to himself. Naturally, Spring would say

that. She had already declared herself to be one of the liberated species of female. She claimed that on her home planet, the women were exactly like men. That had greatly puzzled Herb, who knew Spring was nothing at all like any man he had seen.

It was probably a joke; that was one source of her great attraction for him. Her playful nature, along with good looks, strength of character, intelligence, and honesty. Not necessarily in that order, either. There had to be more to a woman than well-grown limbs to please him. And the longer he knew Spring, the more she had pleased him.

He wanted so much to help, but each time he tried, it had been a colossal failure. Now they were prisoners. Again.

"I'm glad you're here with me, Herb," Spring said, holding his hand tighter. "I mean, no! Of course I'm not."

"Yes," Herb said, misunderstanding. "You wish it was that—that other man you knew. I don't blame you. He could probably have protected you much better than I have."

"Herb! No!" she said sharply.

Herb released the hold of her hands. He should never have presumed such liberties. The misery in his voice was apparent. "I'm sorry."

"Herb! You don't understand anything, do you!" Spring said in exasperation. "I am the one who is sorry. Listen to me. What I said about that man, well, it was just talk. So forget it, okay? I made that up. There's no other man."

Hope, confusion, and anger all collided in Herb's brain. "But why did you say that? Why did you lie to me?"

"Because. Because when we were writing, I didn't really know you then. When I showed up at your house as I did, you might have thought that I wanted to—that I was a—a—" She floundered.

"A passionflower?" suggested Herb.

"That sounds nicer than what I had in mind, but yes.

That's the general idea. I thought if I made up a story, you wouldn't try anything. You wouldn't want me," she explained.

"Whether I wanted to or not, is beside the point. I would never have tried forcing you into anything like that. No male on Paradise would."

"I know that. Now. But not then. I didn't know about your culture. I didn't know how nice you were. And—wait a minute. What about you, anyway? You were reading those sexy zines. That's how you saw my advertisement," she said accusingly.

"Well, yes, but—" he began defensively. "But, I wouldn't have seen it if you didn't write it. What about that?"

"That's different. I found those zines at the retreat. I found them when I dropped a crystal. Never mind. They were a way for me to escape. What's your excuse?"

"I don't need one. I'm a man. Men like to look at pretty girls. What's so terrible about that?"

Spring sighed. "Nothing at all, Herb," she answered quietly. "This was supposed to be an apology. I don't know why I picked a fight. Guess I'm feeling guilty for deceiving you. You've been wonderful all the way, and I know I could never have made it without you. I am so sorry I ever lied to you."

"I know you only did what you had to," Herb said, mollified.

"Another lesson in how lies never pay, even well intentioned ones. In trying to protect both of us, I only hurt us more."

Herb had assimilated everything she'd said, but only one thing was that important. There was no other man. His chlorophyll was surging. If only he had known that before!

"Anyway," she continued. "Another reason I didn't say anything later was because of Lily. If you two planned to marry, you were in love. It would have been tacky of me to intrude, to come on to you just for a hiding place. Just because I found you attractive, after all." But her thoughts were ironic. She found Herb attractive? Only if gorgeous eyes, a slim body, and rakish smile were just attractive. True, his skin was green, but that only made him more special to her. And he was so kind, so genuinely nice, that he'd passed "special" a long time ago.

"Tacky?" Herb asked. That was a term he'd never heard.

"Inappropriate. Besides, I like Lily. Now she's in undeserved trouble, all because of me. I owe her," Spring said, meaningfully.

"Lily is a good person," Herb agreed. "I'm thankful that nothing has happened to her."

"Herb. Everything has happened to her!" Spring exclaimed. "She just hasn't been killed. Yet. Who knows what that crazy old man will do to get to me? I've been thinking about that, too. If I agreed to cooperate quietly–"

"No!" Herb shouted. The thought of Zygote laying just one of his bony fingers on Spring filled him with rage again.

Spring squeezed his hands in hers. "Herb, we can't stop him now. I may as well do what good I can under the circumstances. If I go along, maybe he will agree to let you and Lily go home. After all, once he has the secret, what harm could anyone do him? If what he suspects is true, he will be virtually invincible."

Herb was torn. "If it comes to that, you know I want Lily to be free, but I couldn't stand for you to–to do that. Not with him!"

"Dear Herb," Spring said, pulling him up against the bars, her flesh pressing his in alternate spots. "You are so sweet to care what happens to me, after all I've done to you."

Herb knew it was a lot more than being understanding. It was all over now anyway, so why not confess? "Spring, about Lily—" he began.

"Yes, you and Lily must be together. After all you both have suffered for me, I couldn't bear to be the cause of anything else happening. The love you share mustn't be destroyed by Zygote."

"But Spring. I—"

"Shh. Listen. Someone is coming," she whispered.

Torchlight illuminated the darkness, casting long shadows. They were still holding hands when the giant came to bring them food. Zygote did not intend to starve them, at least.

Larg opened Herb's cell and gave him a small bowl of thick stew, some bread, and a jug of liquid before relocking the door. He then unlocked Spring's and repeated the motions of handing in the dishes. Before she could accept the last one, it flew from his hand and crashed onto the dirt floor. The giant went down with a heavy thud and did not get back up. A round shadow rolled back to them.

"Cling!" Spring cried happily. "You found us!"

He had subdued the giant in the same manner as the goon in the greenhouse on Paradise. Plucking the key from the giant's belt, he tossed it to Herb, who quickly opened his cell. He looked down at the sleeping hulk.

"That's amazing," Herb said. One didn't have to be a giant to defend oneself if one knew the right moves. "You have to teach me how to do that when we get out of this!" he exclaimed. Herb was tired of feeling helpless.

"So sorry to be delayed, but much magic in this castle to avoid," Cling Ling explained.

The trio moved carefully past the small human mountain and up the long stairway. Prepared to fight, they opened the door to the tower room, but it was empty. Where had Zygote taken Lily?

Cling Ling decided to do what he did best, and slipped out the open window to creep along the castle walls. If Lily was anywhere in the castle, he would find her.

Spring and Herb went back down to the first floor to check out the rooms there. For a large castle, it was oddly deserted. They did not see a single servant. Yet Zygote had no family that Spring knew of, and in his line of work he would hardly desire many house guests as witnesses. Still, it must be a lonely life, even for someone like Zygote. Spring quickly upbraided herself. Pity for Zygote? Never!

After searching the entire lower floor, they ascended to the second, starting just below the tower. They were coming to the last few rooms when Spring put a finger to her lips, signaling Herb to silence. She thought she heard faint voices coming from the next room.

Cautiously, she shoved against the door and peered through the tiny slit. A small gasp escaped her lips. Herb pushed past her to look inside.

There was Lily reclined upon a bed, and there was Zygote. He was embracing her. After he had sworn he had never forced himself on her, the liar! Blood boiling, Herb burst into the room despite Spring's attempt to restrain him. This was no time for stealth! He no longer cared what powers Zygote might use against him; he couldn't let Lily be raped by that mad old man.

"Let her go, Zygote!" he shouted.

"Herb!" Lily exclaimed, her eyes wide with surprise and fear. Naturally she was afraid, Herb thought. Who wouldn't be, with that beast pawing her? In her weakened condition, too.

Zygote rose from the bed and faced Herb. Herb dashed forward, but surprisingly, made no headway. Another huge minion of Zygote's had appeared from behind him and clutched Herb tightly about the arms and chest, totally immobilizing him.

Lily looked at Zygote with tears in her eyes. "Please don't hurt Herb," she implored.

Just then, the stained glass of the window broke away as Cling Ling flung himself into the room. One strong roll brought the goon to his knees, breaking the grip on Herb.

"Run!" yelled the Vinese, and taking his own advice, rolled quickly out the doorway. Julep-so he might know, but he was no match for Zygote's magic. The wisest course was to put a wide space between them and the magician before he took action. It was not long in coming.

They dashed down the steps to the floor below, flying out the front entrance toward the gate. The drawbridge had been raised.

"We'll have to swim for it," Herb called. "We'll return for Lily when we can." He removed his shoes and advanced to the water's edge.

"No, don't!" Spring screamed.

Herb looked where she was pointing and withdrew his toes just as a huge, warty, moat creature snapped at it. Sea serpents in a moat? He should have anticipated as much. It was right in line with Zygote's mythical world. Well, mythical it might be, but those jaws were real enough. Zygote did no shoddy workmanship.

Shoving his feet back into his shoes, Herb and the others fled around the side of the castle. Suddenly, they heard the unearthly cry above them.

They looked up. It couldn't be, and yet it was. A mammoth lavender dragon with huge silver wings, bearing down upon them, fire issuing from its toothy mouth.

They needed cover fast, but there was only one place. Back into the castle they tore, the heat of its hot breath scorching their backsides.

"Where can we hide?" Spring gasped, as they stopped to catch their breath in the doorway.

"Hold it right there," came a voice they all recognized. A

thin form stepped out from the shadows brandishing a vapor gun. Without pausing, he aimed and fired. A chunk of the marble floor in front of them disappeared into smoke. He laughed coldly at their fright.

"Elton!" Spring cried.

"Yes, Spring, I have finally arrived. Apparently none too soon. I trust you enjoyed your little charade, for it's all over now." He fired another shot, this time finding a mark. Cling Ling lost a few leaves.

"Stop it. You're insane!" Spring screamed. "I am the one you want. Take me to Zygote. Just put down the weapon."

"It's too late for that, Spring, don't you see? Or shall I call you Lily? How about Mank?" he added with contempt.

"You knew?" asked Spring in a small voice.

"I finally figured it out. How else could you have hidden from me on the ship, except in disguise? You must think you're very clever. I may not be able to have your secret, but neither will anyone else. In another moment you'll all be dust, my dearest."

He fired another blast, ripping a gash from the front of her skirt. Herb grasped Spring in his arms, spinning around to protect her with his body.

"That won't help, hero," Elton said. "This baby can take out a dragon at twenty feet." He smiled insanely.

Spring struggled to free herself from Herb's arms. "Don't. I don't want you to be hurt."

"Whatever happens, Spring, we'll face it together," he said.

Elton rolled his eyes to the ceiling. "Oh please. Spare me. What is this power you have, Spring? One at a time, or two, it makes no difference to me. As long as you die." He raised the weapon again and took careful aim. They knew this was the end. He had only been playing with them before, making them suffer, but knew better than to delay too long.

The vapor gun fell harmlessly to the floor as a huge cockroach went scurrying away. The foot of the giant came down to smash it with a horrible cracking sound.

Zygote stood behind him. "A fitting end. He was always an insect at heart," he said coldly.

The others stood looking on in shock. Zygote had turned Elton into a bug? There was only a greasy smear on the floor where he had stood moments before. Hideous. And yet, he would have left even less of them.

Herb came suddenly to life. Grabbing for Spring, he bolted toward the stairs and down into the darkness. Cling Ling rolled shakily behind, the loss of his leaves throwing him off balance for the moment.

"There's no escape!" Zygote called out from behind them. That might very well be, but they would elude him for as long as possible, Herb thought. He was grateful for Zygote's intervention, but knew it was only to further his own vile purpose. To obtain Spring's secret.

Down past the cells they raced with the slower giant lumbering a small distance behind them. Zygote seemed to have told the truth, however. There were no more doors at this level. Cling Ling had rescued the giant's torch and used it to illuminate the dead end before them. The goon's footsteps grew nearer.

Herb spied a narrow cleft between the two walls at one side. Probably just bad construction, but if they could squeeze between, they might be able to hide for a while longer. Spring tried it first. It was a tight fit, but pressing as flat as possible, they edged inward, one behind the other.

"Oh!" Spring said, tumbling through and out into the other side. A hidden room. Herb entered, followed by Cling Ling. They stood holding their breath as the heavy footsteps of the guard stomped outside. More footsteps joined his. More guards? They did not notice the slit in the wall, so far. Because they were so large, it probably didn't occur to them that anyone could fit through it. After a bit of grumbling around, they heard the giants retreating in the opposite direction. They had bought time.

Cling Ling crept around the walls feeling for secret doors as another exit. His wound was not serious. He had lost leaves and tendrils before and they would grow back. It only hurt a little and the sap had already ceased to ooze out.

"I can't find another way out," he reported. "It would appear our respite is only temporary. Perhaps the guards will conclude we doubled back. While they search elsewhere we could attempt to slip back into the castle." But from his tone, it didn't sound as if he had much conviction of it working.

"It's worth a try," Herb agreed. They couldn't give up hope. He guided Spring toward the dim slit of light in the other room where they had dropped the torch, but stopped short as more footsteps pounded toward them across the dungeon, stopping outside the wall. The pursuers had posted a guard. Then they heard lighter footfalls. It was Zygote!

"I don't know where you are hiding, but it's only a matter of time until we find you," the chillingly familiar voice called. "You may elude us for now, but consider. You have no food or drink, and are weakened from the exertion of this futile escape attempt. I know your gifted friend has overpowered my guards on two separate occasions, but he is wounded. Even if he were not, I seriously doubt he could handle two or three. Think it over. Oh, and Spring, I promise you this. I will be as gentle with you as I would with my own love." With that, he departed. The guards did not.

"Gentle!" Spring scoffed, leaning against Herb's chest. His hand touched her face, finding wetness.

"It will be all right," he said softly, enclosing her in his arms, offering whatever small comfort they could afford.

"I'm sorry to be a crybaby," she sniffed.

"Shhh," Herb whispered, burying his face in her hair. She had been so brave throughout her ordeal, but emotions could not be blocked forever. Herb didn't want her to cry, but it felt good to have an excuse to hold her. She seemed to melt inside his arms naturally, as if she were where she truly belonged.

"Spring, this is impossible," he whispered. "If we give up now, he may keep his word. He may treat you kindly. Perhaps even release Lily. There's no way to prevent it now. You know I would give my life if I could." He released her and moved to the opening to call out for the guards.

"No!" Spring hissed, grasping him. "We can't let him have the secret! I know that now. Even Lily was willing to sacrifice herself to prevent it, and she was right. It isn't just me. If he gets that secret, everyone will lose."

Herb took her gently by the shoulders. "Spring, you know I despise the thought of him touching you, that way, but—"

"It's not that. If it would appease him and free the rest of you, I'd do anything with him he wanted. Only, I can't because there's the secret to protect. He can't get it Herb, he just can't!"

"There's no other way, Spring," Herb said in despair.

"No, you're wrong. There is one."

He was horrified. "You mean death? Oh, Spring, I could never—"

She smiled, somewhat quizzically; he could tell the expression by the tone of her voice. "A fate said by some to be worse."

"Worse? But that's what Zygote means to—"

"With you, Herb. I know it's a gross imposition, considering your relationship with Lily, but perhaps she would understand. I want *you* to have my knowledge."

"To—?" He stared at the place her face should be. "Surely you can't mean—"

"That is exactly what I mean. So as to make it impossible for Zygote to get it. Since it seems I shall have to give it to someone very soon, I want it to be to a good man, and you are that man."

"But you and I aren't—"

"We aren't a couple," she agreed. "But we are united in our desire to keep Zygote from getting this power. Herb, I don't think you would abuse it. I think my father would have approved of you, of your having it, in the circumstances. So, perhaps, if you could just think of me as a—a passing fancy, then we can stop Zygote. I wouldn't suggest this if there were any other reasonable alternative, and I apologize for imposing on you like this, but desperate straits require desperate remedies. So if you can force yourself to—"

"Stop talking as if you're a loathsome creature!" he cried. "You're not. You're a lovely person, in spirit and in body. It would be easy to—in fact, too easy to—if things were otherwise. But—"

"Pretend they are otherwise," she said. "Please."

"But I have no desire to become a superbeing. I want no power."

"That is precisely why I feel I should release it to you," she explained. "It would be safe with you, though for your sake, I wish there were some other way. There isn't."

He realized that she was right: this was the best way out of their dilemma. He had to do it. "I will pretend you are—Holly, my playmate on Avocado. My only interest in her was—this."

"Your only interest," she agreed. "And mine is to stop Zygote." She moved in close to him, and kissed him.

Suddenly he was very much aware of what he had tried to ignore: she was a beautiful creature and a desirable one, in more than one respect. In more than several respects. She was, in a sense it wasn't proper to dwell upon, his ideal woman. But he had to tune that out, and focus only on her purely physical presence. To pretend that the marvelously sexy creature he had discovered one day emerging from his shower was an Avocado playmate fresh from an invigorating victory in ten nets, to be enjoyed and let go.

But that didn't quite work. It was not his way to dally with a mere body; he had to know the whole person. He had mentioned Holly, who had been but a passing dalliance—but she had also been a complete person of her type, enthusiastic about netball, in fact enthusiastic about everything. But Spring was not Holly, and his effort to pretend she was fell flat. In more than one respect, perhaps appropriately.

"Herb, I don't want to rush you, but we haven't much time," she whispered in his ear. "Is there anything I can do to encourage your interest? I—I am not experienced in this."

"The fault is not yours, it's mine," he said. "I was trying to pretend that you are Holly, and it just isn't—"

"I know. Maybe—Lily?"

He tried to pretend she was Lily, with no better success. Meanwhile he heard the sounds of the pursuit-search coming closer. She was right: they had very little time.

"I wish I could help you," Spring said. "You're such a decent person, you don't like doing this, and I understand that, but—"

"You're decent, too," he said quickly. "And you are you, no matter what I try to imagine. That's the problem."

"I'm sorry," she said, her tears beginning to flow. "It was a bad idea."

"It's a great idea. And you're great, too. I'm the one who is fouling up."

"Maybe—I hate to ask this—maybe if you just, well, pretend it's me. I mean, that you and I really care for each other, as we would if we were a couple."

"I'll try." She had given him leave to involve her directly in his pretense. He thought about how it would be to truly love her, without having to pretend he didn't.

Suddenly everything was there, including a passion so great it was as if it had been dammed for weeks. He kissed her, and paradise was on her lips. The oddest thing was that there seemed to be just as much emotion on her part, as if she felt exactly the same about him. She was saying and doing all the right things, with the ring of conviction, just as if they stemmed from wildly overflowing love. Then the dam burst around her and within her, making a tremendous flow that wasn't merely emotional, and it was done.

❧ 26 ❧

Secrets

Herb released Spring and moved away, his face flushed from exertion and shame. Under other circumstances he would have rejoiced, but this—this was an abomination.

He could hear Spring breathing beside him in the darkness. He put out a hand to brush away the locks of hair that had tumbled over her face during their encounter.

"Thank you, Herb," Spring said primly as she reassembled her clothing. "Do you—feel anything yet? What's it like?"

What was it like? The greatest experience of his life! But that was the wrong aspect. "I don't know. I don't feel any different. I don't feel anything." That was true enough; his senses seemed numbed at the moment. "Except for my overwhelming wish that it could have been—" But he could not continue, because it was no proper thing to say to her.

"I, too, wish that, well, that it could have been for love instead of for business. Your pretense was most convincing. But you're right; that's not what we're looking for at the moment. There's nothing else?"

Perhaps he was afraid to let himself feel for fear of what it would be. "It might take a few minutes to start?" he suggested.

If the information was as powerful as everyone thought, they could use it somehow to escape and bring Zygote to a well deserved justice for his crimes. It had been the only reasonable solution to their problem. Spring knew that Herb was a good man, and would never abuse the power, whatever it might be. She knew it was the right choice, so why did it feel so wrong?

Cling Ling had made himself as scarce as possible under the conditions of their confinement. He had squeezed back into the thin crevice as far as he could to give them privacy, his body blocking the opening to leave them in a blanket of darkness. It was a courtesy.

Even if Zygote destroyed them, the secret would die with Herb. He had gone through the motions of lovemaking as quickly as he could to accomplish the deed before they were discovered. What had gone on in his mind wasn't relevant. Already the guards were banging on the walls, possibly looking for secret panels or hollow spots at Zygote's command.

Now Herb lay awaiting the revelations of the secret, whatever it was. And he felt nothing of that nature. That was not strictly true. He felt an abject emptiness. Was it because of the way they had approached it? Sex without love was nothing new to him. How many times had he raised his stalk with a strange flower? Could he ever find pleasure in such an act again? He had changed, but not in the way either of them expected.

Spring sat up in frustration. "I don't understand it. My father said the transfer would happen the first time I made love. You should be bursting with knowledge. I know my father wouldn't lie to me. Not about this."

"Stand back," cried the Vinese, thrusting himself inside just as the outer wall crumbled.

The giants had finally discovered their hiding place and battered down the wall. They stood huddled at the back as one giant threw the light of his torch upon them. There was no escape. Resigned, they crawled over the rubble and were marched back upstairs to face Zygote. Lily stood beside him in the comfortable sitting room.

"Lily. Are you well?" asked Herb, referring to more than the state of her health.

She averted her eyes. "I grow stronger," she answered.

Herb wondered what Zygote had done to her. Perhaps she had given in to his lusts willingly, assuming it would help the rest of them if she appeased him. She had volunteered to do as much before with Elton. There was no shame in such sacrifice.

If anyone should be ashamed, Herb realized it was himself. He had vacillated for months about his commitment to Lily, finally admitting he simply did not love her the way he should. It was a hard truth to swallow.

Zygote turned to Spring. "I would not have you harmed, but there is no other way to obtain the secret. Give me your word you will cooperate, and afterward you may leave with your friends in safety."

"It's too late," Spring blurted. "Please forgive me, Lily, but Herb and I, we—I am no longer a virgin."

Lily's eyes widened with understanding. Zygote looked from Spring to Herb, and back to Spring. "I can test you. I can tell if you're lying. You forgot, I'm a physician as well," he said coldly.

"I'm not lying. We were together. Downstairs, while you searched for us."

"I believe her, Zygote," Lily said. "Spring would not lie about something like that. Not to me." Her eyes met Spring's, now red from tears.

"Lily—" Spring said.

Lily moved forward to hold Spring in her arms, like a comforting mother, though in age they were not that far apart.

"Your eyes. Let me see your eyes," Zygote interrupted, his voice betraying his fear that it was true. He whipped an instrument from his robe and approached Herb, peering through the glass. "You seem normal."

"You're a good physician. I *am* normal. There is no secret," Herb said.

"Impossible!" Zygote exclaimed. He looked at Spring. "Unless you were lying after all."

"Then examine me, if you wish," Spring said evenly. "There was no time to—" she blushed, thinking of the blood that must still stain her garments. They had not even had time to properly disrobe. At the time she had been aware of none of those complications; there had been only love unfettered.

Zygote turned away in consternation. It would be easy enough to check; even the girl knew that. No, she was telling the truth.

"Perhaps there never was a secret," Lily said.

"My father wouldn't lie to me," Spring objected.

"Well, no, but have you considered that his process may not have been complete? Or simply not worked? He may indeed have programmed some information, but—"

"I think I see what you mean," Herb said. "You are saying there was only one way to test it, so no one could be sure about it."

"Yes," Lily said, warming to her hypothesis. "It was surely a desperate move. He must have felt that Zygote or someone else would discover his normal records before he could perfect it. If it was completed, he would have implemented it himself. Why bother to pass on information another could obtain? He could not have expected you to remain celibate throughout your life, Spring."

"No, he wanted me to marry. To have someone to love," Spring said, more confused than ever.

"So—the information you were given was probably preliminary," Herb said. "Yet, in the wrong hands, could have led to the true breakthrough, given time, and luck, and knowhow. In other words, information that would be useful only to your father and perhaps some other trusted person, such as your chosen lover and yourself. His family."

"I suppose. But, in that case, why didn't he just tell that to Zygote when he was being attacked? That the information would be useless without him?" Spring asked.

Lily pondered. "I think he was protecting you then, not his secret. After all, he had not expected Zygote or anyone else to know you had any knowledge at that time, consciously or otherwise."

Zygote turned. "Of course. What a fool I've been! I didn't think he was hurt that badly. Your father must have deliberately—" He paused, remembering. "The choking, the medicine he asked for. It was poison."

"He committed suicide," Lily said. "But not for any great secret. For you, Spring. He must have known that even if Zygote found you, the information would do him no good, yet he was determined not to put you through that. Zygote wouldn't have believed him if he'd told him. He would have—tested for the truth."

"So he died rather than reveal where you were," Zygote breathed. "He knew I could make him talk through magical means, if necessary. That's always dangerous with another magician. He would put up blockades. It could have destroyed his mind, but in the end, I would have won." He turned to Spring.

"Well, my dear. It appears your sacrifice was also in vain, since the information you possessed, if it had taken, would be of no use to me without your father. I have lost. You are all free to leave, of course." He seemed to forget they were there then, and went away to the window where he stood gazing out, his dreams of glory dashed forever. Zygote's shoulders sagged, and he looked all of his age. Herb almost felt sorry for him.

Spring gave a small cry of anguish. "Then I betrayed you for nothing." She looked miserably to Lily and Herb. "Can you ever forgive me?"

Lily shook her head slowly and looked from Spring to Herb. "Forgive you?"

Herb intervened. "Lily, please don't be hard on Spring. It was as much my doing as hers."

"Indeed?" Lily said, an amused smiled crossing her face.

Herb colored. "You know what I mean. We only did it because it was the only way. Or so we thought."

Lily placed her fingertip over his lips for silence. "I cannot defer to you this time, Herb. I cannot forgive what needs no forgiveness. It is obvious to me that you two were meant for each other from the moment you met. I was jealous on Paradise, but now I have had time to reflect. You love each other."

Spring looked dismayed, but did not speak. Herb looked to Spring, but could no longer truthfully deny the depths of his feelings for her, even to spare Lily. His pretense of loving Spring—had been no pretense. Now he could admit that, to himself and others.

"Lily, I never meant to hurt you," he said lamely.

She smiled patiently. "And so you haven't."

Both Herb and Spring registered confusion now.

"Herb, you don't understand even now, do you? I insisted we begin seeing each other again. You were my only love ever since we were saplings. I was certain you cared for me."

"I did. That is, I still do, but—" Herb said.

"But not as lovers," Lily finished. "I mistook those feelings for romance. In reality, we have a special friendship, akin to a brotherly and sisterly love. That's only natural since we grew up together, I suppose. And I believe that is the true reason that I could never bring myself to—to give myself to you, Herb."

"But I thought—"

"That it was my high principles?" She smiled. "I did like to think so. But now I know, when a woman is truly in love with a man, principles are very cold comfort."

"I tried to leave," Herb said, "but I couldn't. Something always drew me back, even though I knew in my heart it wouldn't work." He looked at Spring. "I never knew what love was, until now."

Spring's eyes began to melt. Herb reached for her, but Lily intercepted him. "A last kiss," she said, giving him a warm hug, and kiss. On the cheek. Then she took Spring's hand and placed it in Herb's. "I hope you will be happy in your new love, as I hope to be—with mine."

Flabbergasted, they watched as she went to Zygote and put her hand upon his shoulder. The magician turned about slowly, facing her. She took one of his hands in hers, and placed her other to his cheek. "One door has closed, yet another may open," she said.

"Lovely lady." Zygote smiled sadly, pressing the soft green hand to his lips.

Spring and Herb looked at each other in shocked astonishment. Evidently they had not only mistaken Zygote's relationship to Elton, but his attentions to Lily as well.

"Lily!" Herb exclaimed. "Earlier, upstairs?" He recalled his wild accusations in the bedroom. Rape, indeed!

"But—Zygote?" Spring said with disgust. "Oh, Lily! How could you?"

Lily turned to her with understanding. "Spring, I know it is hard for you to accept after all that has happened between you and Zygote, but he has shown me only kindness since my arrival. I have seen a side of him that you haven't."

"Evidently." Spring didn't bother to conceal the irony.

"You see," Lily continued as if Spring hadn't spoken, "I know you did something to change the time so you could arrive to save me, but for some reason, it did not affect my memory when reversed." She addressed Zygote now.

"Zygote, I know and retain all the memories of what happened during those long days until their ship's arrival."

Zygote visibly blanched. "That—that was to be but an interlude," he said, shaken. "I, of course, knew of the time-warp through my magic. But, when they arrived, that part of it should have been erased as if it never happened to you."

"To us." She addressed Herb and Spring again. "You see, Zygote attended to me during my weakness, and no one could have been more gentle. Then, a young man began visiting me. He was also kind and gentle, and warm. He evoked something within me. Something that had been missing from our relationship, Herb. We talked, exchanging our feelings, and after those days, those wonderful days, I knew that I had fallen in love with him. More than that, I knew he loved me, too."

"A young man? Who? Where?" Herb asked, bewildered. So much had happened so fast!

"He was wonderful. I've never felt that way about anyone before, and that's why I do understand how you and Spring could have become so close. He—he made love to me, and I have never known anything so beautiful. Then, you arrived, and I was confused because at first it all seemed like a dream—"

"A dream," Zygote said. "You were ill. There is no young man here."

"But there is. I can't go on without him now," she protested.

"You should not have remembered," Zygote said rubbing his thinning hair with one hand. "I would not have you suffer a loss."

"I'm glad I remember. And I feel no loss. Do you think a woman does not know the man she loves?" Lily smiled, embracing Zygote warmly.

"Lily," Zygote said, seeming appalled. "You don't know."

"Oh, but I do. I know that young man was you, Zygote."

"A spell," Herb cried. "He used a spell on you, to have his way." He moved in to punch out Zygote. The man was unspeakable!

Lily blocked his way. "Only to change his appearance. He didn't expect me to remember any of our time together. What we felt was in need of no spell. From the time your ship arrived, he put all that behind us. He has treated me as an honored guest and nothing more."

"What about what I saw upstairs?" Herb asked, referring darkly to the incident in the bedroom. "I saw his arms around you."

"He was helping me into bed. To rest. I am the one who embraced him. I was determined to reveal my memories and ask him to release you, but then you burst in to save me." She smiled.

"But, this is too crazy!" Herb said.

"Herb, you never needed me. Zygote does. He's been a lonely man despite his power. Would you begrudge me happiness now that you've found yours?"

"No." Herb was torn. He wanted Lily to be happy, but how could she find that with a man like Zygote?

"I think our love could flourish. The love of a good woman has brought forth the good in many men; I know many women who would envy a fairy tale life with a brilliant, reformed, mad magician." She looked at Zygote questioningly. So much depended upon his answer.

Zygote raised an eyebrow and considered. It seemed that he was being proposed to by a beautiful young woman. And at his age. His age! Quickly, he cast a silent spell and looked younger as the lines began disappearing.

"Quite reformed," he affirmed, his eyes glistening with a slight moisture.

"But not too much," Lily said, noticing the character lines fading from his features. "I love you just the way you are," she said, tracing a smile line with her fingers.

The process stopped abruptly, and they stood gazing into each other's eyes with a silent communication, forgetting the other three. The magician enclosed Lily in his arms—where she seemed quite content to remain.

"Let's leave," Spring whispered to Herb and Cling Ling. "We aren't wanted here now."

Herb looked at the unlikely couple lost in their embrace, then shrugged and went along with the others. This time no giants pursued them; no dragons dive bombed from the skies. Cling Ling wandered away to search for transportation.

"We can't just leave her here," Herb insisted. "Zygote is too old for her. And besides, he's evil. Look at everything he did to you."

"I'm not forgetting, Herb. I have no love for Zygote. True,

he didn't kill my father, but he caused that death. Zygote's failure has been a small punishment. But, I do owe Lily, and crazy as it is, if she wants to stay with Zygote, I won't deny her that choice. I have to go on. I want my life back."

"Why do you think she retained all those memories? It shouldn't have been possible. It's not—not scientific," Herb muttered.

"I don't have an answer, but this is a magical realm. If anyone deserves to live happily ever after, it's Lily," Spring said.

"Yes, but—"

"Shh," Spring said silencing him with a kiss. "Love casts its own spell. That's all we need to know."

"I think I feel some of that magic now," Herb said, kissing her again. And again. And again.

The noise of a throat being cleared sounded behind them. Cling Ling had returned. He had rounded up a sleek spaceship with a robot pilot at the modern, private port behind Zygote's castle. The magician might have preferred days of old, but he wasn't a fool when it came to modern comfort and convenience.

The new ship was nothing close to the bucket of bolts they had travelled in with the Txnghc. It had luxurious accommodations with good food from well stocked nutrition units, and even separate sleeping compartments.

Cling Ling sat in the front of the ship with the metallic pilot while Spring and Herb shut their compartment door for long awaited privacy.

"What did your father say when you called to tell him you were bringing home a bride?" Spring asked. "Was he disappointed it wasn't Lily? Does he know I'm not—green?"

"My family loves Lily, but they understand. They are happy for us, so don't be afraid. Cross-pollination is not unknown on my planet, after all. You are beautiful, and they will love you as much as I do." He took her in his arms and squeezed to make this point. And also because he enjoyed it.

Spring snuggled close on the small bunk, and reminisced. "Lily was a beautiful bride. I'm glad she came after us. I never thought I'd be married in a double ceremony. Especially with Zygote as one of the grooms."

"Love conquers all," Herb said.

"Did you just make that up?" Spring teased. "So much talk. What kind of honeymoon is this, anyway?"

"This kind," Herb said, with an immediate demonstration. Spring heartily endorsed the suggestion. This time around there were no giants pounding on the walls. There was no need to rush, so they went slowly, getting to know each other as lovers, as well as friends. "But you know, it was almost better when we were pretending, there on Kamalot."

"Who was pretending?" she demanded with a mock frown.

He laughed. "When we pretended we were pretending."

At the wonderful moment of union, Spring cried out her deep love for Herb. As Herb reciprocated the sentiment, he felt a tremendous wave—of knowledge.

"Spring! Oh, Spring!" he cried. "It's working!" he gasped as his mind was filled with—practically everything.

"Is it ever," Spring sighed, misunderstanding his meaning.

"No. I mean the transference. The secret. Don't you see? The first time, we held back our true feelings. We pretended it was just sex. But now it's love. No pretense. Love is the answer!"

"It always was, darling," Spring said, covering his face with kisses. She relaxed in the afterglow, feeling truly happy for the first time since the loss of her father. She wanted to stay in Herb's strong arms forever.

"You don't understand," Herb said gently. "I have all the information now. All of it. And Lily was only partially right about your father and why he did this. This secret is your legacy. You see," he continued, assimilating this aspect, "your father loved you very much Spring, but he—he was dying. Of an incurable malady."

"Dying? No!"

"This was the only way he knew to be sure you would have this knowledge, in the arms of someone you loved. He knew you would need someone."

"I never—" She swallowed, still in shock. "I never even suspected that anything was wrong. He would have left me anyway." She tried to remember if there had been any signs, but there hadn't been. He had spared her even that. "Then, it wasn't Zygote at all? It would have ended the same way, even if he hadn't taken the poison. I've been so wrong about so much! Lily—somehow she sensed it."

"I feel better about Lily, knowing this. Perhaps now it will be easier for you to—to let go, Spring," Herb said, knowing how close she had been to her father. It was still a lot to ask.

Spring looked at Herb and realized that he was right. The old life was over. It was time to move on. Her father had been a wonderful man, but now she had another. "Kiss me Herb," she implored as if they had never done it before. "Kiss me."

Herb gladly complied, and another shock wave of information rocked his brain. "Spring! Every time we kiss, I learn something new. You wouldn't believe some of the things I know how to do now."

"And I can't wait to find out," she said mischievously.

"Tell me, is it true what they say about plant men?" She cupped her hands and whispered in his ear.

Herb blushed a bright lizard green but smiled broadly. Some secrets were better when shared. As for the rest, it would take time to learn, but he was an eager student.

AUTHORS' NOTES

Piers Anthony

I have known Jo Anne Taeusch since 1987, when we met at the World Fantasy Convention in Nashville, Tennessee. She really didn't make much of an impression on me then. As I recall, she was a tiny figure under a mass of orange hair who came to one of my autographings and to my reading. It wasn't until she started sending me cute letters that I delved into the recesses of my cranium to reconstruct the lost memory. She also sent me cards for holidays, always clever, and sometimes little gifts.

I should clarify that I try to discourage too many letters from readers, as I have been answering an average of 150 a month for several years, and it strains my time. I especially try to discourage gifts, because I really have everything I need, and feel that my contact with readers should be via the printed pages of my novels. I seldom give gifts, other than the words in my fiction, to any of my readers, as part of a similar principle. But Jo Anne was one of three who would not be gainsaid in such respects. I am not the fastest study in such matters, but eventually I realized that something more than mere generosity was motivating these three, all married women, in this respect, and concluded that it was best to let the matter be. So I have a growing collection of gifts in my study, some of significant value, and they do remind me of their donors. I have met each of them, at some event. And I do use the novel solar calculator Jo Anne sent (it had blue fluid saturating its works; eventually that evaporated, leaving it empty, but it still works nicely), and the Samurai sword letter opener on those hundreds of other letters that pile in. This year it was a toy computer that blinks MERRY CHRISTMAS.

So I was there, as it were, during Jo Anne's ups and downs, watching somewhat helplessly from the sidelines as her marriage failed, debts she hadn't incurred bankrupted her (our legal system is at times an ass), and illness led to depletion and surgery. But her cute outlook remained. Once she remarked that she had just turned forty, and was still mad about it. I watched as she slowly put her life together again, though it was clearly no joyous existence. I hear from many whose lives are, as I put it, subdivisions of Hell, and many more who seem to be skidding on thinning ice over a threatening abyss. I'm depressive; I felt that my own life was not a pleasant one, until success came by luck and tenacity and drove the wolf from my door. But it has become clear that I never faced the trials some of my readers endure.

When Jo Anne asked whether I would critique her failed fantasy novel, I knew it was payback time. I don't claim to know a lot about much, but I do know something about commercial fantasy. So I gave her my usual warning about the likelihood of having to tell her all the ways she was going wrong—maybe there are those who enjoy that, but I don't—and agreed to read it. Thus came *The Secret of Spring*. Therein I found all the cute cleverness formerly evident in her letters, plus a pretty good entertainment science fantasy novel. It did need work, and I told her what I felt it needed. But I also advised her that I was doing an experimental series of collaborative novels, and could do the work I recommended myself, if she wished. I'm not eager to get into more collaborations, as I have more than enough of my own writing to do, but I judge each case on its merits, and I felt *Spring* deserved her chance.

Thus this volume, my 21st collaborative novel, and 104th overall book. I've done two collaborative anthologies, too, but on reconsideration I decided that they don't count, because they represent the work of other writers. This will be Jo Anne's first published novel, but perhaps not her last. I think there is a place in Parnassus for cute, clever stories like this one.

So why am I talking about Jo Anne, instead of myself? Well, my life is dull; all I do is sit in front of a red screen with yellow print and type fiction. But perhaps one interesting thing is happening to me now: I'm being sued. No, it's frivolous; someone is trying to get the commissions I paid my literary agent. But the legalistic vilification in the suit is something to appreciate. There must be a fiction writer in the works.

Remember, those interested in more of my works, can visit my web site www.hipiers.com. And no, they won't give you Jo Anne's phone number.

Jo Anne Taeusch

I had a lot of fun writing this story, which was one reason why I did it; there hasn't been nearly enough of that in my recent history. But that aside, I believe, like most folk who do this, I wrote because I had to. There's still a soft callous on my middle finger from holding a pencil so often as a child.

Due to family illness and other circumstances I was encouraged to be quiet and entertain myself. Thus began a lifelong love affair with books; even the means of earning my living has revolved around them, as I've been in library services for more than thirty years.

The Secret of Spring is my first published work, but not my first effort. Over the years I've penned poetry, written short stories and even puppet plays, but when going through an especially difficult period around the time I met Piers Anthony (no connection) it was time to tackle "The Book."

It served me well as therapy and although not published, has proved profitable, since it was from a minor character came the notion for the plant people. So while I'd love to claim a green thumb and say inspiration came naturally from my great storehouse of knowledge about plants, the truth is that grass turns brown where I walk. I also wanted to explore communication differences between the sexes without losing the humor, and this story seemed a natural vehicle.

Some have said the pun is the lowest form of humor, but I've always enjoyed them; the worse, the better. I truly believe that Piers Anthony's Xanths are the highest form of pun-ishment. Whenever I've needed a lift, his wonderful books have been there to turn to, and he has been my favorite author for many years. In spite of the pest (I read his Author's Note) I've made of myself, when I asked for an opinion of my story he was kind enough to look it over.

The result has been an opportunity beyond any I could have hoped for or expected. *Spring* is here!